THE DYING LIGHT

ALSO BY DANIEL AUBREY

Dark Island

THE DYING LIGHT

by

DANIEL AUBREY

Harper North

HarperNorth
Windmill Green
24 Mount Street
Manchester M2 3NX

A division of
HarperCollins*Publishers*
1 London Bridge Street
London SE1 9GF

www.harpercollins.co.uk

HarperCollins*Publishers*
Macken House,
39/40 Mayor Street Upper,
Dublin 1, D01 C9W8, Ireland

First published by HarperCollins*Publishers* Ltd 2025
1

A catalogue record for this book is available from the British Library.

HB ISBN: 978-0-00-862443-9

Set in Adobe Caslon Pro by Amnet

Printed and bound in the UK using 100% Renewable Electricity by CPI Group (UK) Ltd

For DD
you gorgeous human

ORKNEY

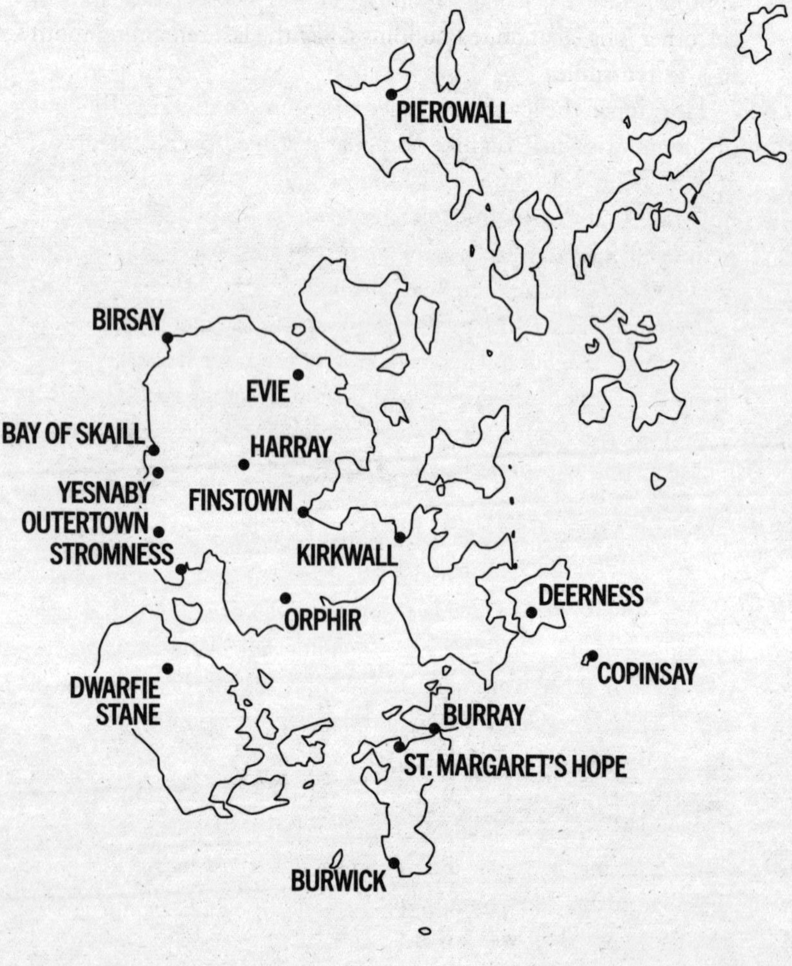
PIEROWALL
BIRSAY
EVIE
BAY OF SKAILL
HARRAY
YESNABY
FINSTOWN
OUTERTOWN
STROMNESS
KIRKWALL
ORPHIR
DEERNESS
COPINSAY
DWARFIE STANE
BURRAY
ST. MARGARET'S HOPE
BURWICK

Saturday, 21st June, 1997 - 12.07 a.m.

It was after midnight, but still light enough to see the farmhouse on the shore. Michael spotted it from the boat as they approached, a black mass looming above the jagged shapes of the other long-abandoned buildings, like the last remaining tooth in a rotten smile.

He gripped the icy railings, tried to suppress a shudder. Thought of his mum saying 'It's like someone's walked over your grave', and suddenly felt a wave of sadness, followed by a longing to hug her that he hadn't felt in years. It surprised him, and hammered home what he already knew but was trying not to admit: this was a huge fucking mistake.

A glance back at the others. Nobody else seemed to share his concern. He needed to get a grip, not let them see he was starting to panic. His chance to protest had come and gone an hour since, when they had been sat in Rabbie's chilly barn, getting blootered on bucky and weed and listening to 'What's The Story, Morning Glory?' on repeat. Not his choice; he would've agreed to anything not to have to hear 'She's Electric' for the fifth or sixth bloody time. But he told himself that, even if he had said anything then, he'd have been outvoted five to one. Rabbie, Jake, and the three girls all wanted to go. He'd have looked a right fanny. Plus, there was the look Alice was giving him with those big, beautiful hazel eyes of hers. He was seventeen now, not a bairn anymore. Probably the last of his pals to get laid, if their stories were true. It was honestly mortifying. And it was rare for Alice to get a night away from home; this was their first chance to spend some proper time together alone. So, when Rabbie, pished as fuck, had yelled they should steal his dad's boat, sail it to Copinsay and spend a night getting out of their tree on an uninhabited island, he'd whooped along with the others.

'Let's fucking do it!' he'd cried.

Might even have uttered: 'What's the worst that can happen?'

The rim of the northern horizon still glowed yellowy green. The sun was only briefly hiding below it; it would rise again in less than four hours, at the dawn of the year's longest day. High above the island, a dome of deep blue was light enough to conceal all but the brightest stars and a tiny sliver of moon. Rabbie cut the boat's engine and the vessel drifted silently towards the small wooden jetty that came off the beach. From the deck, Michael could see they were coming in too fast, and they clattered into the jetty with a sickening crack. Rabbie was a bloody liability and he couldn't sail for shit, even if he had been sober. Copinsay was less than an hour's sail from South Ronaldsay, but they never should've attempted it without checking the conditions first. Michael kept his mouth shut though. He didn't query how Rabbie's dad could afford such a vessel either, or why a supposed cattle farmer would even need one. Rabbie was more a friend of a friend, they hadn't known each other that long, but he already understood that, when it came to him and his family, it was best not to ask too many questions.

He hopped off the boat, hoping not to go straight through the remaining rickety planks that hadn't been stepped on in decades, shot a look at the hull for damage as he did, then he held out his hand for Alice. The pier swayed beneath his feet like a rope-bridge as Jake jumped down too. Jake quickly turned back to help Kelly off before Rabbie could, leaving Michael and Alice to help Isla. From the look on Isla's face, he realised that, if he had spoken up earlier, he might only have been outvoted four to two.

'Last one in the house has to fuck Isla Gunn.'

Rabbie's voice cut through the half-light, followed by a splash seconds later as the radge bastard launched himself into the water. The island rattled with the cries of seabirds, a black cloud of them launching into the luminescent sky at the sound of intruders.

'Prick,' Isla muttered. She dropped her head, her blonde fringe falling over her eyes as she fiddled with the silver bracelet on her tiny wrist. Rabbie took off down the narrow strip of sand that led to the bulk of the island. The sea was coming in either side of it. Kelly and Jake were ahead of him, walking towards the old farmhouse at the far end of the beach. Isla and Alice hung back while Michael checked the ropes, then checked them again. Coming here was bad enough; getting stuck here would be a nightmare.

'I wouldn't shag Rabbie Cleat if he was the last man on Earth,' Isla said.

'Don't compliment the silly wank,' said Alice. 'He's hardly a man. Especially not if what Sally McGregor says is true.'

The two girls laughed in that conspiratorial way that made Michael's balls shrink.

'First time you've cracked a smile all night,' Alice said, looping her arm over Isla's shoulder.

'Aye, well, the night's hardly going as planned, is it?' Isla nodded to the trio further up the beach.

'You and Jake? Fuck, is that why you agreed to come out tonight?'

'Well, I'm not here for that bawbag Rabbie, am I? And this one here's taken.'

Isla glanced at Michael, walking up the sand beside them in silence, and the two girls laughed again.

'Jake won't go for a girl like Kelly,' he said.

'Aye, that's right, you two are best pals, aren't you?' Isla replied.

Michael shrugged. 'We're pals, sure. I don't know about best pals.'

'Ah, come off it, the two of yous are always going around together at school. You're joined at the bloody hip.'

Michael felt his cheeks flush. He hoped in the half-light that the girls wouldn't see.

'Does he ever mention me?' Isla asked.

'You?' The word almost caught in his windpipe. Jake Drever talked about a lot of girls a lot of the time – it was fucking tedious, to be honest – but Michael didn't think he'd ever heard mention of Isla.

He couldn't be the one to extinguish the dim flame of hope that had lit in her eyes, though.

'I mean, yeah, he's spoken about you before. He likes you.'

The pale light caught the whites of Isla's eyes as they flicked between his. She turned to Alice. 'If he shags as well as he lies, you're in for a shite night as well.'

Michael felt blood heat his face again.

They caught up with the others. The beach split in two and ran either side of a triangular outcrop of land where the farmhouse had been built, along with a couple of other smaller houses. Steadings for the farm workers who had lived here when Copinsay was still a thriving community. Michael had heard the family that used to farm the land had thirteen children and there was even an old schoolhouse here somewhere. Metal cages covered most of the empty windows. Weathered signs implored them to keep out.

They didn't heed their warning.

Jake tried the front door of the farmhouse. This building at least was still intact, with glass in the windows and in remarkably good condition considering its last occupants had left over forty years ago. The wooden door was unlocked but stuck. Jake was about to put his shoulder to it when Rabbie steamed in from behind, beat him to it. The wood shattered and splintered as the door burst open. Rabbie went face first into the hallway floor, then exploded in a burst of that hyena-like laugh. Michael was standing behind the others. He watched as nervous chuckling spread through the group. It didn't reach him. One by one, they disappeared inside, leaving Michael standing alone, listening to the wind as it whistled between the buildings where the eerie half-light cast impenetrable shadows, and to the constant background sigh of the sea which seemed to wrap itself around him. Every now and then, a deep boom would rattle across the landscape, like cannon fire from a nearby battlefield. He realised it was the relentless march of the North Sea, pummelling the cliffs on the far side of the small island. It was strange being in a place where you knew there were no other people. He supposed this was the first time in his life that he had experienced it. His eyes were drawn to the black holes on the decaying steading opposite the farmhouse, and he tried to picture what it would've been like when people lived here. His imagination ran riot with visions of all the souls who had been and had now gone, and a shiver ripped through him again.

'Everything okay?'

Alice was hanging back in the doorway. She swept a strand of her auburn hair from her face.

He nodded. 'Just wishing I'd brought a jacket.'

Alice stepped closer. She smiled as she took his hands and wrapped them around her waist. 'You can cuddle up to me, that might help.'

When she kissed him, he felt a charge of electricity course across his skin, followed by movement in his trousers he hoped to God Alice wouldn't feel.

She began to giggle, her lips still pressed against his.

'Feels like you're warming up,' she whispered, and that only made things worse.

Fucking hell, this was incredible. He tried to clear his head, just be in the moment for once and enjoy it, but he was flooded with conflicting emotions. He wanted Alice so badly, he really did. But if that was the case, then why did he also feel the way he did about—

The sound of wood snapping inside the house, followed by Isla's shrill cry, split them apart.

In the living room, someone had put the battery-powered lantern from the barn on the window ledge. It flicked long spindly shadows across a sparsely furnished room where the air hung thick with damp under a claustrophobically low ceiling. There were curtains still half drawn across the windows, an armchair and a wooden rocking chair pushed close together, and in the corner of the room a table with three chairs. The fourth was in pieces at Rabbie's feet.

As Michael and Alice ran in, Jake picked up another of the chairs and swung it with all his might against the wall where it too exploded with a bone-crunching crack.

Isla screamed again, her hands over her ears. Kelly was laughing.

'The fuck are you playing at?' Alice yelled.

'It's bloody Baltic in here,' Jake said, picking up a third chair. 'We need firewood.'

'Are you being serious right now? This belonged to people. It was their furniture.'

'Aye, well I don't think they'll be coming back for it any time soon, do you?' Rabbie said, that God-awful laugh of his filling this hole of a room.

Michael flinched. Another belonging burst into pieces.

Rabbie picked up the final chair. Alice marched across the room, and grabbed his wrist as he was about to launch it at the wall where, in the pale blue light of the lantern, Michael could see discoloured patches where pictures had once hung. He wasn't sure what had happened – maybe her nails had dug into his skin – but Rabbie cried out, dropping the chair. Kelly howled again, but Michael knew this was no laughing matter. Anger flashed across Rabbie's face like accelerant catching fire.

Someone gasped as he slapped Alice, the sound of it like the crack of a whip. In the shock of it all, Michael stayed rooted to the spot. He should have reacted, but he didn't. Instead, it was Jake who leaped forward, grabbing Rabbie by the arm.

A chorus of yelled voices and the things she had brought into their life as a result followed. Another scream.

'The fuck are you doing, man?'

'Get your fucking hands off me!'

'Rabbie, stop!'

The ceiling seemed a foot lower. The electric light from the lantern was painfully bright.

When everyone calmed down, Jake stood between Rabbie and Alice, the three of them panting, Jake holding Rabbie back, Alice holding a hand to her cheek. Michael felt his throat close as Rabbie turned his gaze to him, the whites of his eyes gleaming in the blue light.

His lips curled into a sneer. 'You wanna come get your bitch, Wishy Washy. Put her back on her leash.'

He should've said something, he knew he should.

But he didn't.

Alice turned. She didn't look at Michael. She stormed past him, out of the room, without saying a word.

He followed, chasing the sound of her stamped footsteps up the uneven wooden stairs. He found her in the bedroom at the end of the landing, sitting on a bare mattress on an old iron frame. There was a window across from her, but the glow from the twilight sky was too weak to force its way through the salt-crusted glass. He could barely see Alice's face, but he could hear that she was crying.

The bedframe groaned as he sat beside her, but the mattress was still surprisingly firm.

He placed his hand on hers. She snatched it away.

'Why didn't you say anything?'

Michael sighed. 'I'm sorry.'

'Seriously, that's it? "I'm sorry"?'

'I … I don't know what you wanted me to do. It's his boat, we can't—'

'So, he can do what he wants? He can hit me because we need his boat to get home?'

'No, of course not, I just mean—'

'Save it, Wishy. You're all the fucking same.'

'Who are?'

A dim light swept through the room; the beam from the island lighthouse on the nearby clifftops. It caught on the tears on Alice's cheek as she looked towards the window. She wiped them away with her sleeve. 'Men. You're so full of talk, but the minute anyone actually needs you…'

Michael's mouth swung open to protest, but he had thought better of it, and so he decided against it. He hauled himself up off the hard mattress and walked over to the window, leaned his head against the abraded glass and looked out at the crumbling old buildings around them and the fields beyond. Four hours until sunrise was going to feel like forever. He wished he could go back to the fight, say something. No, fuck that, he wished he could go back to the barn, speak up then. Or maybe earlier in the night, when he'd first met up with Alice, when he could've decided to spend the night with her instead of calling in on Jake. The lighthouse blinked again, and as it did, Michael caught sight of something written on the wall along the edge of the window. He leaned in close. There were faint lines and marks etched in pencil on the peeling wallpaper.

It took him a moment to realise what it was.

'No way! Alice, come see this.'

She didn't move.

He turned back to the markings on the wall. Lines and letters, barely visible in the low light. S. Groat, '23. C. Groat, '27. Initials and surnames of the people who used to live here. Must've been the children who'd occupied this room.

'Someone's written on the wall here,' he said. 'It looks like they've been measuring how tall the bairns were growing. Jesus, I can't believe these are still—'

He stopped.

For a brief few seconds, he thought he'd imagined it. Something shifting in his peripheral vision through the window.

Then he saw it again.

'Alice.'

No sound.

'Alice, seriously, come—'

'Piss off and leave me alone.'

'There's someone outside.'

His voice was still barely above a whisper. This time, he heard the creak of the bedframe.

Seconds later he felt Alice's breath on his cheek. 'What?'

Michael didn't take his eyes off the window. Off the spot where he had last seen the dark shape disappear after flashing across the open space between the buildings.

'Stop fucking around, Mike.'

'I'm not, I swear on my mother's life I saw—'

There it was again. A person. No doubt in his mind.

Whoever it was, they ran from behind the derelict steading and into the old schoolhouse.

'There! Tell me you saw that!'

He turned to Alice, her face as pale as bone in the low light. She said nothing, but the way the blood had drained from her skin spoke for her. He hadn't imagined it.

They weren't the only people on the island.

THURSDAY, 5TH JUNE. PRESENT DAY.

1

It was the silence that unsettled him. It seemed unnatural, even out here, like the hills themselves were holding their breath.

DI Fergus Muir stepped away from the gaggle of police vehicles blocking the single-track road to Rackwick and stood at the edge of the tarmac, his hand to his brow, screening out the early morning sun so he could see the large boulder in the distance across the lush moorland. There was no wind, that was the issue. The sea was only a mile or two away in either direction, but the crisp June air seemed remarkably still. Even with the melee of men and women in uniform, buzzing around the road and the path out to the Dwarfie Stane like the insects among the heather, there was a discernible hush over the valley. Like the peace here was so thick even a crime scene couldn't penetrate it. It made Fergus wonder if that was what had brought the man out here to die.

'You on the lookout for trowies, aye?'

Fergus smiled at the sound of the approaching voice. He didn't need to turn to face them to know who it was. If a silence could ever be shattered, PC Jim Brannigan was the man to do it.

'It's a bit bright the day,' he said. 'Don't think I'll have any luck.'

It was still early, a little after eight, but the sun had long since risen above the cliffs on the far side of the valley. It wasn't yet strong enough, however, to burn off the effects of a poor night's sleep. The call had come a little over two hours ago and Fergus had jolted awake, surprised at having nodded off at all. Sleep had still eluded him a few hours earlier, when the rain had started and the first shafts of sallow daylight had begun to creep between the curtains, the pain in his stomach gnawing at him again. He had glanced at the bedside table, seen the near-spent blister pack of aspirin and the empty glass and decided this time he would swallow two of the powdery tablets dry rather than climb out of bed and fetch water.

Now, he ran his hand through his thatch of slate-grey hair as he kept his gaze on the huge slab of sandstone a few hundred metres away. To anyone unfamiliar with this lonely part of Orkney, the massive rock would look much like any other dumped along the vast valley floor by the glacier that had carved out these looming hills and sombre cliff faces several millennia ago. But this rock was different, special. Even before the events of this morning.

'Maybe that's who's to blame for all this kerfuffle,' Jim said, coming to stand alongside him. 'A trowie, or a giant, perhaps. There's folk living not far from here who'd probably believe that, ye ken.'

Fergus grinned, glanced at his colleague. Jim flicked away a strand of the unkempt grey hair that was falling onto his face from under his hat, and looked at Fergus with weary eyes. Possibly the result of a long night shift made longer by an unexpected trip to Hoy, but Fergus knew better. PC Jim Brannigan always looked like shite warmed up and left out to cool off. But he was a stalwart of the Orkney police, had been around as long as Fergus. Much longer, in fact. Fergus swore Jim had been an old man back when he'd joined the force over a quarter of a century ago now. He was never going to be the man picked to be the face of one of Police Scotland's recruitment drives, and he was a peedie work-shy bastard, no doubt about that, but Fergus couldn't help but like him.

'You were first on scene, I take it?' Fergus asked.

'For my sins. Want the run-down yet, or do you need a minute longer with your thoughts?'

'Let me have it.'

Jim began to fill him in on what they knew so far. A 999 call had been placed a little after 6 a.m. by tourists who had found a man lying unresponsive inside the Dwarfie Stane, a Neolithic tomb cut into a giant slab of sandstone hollowed out over six thousand years ago by nothing more than stone tools and bloody-minded determination.

'They'd camped out here overnight,' Jim said, nodding towards the small parking area off to the side of the road twenty metres away. There was a green VW Transporter campervan with a couple in their late thirties standing beside it, looking rather shellshocked amidst the fleet of police vehicles now surrounding their van. 'They wanted to be the first ones out there at the tomb, apparently, get the place to themselves. Looks like they didna manage it.'

'Who came out from the hospital?'

'Irishman by the name of Keogh. I'd not come across him afore now.'

Fergus shook his head. He didn't know the doctor either. He thought he'd have worked with them all by now.

'The doc had pronounced him dead by the time we got here.'

He looked up the valley. There was no sign of the air ambulance that would've been dispatched. Not the kind of thing you'd miss.

Jim read his mind. 'There was nothing else for them to do here, and they had to get the chopper away back to base, in case it was needed elsewhere. They're sending a regular ambulance over for the auld fella. It's not been requested just yet. We knew you'd want to be taking a look first.'

'Any clue who he is?'

'I've not seen him. You didn't think I'd be trekking all the way up there at my age, did you?' Jim nodded towards the tomb. 'I sent Kate up. She's secured it all off. She's still up there now, keeping watch. Best I can tell you is our man's a white male, looks to be maybe late fifties. Doc said from the colour of him he'd likely been dead only a few hours by the time the couple found him.'

'Any ID on him?'

'We've not checked. Kate's by the book. She'll not touch him or let anybody else near him till you give the say so.'

Fergus nodded. He knew PC Kate Flynn well, was glad she was in charge of managing the inner cordon instead of Jim. 'You thinking this is a big fuss over nothing?'

Jim shrugged. 'Ah well, you ken me well enough, Fergie boy. Ever the pragmatist.'

Fergus smiled to himself. 'Lazy shite' was the term more commonly associated with Jim down the station.

'The doc couldn't say for certain what had done him in solely by looking at him, but he's thinking natural causes,' Jim said. 'There's no obvious cuts or bruises, not a single suggestion of foul play. He said he looks like he climbed inside that stone for a nap and never woke up.'

Fergus looked back towards the car park. The couple were still standing by their van. 'You'll have spoken to those two already?'

'I have indeed. An English couple up here on their jollies. The Bothamleys. Lorna and Craig. Lovely people. Lorna there's a nurse. She called it in.'

'You said they slept here last night. Did they not hear or see anything?'

'They say not.'

'Are they up to a chat with me, do you think?'

'I should think so. The wifey especially. The doc checked them both over afore he left, said there was no sign they were in shock. We kept them here for you.'

Fergus glanced again across the valley, beautiful in the soft morning light. Behind them, the green slopes of Orkney's highest peak rose steeply into a blue sky with barely a blemish while, across the moorland, a wall of granite cliffs, the Dwarfie Hamars, presented a dramatic backdrop to the Stane itself. A chill lingered, the bright June sunshine yet to take the damp out of the air from last night's rain, and the slight breeze now coming up off the Hoy Sound carried a bite with it. A keen reminder of how far north they were.

'Whoever he is, he's an awfully long way from home,' Jim said, reading Fergus's mind again. 'We must be three mile from Rackwick, a good two mile afore you reach any houses going the other way. And you'll have spotted there's no other vehicles in that car park. It's a fair ways to be walking in the middle of the night.'

'You don't find that odd?'

'You ken well enough, odd's our bread and butter. Doesn't mean it's anything suspicious. Maybe the auld fella had dementia and was out here wandering. I've seen that afore now.'

It was a fair point. Fergus had too. They'd soon know if that was a possibility once they found out who he was.

'Did this Dr Keogh tell you anything else?'

Jim shook his head. 'Wasn't a lot he could say. I suppose we won't know for certain until we get the postmortem.'

'I take it you told him to come by the station later and give a formal statement?'

'I did, aye,' Jim replied. 'He seemed quite excited. Said he'd only been in Orkney a couple of weeks, thought he was coming here to be put out to pasture. His missus talked him into it. Open spaces, beaches. A slice of the quiet life and all that.'

Beyond Jim, he saw he was being gestured to by DS Eilidh Murray. She had her phone to her ear and did not look happy.

A memory tweaked the corners of Fergus's lips into a smile. He laid a hand on his colleague's shoulder as he walked past him. 'You know, Jim, I've heard that somewhere afore now.'

2

Eilidh was standing by the bonnet of Fergus's black Volkswagen Passat, phone to her ear, telling some poor unfortunate soul on the other end they were '...clearly taking the piss.'

Fergus grinned as he approached from the rear of the car, not wanting to disturb her while she was in full flow. It couldn't have been more than three months since Eilidh had arrived in Kirkwall, having been working previously in Perth, and she was probably the first new recruit to have joined the Orkney CID in years. The woman was a bloody force of nature. Exactly what the stale team needed.

She put her phone away as Fergus neared. 'Forensic services. They're claiming it'll be two to three hours before a pathologist can get here.'

'It's a fair trip from Aberdeen, especially with the additional ferry thrown in to get across from Mainland. Then the drive over from Lyness. I'd be surprised if it's less than four.'

'Jesus, how do you get anything done here?'

'We've managed okay until now.'

Eilidh raised an eyebrow. 'That's not strictly true, is it?' She nodded over to the Bothamleys, changed the subject. 'Did you speak to them?'

'Not yet, boss.'

Eilidh grinned. 'I should have your job. You know that, right?'

'You're welcome to it. Soon as I retire.'

'I'll not have long to wait then. Shall we?'

'After you, ma'am.' Fergus kept a straight face as he raised an arm, let Eilidh lead the way.

The Bothamleys' VW van was the only civilian vehicle in the parking area, as Jim had noted. The surface was tarmac, same as the road, and was completely wet from the rain overnight; there were no dry patches, where any other vehicles might have been parked, except for under the Bothamleys' van. Eilidh led the introductions, showing the couple her warrant card. Fergus then did the same. He was happy to allow his colleague to take the reins on this one. His mind drifted easily to that retirement Eilidh had mentioned; he'd been counting down the days for months now and was only another half a year away. He didn't yet know what he planned to do with his free time, but he was sure he'd find something to keep him busy.

The Bothamleys seemed happy enough to answer questions a second time. They had already given a statement to Jim, but Fergus knew Eilidh would want to hear it for herself. She could then compare what she was told to the statement they had first given. It was a tactic Fergus had employed himself before now. Not that there was any reason to distrust the couple or to suspect them of anything. Fergus wasn't even sure yet if there was anything to suspect them of; it sounded like Dr Keogh had been pretty clear that there were no obvious signs of foul play.

'We'd camped here overnight,' Lorna was saying. 'We thought this place would get busy during the day so we wanted to be the first ones out here to visit the tomb this morning, but it looks like someone beat us to it, eh?'

She laughed, the dark humour of someone who worked around death and saw it every day. Her husband gave her a look as if to say 'Are you fucking kidding?' Fergus couldn't help but smile.

'Did you see or hear anyone else during the night?' Eilidh asked.

'No. No one. I'm not even sure any other cars came past on the road,' Lorna replied.

'What time did you turn in?'

'We pulled the blinds down at about … what time was it, Craig?' she asked her husband, who still looked pale.

'Eleven thirty.'

'It was still light,' Lorna added.

'And had anyone come and gone before then?' Eilidh asked.

'No. We had the place to ourselves.'

'Did you walk over to the tomb last night?' Fergus asked. 'Before turning in?'

Lorna explained how they had arrived at the car park quite late, having spent the evening hiking from Rackwick up across the clifftops to see the Old Man of Hoy at sunset. 'But we didn't realise how late sunset would be, so we gave up and came back. Plus, it had gone cloudy. Didn't seem worth sticking around up there. Bloody windy too. Then, by the time we parked up here, we were shattered and thought we'd save it till morning.'

'So, what time did you pull up here?' Eilidh asked.

Lorna looked to Craig again. 'It wasn't long before we closed the blinds. Maybe eleven-ish.'

Fergus made a mental note to check what time the last tour guides had come by here. That would give them a loose window.

Eilidh checked the Bothamleys had given the first officer on scene details of where they would be staying next and when they would be returning to England, then she thanked them for their time.

'There is one other thing,' Lorna said. She looked again at her husband. 'There was that car as we got here, wasn't there?'

'The one ahead of us along the road?' Craig replied.

'Yeah, it wasn't in the car park, it was driving away as we arrived. But slowly, like it might've just pulled out.'

'Can you describe it?'

'It was hard to tell in the twilight, but it was a light colour. Could've been white. Or silver,' Lorna said. She looked at Craig. 'It was definitely a newer model. One of those electric ones your cousin's got. You could tell from the funny lights across the back that look like a staple.'

'A Polestar,' Craig added. 'Yeah, it could've been.'

Fergus glanced at Eilidh, who was looking at him. He'd never bloody heard of a Polestar, but it had to be easier to track down than a Fiesta or a Corsa, even without a registration plate. It was only a crumb, but it was something.

As they left the Bothamleys and walked back over to Fergus's car, Eilidh unclipped her phone from her belt. 'Okay, so I'll send a couple of uniforms out looking for a light-coloured Polestar. We should get someone on to the ferries too, see if any have been booked on any crossings. It's either got to be a local or someone travelling in, and no boats will have left between last night and now, so they'll still be on this island somewhere. If this thing's an EV, it'll be worth finding out where the charge points are too. If we can trace who was driving, we can get their story, maybe narrow down our window of when this guy crawled inside that tomb for one last nap. Is there anywhere around here where it might've been picked up on CCTV? I'm not even going to ask about ANPR.'

She noticed Fergus's grin.

'Sorry, want me to pretend I don't know what I'm doing and let you tell me what's next?'

'You seem excited.'

'Aren't you? Aren't your spidey senses telling you this is all a bit off?'

'My what?'

'You're such a grandad. Like a sixth sense, telling you something isn't right. Like, where has he come from? Why was he here, alone, late at night, with no vehicle? Where's the closest thing to civilisation from here?'

'It would have to be Rackwick at the end of the road here. Or Linksness coming the other way. I'd say that's more likely.' Something occurred to him then. 'There's a hostel there, not far from where the foot passenger ferry docks—'

That pain that had been growing more frequent and more violent these past few weeks bit again, cutting his words short. Instinctively his hand went to his stomach.

'What's wrong?' Eilidh asked.

'Nothing. My breakfast isn't agreeing with me.'

'I didn't think breakfast was your thing.'

'It isn't, for this very reason. So, what's your take on involving CSI, ma'am?'

Eilidh would have spotted the deliberate change of subject and the weak joke, Fergus was in no doubt, but she didn't say anything. She puffed out her cheeks, surveyed the valley. 'The rain last night will have washed anything away. That's if there even is anything out here to find. We've nothing yet to suggest foul play.'

'Other than your spider senses.'

'Spid-ey.'

Fergus opened his car boot, took out two sets of forensic paper overalls. 'Aye, well, whatever they're called,' he said, handing a pair to Eilidh. 'Let's see if they're on to anything.'

They pulled on the forensic suits, covering their clothes and shoes, and set off towards the boggy path between the road and the Dwarfie Stane in the middle of the valley.

Before they reached it, Fergus stopped.

Eilidh turned. 'What is it?'

'You go on ahead.'

'Problem?'

Fergus shook his head as he headed back to his car. 'Just need to fetch something. I'll catch you up.'

'The shape you're in, I doubt it.'

'Thin ice, Murray.'

He had to smile when she winked at him before turning and carrying on towards the giant sandstone boulder in the distance.

Fergus opened the passenger side door of his car and, quickly checking nobody was looking, took out the burner phone he kept in the glovebox.

He fired off a hastily written message.

Change of plan…

3

She was late. As usual.

Chief Inspector Magnus Robertson, the Area Commander of the Orkney Police, was already in full flow by the time Freya Sinclair pulled into the large car park at Evie Primary School. There wasn't time to sit and gather herself, or to plan the wording of the questions she wanted to ask. She would have to do that while he spoke. She wasn't intending to listen to whatever shite he had to say before she asked her question anyway.

Magnus was trying to look casual, with his uniform jacket and hat removed and the sleeves of his crisp white shirt rolled up to the elbows. He was standing next to a police car, a woman wearing a smart suit and a painted-on smile positioned beside him. Freya guessed she was the school headteacher. They were faced by a group that outnumbered them only by one. She recognised Iain MacKay from BBC Radio Orkney, and there was a photographer eagerly snapping shots from various angles as the Chief Inspector spoke, his back to the main road and the lush green fields rolling down to the Eynhallow Sound in the distance. They must've been someone from Police Scotland, getting images for the media team. Her heart sank at the sight of the third member of the small huddle – Gill Irvine. Freya had known she would be here, but she had hoped there might have been more people present so she could hide.

Gill scowled at Freya as she picked her way between the small children in hi-vis vests, who were wobbling round and round the car park on bicycles. She did her best not to return Gill's stare as she joined the others. The point of this peedie get together was to launch a new local policing initiative to try and improve road safety, hence the location next to the A road, and the gaggle of small humans in crash helmets going through the motions of a cycling proficiency class.

'In these islands, we police by consent,' Magnus was saying as Freya joined the group. 'We're not only here for the community, we're a part of it ourselves.'

Freya fought hard not to roll her eyes. Magnus Robertson spoke solely in soundbites; she'd heard nothing but this kind of guff out of him and the Police Scotland media team for the past few months. They'd been on a PR offensive since the Professional Standards Division had launched an investigation into the Orkney Area Command in the spring. Policing by consent and Part of the community were two of the most common lines to get rolled out. Every press conference or press release now felt like a game of Bullshit Bingo.

'Keeping our loved ones safe is more than just a job to us,' Magnus carried on. Freya bit back the urge to cry out House! 'And that's why today, as part of our long-term road safety strategy, I'm immensely proud to be launching our Safer Roads, Stronger Communities programme – a multi-faceted campaign combining community-led initiatives with education and awareness, as well as collaboration with our officers, who'll be a more visible presence on our roads over the coming weeks and months.'

Meaning they'll be out of the station and away from the PSD detectives, Freya thought. Very convenient.

The officers themselves were sure to be thrilled about it, too. She remembered her dad referring to traffic cops as 'Black Rats' when she was a bairn. It had been such a surreal image, it had always stayed with her.

'It's because nobody's safe from them, not even the rest of us cops,' he'd explained to her with a playful grin. 'So that's why we call them black rats, because they eat their own.'

The sound of a horn blaring startled the group, and caused a number of the children taking the staged cycling proficiency class to scream. Everyone turned to see a black BMW on the wrong side of the main road, overtaking a tractor just as a campervan had started to pull out of the junction from the lane leading down to the Broch of Gurness. It looked like the campervan had braked, sounded the horn. The car swerved back in with only inches to spare before colliding with it. It could've been nasty.

Magnus turned back to the group. 'Right on cue, as if to prove how important this is,' he said with a shake of his head. 'Anyone would think we'd planned that.'

There was muted polite laughter from the handful of people present, but not from Freya. She wouldn't have been surprised at all if he had staged such a stunt.

The Chief Inspector finally opened things up for questions, and Gill Irvine dived in first.

'Chief Inspector Robertson, Gill Irvine from *The Orcadian*,' she began, announcing her full name and job, even though he knew full well who she was. 'Could you assure my readers this scheme of yours won't be taking police away from the essential duty of keeping folk in these islands safe from crime?'

Gill's question, as always, came across as aggressive and combative, but Magnus didn't get rattled. He never did. 'I can assure everyone that this programme, which belongs to the whole community, is perhaps one of the most important things my officers can do to keep everyone in these islands safe. Orkney, sadly, has one of the highest rates of deaths per miles driven in all of Scotland, a figure which none of us are proud of, but which all of us can actively work to change.'

Iain asked a question next, something to do with what regular folk could do to play their part in the programme, but Freya had stopped listening. She was distracted by the muted sound of her phone buzzing. She surreptitiously pulled it out slightly from her coat pocket, pressed the cracked glass to bring the screen to life. Over the photograph of Tom and their two dogs, Luna and Thorfinn, there was a text from a mobile number with no name assigned to it, but she knew it belonged to Fergus. Without opening it, all she could read were the few words in the preview:

Change of plan, something's come up. Can't meet as . . .

She felt a weight dragging in the pit of her stomach, but couldn't say why.

'And you, Freya?'

She looked up. Magnus Robertson and everyone else was looking at her.

'I assume if *The Orcadian* has felt this event is important enough to send along two of its reporters, you'll want to ask a question,' he said with a fake smile.

Freya put her phone back in her pocket, fought the urge to reach for the piercings in her ear, counted. and pinch them in order. She'd been distracted, hadn't planned the wording of her question at all, and hated being put on the spot. She could feel everyone's eyes on her, like grubby fingers on her skin.

'I was hoping to get a comment from you about the death of Trevor Scott.'

Did Magnus's right eye twitch slightly, or did she imagine it?

The Chief Inspector seemed to take a millisecond or two longer to respond than he usually did, but he was soon back on form. 'The tragic death of sergeant Scott has saddened me greatly, as it saddened everyone who knew him and everyone associated with policing in these islands. I worked with him for a number of years.' He paused, swallowed. 'He was a good man.'

Freya genuinely couldn't tell if that was heartfelt or simply more good acting.

'Had detectives from PSD been talking to Trevor before he took—'

'Mrs Sinclair, I don't think now is the moment to be drawing speculative connections between Trevor's tragic passing and ongoing investigations that are yet to reach any conclusions.'

Freya felt her cheeks burn as red as her hair. 'I'm not, I'm simply asking if anyone from Professional Standards had spoken to him before he died. It seems like he would be someone who could help their investigation. He was with the force a long time before he retired, he'd worked under Allan Tait—'

'As did I, and a lot of folk besides, including your own father,' Magnus cut in again.

'Nobody, least of all I, will try and defend our former chief inspector, but there will be a time and a place to talk about the

PSD investigation, and it isn't here. Today is all about the work we're doing with our partners in the community to keep people from harm. And with that in mind, I think it's time we hear from Mrs Wilson about what she and her colleagues have been doing to teach pupils about staying safe out on the roads.'

'Thank you, Chief Inspector Robertson . . .'

The headteacher launched into her prepared speech. Freya felt her hands balling into fists. She spotted the look Gill was giving her out of the corner of her eye, decided it was time to leave. The last thing she needed was Orkney's self-appointed senior reporter having a pop at her as well.

She walked back to her car while the others stayed behind to listen to what Mrs Wilson had to say. As she reached the turquoise Hyundai, she glanced back at the small gathering outside the school, just caught the glare Magnus was giving her before he saw her looking over and turned away.

So much for him never getting rattled.

4

Freya killed the engine and sat back in the driver's seat, listened to the occasional low rumble of vans and lorries going past on the main road on the other side of the building. She needed to get inside, but her limbs weren't listening; her body and brain had both decided to take a beat before braving the newsroom. She sat in her car in her parking space, that wasn't her space at all because none were assigned, it was simply the best one because other cars usually shielded it from view. That meant anyone coming or going from *The Orcadian* would likely not see her or come over and try and talk to her. It was also the furthest from the door, which meant it was often free, so she could park in the same place every time. And it had grass on one side of it, so she halved her risk of some idiot parking too close beside her.

She closed her eyes and tried to process the morning so far, but she knew it was pointless. She felt nothing besides the familiar tightness in her chest she couldn't name. Anxiety? Guilt? She doubted that as she had nothing to feel guilty about. She took her phone from her coat pocket, read the message from Fergus again: 'Change of plan, something's come up. Can't meet as planned, will txt u later.' The meaning of the words sank in slowly, like sediment settling in water. It did nothing to ease that knot in her chest. If anything, it only made it worse, but she wasn't sure why. All this meant was her day wasn't going to be exactly as she'd planned it, but she would still catch up with Fergus at some point, as they had regularly done for the past couple of months. It was no big deal, other people didn't get so wound up about such insignificant things, so why did she? What she should have been feeling was curiosity about why Fergus needed to cancel their catch-up this lunchtime. Surely it meant something had happened at his work, something that needed the attention of a detective inspector. There was a story there and her journalistic instinct should've been kicking into hyperdrive, but the truth was she couldn't have cared less. She hadn't felt the urge to chase a story in months. If she should be bothered about anything, it was that she really wasn't fussed if she never felt that urge again.

Her phone buzzed in her hand as she stared through it, making her jump. A text from her boss.

Care to join us this side of Christmas?

Freya looked up. Kristin was watching her from her small office window.

She was going to need a new parking space.

Kristin was leaning against the frame of her office door when Freya walked into the newsroom.

'Freya, a word.'

There was no smile, no use of her preferred pet name, chick.

Freya glanced at the large desk in the middle of room as she walked past, around which the small team that made up *The Orcadian* sat. Keith hid his face behind a mug of steaming coffee, stared into his laptop, wanting no part in whatever was going on around him. Sophie bit her lip, looked concerned. She tried to give her colleague a reassuring thumbs up, but didn't quite pull it off.

'Everything okay?' Freya asked as she stepped inside and closed the door behind her. It made the small space even more claustrophobic.

Kristin motioned for her to sit in the chair across her desk. 'Not really.'

Freya squirmed in her seat, unable to get comfortable. Every time she sat in the editor's office, she felt like a school kid called in to see the headmistress. The feeling had been even worse of late. She had always misread tone and body language and, in the absence of being able to tell how people were feeling without them telling her directly, she often simply assumed everyone was mad at her. It was something she was trying to get better at. But there was no mistaking her boss was pissed off now, and seemed to have been for months. She noticed Kristin's desk had become more cluttered since the last time she had been in here – copies of other local papers and a growing collection of mugs from the equally cramped kitchen next door were spread between her laptop and the framed photos of her two teenaged children. Freya knew Kristin had been under increased pressure of late due to the sale of the paper by its late owner's family. Alistair Sutherland's widow and adult children had inherited it and wanted nothing to do with it. They saw it as part of Alistair's legacy and, as such, wanted to wash their hands clean of it. They had abandoned all their properties and businesses in Orkney within weeks of the news breaking that Alistair had been involved in a grooming ring, and they were desperately seeking buyers. Unfortunately, none had yet come forward for the paper. The only thing keeping it afloat was the fact it wasn't losing the Sutherlands any money.

Yet.

'Where have you been?' Kristin asked.

'Magnus Robertson was doing a press event at Evie, I was there.'

'It would've been nice for you to tell me.'

'I did.'

That came out more defensive than Freya had intended, but she was sure she had mentioned it. Though there was every chance she had forgot.

'You didn't, Freya. Because if you had, I'd have told you Gill was going. What was the point of both of you being there?'

'I wanted to get a line from him for the Trevor Scott piece.'

'And you couldn't have asked Gill to do it?'

She could have, she supposed, but she didn't want to. She didn't trust her to do it. She knew it was silly for them both to go, but she needed to do it.

Freya said nothing, and

Kristin released a slow puff of air. Her foundation couldn't disguise the bags under her eyes; she looked several years older than the woman Freya had first met six months ago.

"It doesn't matter now. That's not even what I wanted to talk to you about,' Kristin said. We've had a complaint about you.'

'Me?'

'Apparently, you "accosted" a member of the board of NHS Orkney out with The Balfour the other day. His words not mine.'

The strip lights in the ceiling clicked and hummed. Freya's mind raced. 'Are you talking about James Cooper?'

'So, you're not denying it?'

'I didn't accost him, I asked him a question. That's my job, isn't it? And it was a public event, I had every right to be there.'

She caught the sound of her tone again and there was no mistaking that either. She still sounded overly defensive, guilty. She didn't mean to.

'So, this is for a story?'

Freya blinked. 'Yes.'

'Then why is this the first I'm hearing about it?'

'Because I ... It's something new. I was going to mention it this morning at the meeting.'

Kirstin pinched the bridge of her nose. 'Freya, have I or have I not shown you by now that I'll have your back?'

'Aye, of course.'

'Everything you've done on the Ola and Liam case, all the stuff around what's going on over at the police station, the Trevor Scott story – it's not the kind of clickbait shite that's going to appeal to any new owners, but it is the kind of thing we should be reporting on, so I'm backing you. But you have to involve me, right from the start. You can't be running off on your own again.'

'I'm not, I'm...'

She stopped, uncertain of what to say next, because running off on her own was exactly what she was doing. And Kristin was right, she had been supported this whole time while she had been reporting on the fallout of what had happened six months ago. The previous chief inspector of the Orkney Area Command, Allan Tait, had been exposed as a key player in a grooming gang that had organised sex parties with underage girls, parties which were attended by the newspaper's former owner. That had put the paper in a very dicey position, but Freya had been instrumental in bringing the truth to light and, after some time off to recover, had continued to tell the stories of women who had been victims all those years ago, one of whom was Kristin herself. Due to Tait's involvement, Police Scotland's Professional Standards Division had been given the go-ahead to investigate historical and possible ongoing corruption within the area command, and Freya and Kristin had made sure any developments were thoroughly and properly reported, even though it hadn't been without consequence. The usual trickle of information that came from cops when they needed something out in the public domain had stopped, everything coming formally now through Police Scotland's press office, hundreds of miles away to the south. It had certainly made life harder for them, at precisely the time when they needed things to be easy.

Freya knew she owed Kristin a debt of gratitude. She knew she should involve her in whatever she was working on. But she couldn't tell her why she'd been trying to talk to James Cooper, because the truth was it had nothing to do with a story.

Kristin must've grown bored of waiting for Freya to say something, because she said, 'It's this simple: if you don't let me know what's happening, I'll have to uphold the complaint and keep you away from him. This is serious. He's threatening to go to the police.'

'And report me for what?'

'Stalking.'

'For it to be stalking, he'd have to prove fixation and obsession, which he can't. It's harassment at best.'

The face Kristin pulled made Freya shudder. It was the same look her mother always used to give her as a kid. 'You always have an answer for everything, don't you, little missy?' she'd tell her. 'One day it's going to get you into trouble.'

'That's not any better,' Kristin said. 'You realise that, right?'

Actually, harassment's a lesser charge, and as such carries a lighter sentence, so technically it is better than being charged with stalking.

Freya had opened her mouth to say that, but she decided to heed her mother's advice for once.

'As soon as it becomes something, I'll let you know,' Freya conceded.

'And in the meantime, you'll back off.'

Freya wasn't sure if it was a question or a command. She nodded.

'What time's your interview with Angus Scott?' Kristin asked, changing the subject.

'Half eleven, in Stromness,' Freya replied. 'I'll have to set off straight after the meeting.'

Her boss nodded. 'Well, hope it goes well.'

Freya felt that twisting sensation in her stomach again. It happened any time Kristin was upset with her. Or whenever anyone was, for that matter. Yet another thing she needed to work on.

'I might have something else.' She blurted that out, started the sentence without knowing where it was going. She paused a moment to think.

'Is it something you care to share?'

'Aye, I was … … I was meant to meet Fergus Muir later today, but he cancelled on me and said something had come up.'

'A work something?'

'I reckon it would've been, for him to know he was going to be busy all day. I just don't know what yet. But I'll make sure we're the first to know.'

A chick was perhaps too much to ask for, but she'd hoped that would at least earn her a smile.

It didn't. Simply another nod.

'Glad to hear it,' Kristin said. 'Close the door on your way out.'

5

'You took your time.'

Eilidh was standing at the inner cordon, at the boundary of the plateau on which the Dwarfie Stane sat. PC Kate Flynn was beside her inside the blue and white tape, clipboard in hand, blonde hair in a tight bun beneath her police hat, watching Fergus approach. In her early twenties, Kate had only been on the force a matter of eighteen months, but she'd made great strides in that time. She was aiming to climb the ladder and didn't keep her intentions a secret, which rubbed the wrong way with some of the auld guard, but Fergus admired it. Not that it had ever been his approach – he'd ascended to the rank of detective inspector more from a lack of ambition than anything else. He'd lived in Orkney all his life, had never given any more than a passing thought to moving elsewhere, so when those above him had either retired or passed away, the job had fallen to him. He'd worked with Kate often enough now to know he had a lot of time for her. Though there weren't the numbers for cops to always work in twos, whenever she did get paired up with someone, it always seemed to be with Jim, possibly because he was technically the most experienced officer on the force in terms of number of years worked. Fergus had once offered Kate the sage advice that she should closely observe everything PC Brannigan did, then do the exact opposite. It appeared to be working out well for her.

The two women were framed by the dramatic backdrop of the dark cliffs behind them and the blue sky above. On a morning like this, there were few places more breathtaking in all of Orkney, but in the simmer dim – the eerie half-light of the summer nights this far north – he could imagine it would be a foreboding spot. The landscape would take on a life of its own then, the light playing tricks on you. There was a reason tales of dwarves and giants abounded here.

Coupled with that, the route to reach the tomb had not been easy. The path was uneven and climbed steadily, and last night's rain had made the track boggy, adding to the challenge. Fergus told himself in drier conditions he'd manage this just fine, but more than once on the short hike he'd had to stop, each time turning to look down the valley towards the glittering sea in the distance and try discreetly to catch his breath.

'Out of puff?' Eilidh asked as Fergus ducked under the tape.

'I was admiring the view.'

'By the view, you'd better not mean my arse.'

'You're not my type, Murray.'

'And young enough to be your granddaughter.'

She laughed and turned away while Kate handed him the clipboard to sign the scene log. She smiled uneasily at the back-and-forth between the two detectives.

'Have you had a look around here?' Fergus asked.

'I have, sir, aye. I've had the body cam on and recording since we got here too, but there's nothing of note.' She pointed behind Fergus, to the northwest corner of the stone. 'There's a small opening under the rock at the far side there. I shone my torch in but couldn't see anything that might've been discarded. No drug paraphernalia et cetera. There are footprints all over, but there's no telling when they're from. I've marked out my route on here in any case.'

She handed Fergus another piece of paper with a hand-drawn map of the scene, dotted with small Xs.

'I've established a common approach path,' she said, pointing at a line drawn on the paper from the cordon to the tomb entrance. 'It all looks pretty innocuous, but I didn't know if you'd be wanting to call in forensic services.'

'Thanks, Kate,' Fergus said with a smile. 'We'll see what the boss decides.'

Eilidh was crouched down at the small passage carved into the solid boulder, peering inside. Fergus joined her. The tomb wasn't deep. Enough light crept in from outside to make out the dark hair of a man lying on his side, his face to the entrance, eyes closed. His head was resting on a ridge inside the chamber, like it was a pillow. Like he'd crawled inside to take one last, very long nap.

He was pale to the point of appearing blue, his skin translucent, almost marble-like, but there was nothing in his expression that suggested he had died in pain.

Eilidh was snapping on a pair of blue nitrile gloves. 'You okay with me taking a closer look?'

'I'm amazed you asked for permission.'

'Is that a yes?'

'Be my guest.'

Eilidh got on her hands and knees to crawl inside. The tomb was carved inside a giant slab of long, flat sandstone. Another sandstone block, far too heavy for a single soul to lift, lay just in front of the entrance. This had once sealed the opening to the tomb but had been removed at some point in the last five hundred years for reasons and by means unknown. Fergus leaned against it, tried to discreetly rest a hand on his aching stomach, and peered inside. Past Eilidh, he could see the man was lying with one hand draped over his stomach too. He was wearing dark trousers and a white shirt with a light brown flannel coat over the top. It wasn't too different from what Fergus was wearing under his white forensic overalls. He looked more like he was dressed for a shift in an office than taking a night hike.

Fergus looked around at the ground outside. There were several footprints in the muddy ground, as Kate had said, but so many people visited this site every day it would be impossible to use any as evidence. Instead, he looked for any signs of a struggle – scuff marks in the mud, scraps of material pulled off clothing, spots of blood. Failing that, there might be used needles, empty packets of pills.

Yet again, as Kate had said, there was nothing.

'How do his shoes look?'

'Sorry?' Eilidh's voice carried a slight echo.

'His shoes? Are they muddy? Scuffed?'

'Not really. What time did the rain start last night?'

'Around two-ish.' He realised the only reason he knew that was because he had been lying awake, unable to sleep. His colleague was a good detective, she'd pick up on that. 'I got up to pee,' he added quickly.

Fergus was expecting another quip about his age, but none came.

'He's bone dry,' Eilidh said. 'Hair as well as clothing.'

Fergus nodded, though Eilidh couldn't see. The inside of that tomb was cold and damp at any time of year, and the temperature last night had dropped into single figures as the rain had set in. The fact it was early June didn't mean anything other than it barely got dark. The shifting of the seasons in Orkney was marked more by the ebb and flow of the light than any significant change in the temperature. If he had been soaked by the rain when he had crawled in there, he would still be wet now.

'That gives us a window,' Eilidh's disembodied voice said from inside the tomb. 'Unless whoever was in that EV killed him and dumped him here, he crawled in sometime between eleven thirty and two.'

'We'll need to check with the Met Office. The rain started at two in Tankerness. It might have been different here. Probably will have been.'

There was the flash of a camera as Eilidh took photos of the position of the body before touching it. 'I'm going to check his pockets for ID.'

'Right you are.'

The machine-gun call of a hen harrier echoed off the vertical sides of the valley and ricocheted around the rocks. Other than that, and the slight ripple of the police tape in the light breeze, there was barely a sound.

'We've got a phone,' Eilidh said. 'A basic one, mind. Looks like the very definition of a burner to me.'

Her hand appeared at the tomb entrance, holding an evidence bag with a small phone sealed within it. Fergus leaned down to take it. It was a Nokia, but not an old one. The kind of cheap model he'd seen in the Tesco in town.

'Anything else?'

'Looks like cash here, but no wallet,' Eilidh said, still rummaging through the dead man's pockets. 'No keys, no ID, but he's carrying …' She paused while she counted. '… a hundred and fifty quid in notes.'

As with the phone, she dropped the money into a clear, zip-loc bag she took from the pocket of her forensic suit, and passed it to Fergus.

'So, it wasn't a robbery, then,' he said. 'Or some kind of drug deal. It's hardly Pablo Escobar quantities of cash.'

'Unless there was more and someone took the rest of it, left this and the cheap phone to make it look like…'

'Like what? I think you're grasping now, Murray.'

Eilidh didn't reply. Fergus ducked his head inside the tomb entrance again. Eilidh was sitting on her feet in the gloomy chamber, her head almost touching the ceiling despite being bent over. She had pulled the man's right sleeve back slightly to reveal a watch on his wrist.

'Something interesting?'

'Aye, this.'

'The watch on the right wrist instead of the left? That's not all that odd, you're left-handed, aren't you?' Fergus grinned before adding, 'On second thoughts…'

'Do you know what type of watch that is?'

Fergus looked. It was a small black square on a rubber strap with no clock face. 'Looks like an Apple Watch. Or a rip-off of one. I'm not that old and past it.'

'Exactly, it's an Apple Watch,' Eilidh said. When the significance didn't register with Fergus, she explained, 'It pairs with an iPhone. And only an iPhone.'

'Which he doesn't have on him?'

'Right. He's got that cheap thing instead.' She pointed to the tiny phone in the plastic bag in Fergus's hand.

Fergus ran his free hand through his hair. If he was honest, he thought his colleague was getting carried away, looking for something that wasn't there. He leaned forward to get a better view of the man's face: eyes closed, a peaceful look settled over him. He was maybe a little older than Fergus, late fifties. Not an old man by any means, despite Eilidh's constant barbs. He seemed slim and in shape. Nothing definitively pointed towards foul play.

And yet, he had to admit, the location, the time of night the man had come out here, the way he was dressed … he had a nagging feeling something was off.

'Bastard,' Eilidh said, snapping Fergus from his thoughts. She was tapping a gloved finger on the screen of the watch, which stayed black. 'Battery must be dead. But, if we can get this thing charged and get into it, even without the iPhone we'll be able to see from the activity tracker what time he walked up here, what time his heart stopped beat—'

'Hold on a blink.'

Eilidh glanced up when Fergus cut her off. She had been pulling the man's sleeve higher to get a better look at the watch, turning his arm in the process. Her eyes tracked a line to where Fergus was pointing.

To the three words scrawled in ink on the dead man's forearm.

6

The Ferry Road car park in Stromness was almost completely full. Most of the vehicles parked along the harbour's edge were campervans of various sizes, some of which took up more than one space, which meant Freya had to drive up and down the street twice before she found a spot. She pulled up facing the town, looking along the road to the passenger terminal; there was no Northlink ferry in the dock, meaning her view across the water to Hoy was unimpeded. The sun was high in a powder-blue sky dotted with spun-cotton clouds and the day had warmed up quickly. Her weather app said it could get up to around 20°C by the afternoon. Hardly taps aff, as they'd say where she used to live in Glasgow, but sadly it was definitely warm enough for her to have to abandon her coat.

Try as she might, she couldn't ditch the dragging feeling in her stomach that her earlier chat with Kristin had left her with. Her boss hadn't cheered up much during the editorial meeting either, shooting down several pitches for stories from across the team. But at least on that occasion her ire had been aimed at everyone. And it had almost been worth taking a bollocking just to see the range of colours Gill's face took on when Kristin had torpedoed her wild camping story.

'Where's the balance?' Kristin had said. 'You can't bang on about "bloody tourists", as you call them, without looking at any benefits they bring. They contribute a lot of money to the local economy.'

'They're showing up on folk's land in their vans, Kris, with no respect at all for private property,' Gill had shot back, her cheeks a rare shade of purple. 'How's that contributing money? My pal, Graeme, over at Outertown, says there's been at least one van there on his land all summer. This latest one's been there for nearly a week. He's asked them to move on and they've not.

There's a campsite at Point of Ness not more than two miles away they could be using and they're—'

'Balance it,' Kristin had said, cutting Gill short. 'Do a piece on the impact of wild camping by all means, but I'm not printing a rant on behalf of your pal Graeme, do you hear me?'

Freya wasn't sure how to describe the shade Gill's face had taken on then, but she imagined it was the colour people turned at the onset of a heart attack.

She rubbed her eyes, looked again along the street, and thought about getting out and walking along to the cafe where Angus had asked to meet. She wasn't relishing this at all. Angus Scott was the brother of a recently retired Orkney police sergeant, Trevor. Soon after word had got out that the CAAPD had given Police Scotland's Professional Standards Division the green light to investigate the Orkney Area Command, Trevor Scott had taken his small fishing boat out of Kirkwall harbour into the deeper waters of the Stronsay Firth, filled his pockets with rubble and stepped into the sea. His craft had been found drifting into the shipping lanes. Onboard, a note was found pinned beneath a rock. All it said was: 'Forgive me for everything.' It didn't take long for the rumour to spread that Trevor had taken his own life because of something that was going to come out in the investigation.

The inside of her car was beginning to heat up, but still she didn't move. She preferred to stay there, sweat pooling at the base of her back, than go and talk to a man about his dead brother. The pavements outside were busy with tourists cradling rapidly melting ice-creams and sweating cans of cold juice, and the cafe would no doubt be hoaching too. None of it appealed. She checked the clock on her phone, saw she still had ten minutes. She could use that time to do some preparation for the interview, seeing as she hadn't done any yet. But instead, her mind went somewhere else.

She reached over and opened the glovebox, rummaged among the junk and the twisted cable of a phone charger Tom had insisted she keep in there, and pulled out an old notebook. She opened it to the first page, ran her finger lightly over the ink scrawled on the lined paper, breathed in its musty smell. The rest of the notebooks like this one were locked away safely at home. She had images of them stored on her phone, but Freya liked to keep this one with her. She wanted to be close to it.

The handwriting wasn't too dissimilar to her own. At the top of the page was the date these first entries had been written – October, 1997. Beneath it were the now familiar but still undeciphered notes and initials her father had filled most of these pages with:

> AT uses phone box c/o Cragiefield and Work, 3/31
> AT meets SC @ Windwick, 22:49, 04/07
> TDL @ Burwick, AT, SC, GL present, 00:19, 07/07
> AT uses phone box c/o Cragiefield and Work, 4/31
> AT meets SC @ Evie Sands, 23:30, 10/07.

It was six months now that she'd had these pages in her possession. For the first three, she'd struggled even to look at them. She'd struggled to do anything, in fact. But, since around Easter, she'd started to read them on a near daily basis. For the past two months, she had been actively throwing herself into resolving their mystery.

But she was chasing a ghost. It had been almost thirty years since her dad, Neill, had penned these notes. He'd been the detective inspector heading up Kirkwall CID at the time of his death shortly before Freya's eleventh birthday. These notebooks were personal, though, not official police issue. They had been gathering dust in a box until about a year ago when her mother had found them in her loft and handed them to Fergus, thinking they were related to his work. But whatever Neill had been doing was off the books; he had never told Fergus about any of it. Freya longed to know what they meant, to understand what her dad had been trying to uncover at the time of his death, but it remained infuriatingly out of reach. She still didn't know what all the letters and numbers meant, much less why her father had written them down and kept them hidden away.

Some of the initials had been deciphered – she could be fairly certain that AT stood for Allan Tait. GL was Graham Linklater, whose portfolio of properties had provided the venues for the evil rich perverts who had paid to have schoolgirls drugged and delivered to them for sex. The thought of it still brought sick to Freya's throat. The third set of common initials – SC – remained a mystery. The only negative thing about Tait and Linklater being dead was it meant they couldn't beat the identity of SC out of them. With Fergus's help, at least she had an idea of who it might be: Simon Cooper, a disgraced former local politician who Freya's dad had arrested in the late nineties for fraud and embezzlement. Simon, too, was no longer on this mortal plane, having died in prison some years ago, but his son was still alive, and still living in Orkney. James was proving difficult to reach, however, and it seemed like he would be even further out of bounds after this morning. But at least it was a lead. After two months of guesswork and off-the-books investigating, they were still no closer to decoding the less frequently used combination of TDL.

Even so, the sight of her father's handwriting, those same loops and scrawls she remembered from birthday cards and little notes inside her school lunchbox, made her feel close to him, if only for a moment or two.

She jumped out of her skin, startled, when her phone rang.

Fergus.

Her hand didn't move. The phone buzzed near-silently across the passenger seat, but she didn't answer the call. She wanted to speak to him, but like the change of plan this morning, this was unexpected. It hadn't been planned for, and so it was like some force within her was pushing her back, stopping her from answering. The same force that stops you from intentionally stamping your bare foot on an upturned nail or slamming your hand down on a lit stove.

Her mind drifted again, this time to thoughts of the autism assessment she'd undergone in last November. Even though the clinical psychologist had concluded she displayed a lot of the characteristics of being autistic, they had decided they did not cause her 'persistent difficulties', and so she had not met the threshold to be diagnosed as autistic, they had said she displayed a lot of the traits. And yet here she was, sitting in a red-hot car with her coat zipped up to her chin, unable to answer a bloody phone.

Not 'unwilling' to; she was actually physically unable to make her thumb swipe the screen.

The stories she'd read and heard from autistic people online, describing their experiences, still resonated strongly with her. It all made a lot of sense. But then she also wondered if maybe the assessment had been right, if maybe she could try harder not to let things affect her. And she was trying, but times like this, it felt impossible, and these were the times when she considered seeking a second opinion, but then the thought of putting herself through that whole soul-crushing process again was simply unbearable.

The buzzing stopped. Seconds later, a text arrived: **I forgot you don't answer your phone. I'll try you again later.**

Fergus would have been calling from his burner phone. He'd have to wait until the coast was clear again to call back.

Suddenly her limbs unlocked. Her hand shot to the phone.

She got the dial tone, meaning he hadn't switched off the phone yet. It rang only twice before he answered.

'Did I just miss you?' Fergus's voice was hushed with a slight echo, like he was standing in an empty room.

'Aye, my phone was on silent for work, sorry. I didn't hear it until just before you hung up.'

Lying was certainly an unhealthy habit of hers. But it was easier than saying, I didn't answer the phone because for some reason my brain wouldn't let me.

'Not a bother. I've not got long, just wanted to give you the heads-up there'll be a story coming your way soon.'

'Okay.'

'Okay? You could at least pretend to be interested, Red. Or are you already all over it, solved the case already?'

Freya thought she could hear the smile in his voice. And when he called her by the nickname her dad had given her – Red, on account of her hair – it was always a good sign. It was always a good sign when he used it with her. She knew this was going to give her a way back into Kristin's good books, and without her having to trawl through mountains of Facebook posts from curtain-twitchers on the local community pages to find out what Fergus had been up to today.

'Sorry, I was just … I was a little distracted,' she said.

'Everything okay?'

'Aye, it's good. What have you got for me?'

Fergus filled Freya in on the highlights. Her interest was piqued by the lack of any vehicle, and by the presence of an Apple Watch with no accompanying phone. 'So, are you thinking natural causes?' she asked. 'If there was no vehicle left behind, he either walked or…'

'Or someone left him there. It's a line of enquiry we're pursuing.'

'You're treating it as suspicious?'

'You know the drill; all deaths have to be until we can rule it out.'

'But there was no obvious indication of what killed him? No drug paraphernalia or—'

'You're as bad as my co-worker. Don't tell me this has got your spidey-senses tingling too?'

Freya was a little taken aback that Fergus knew such a phrase. She grinned to herself, but didn't answer.

'So, in all likelihood, this'll be a natural death,' Fergus continued. Though what he was doing out there is anybody's guess. And there were a couple of—'

A voice in the background cut Fergus off. A woman's voice. Freya assumed it was the DS Fergus worked with, Eilidh Murray, but the sound became quickly muffled and she couldn't hear what was said. Fergus replied, said something too, but she didn't hear that either. Sounded like it might've been, 'I'll be right there.'

'I've got to go,' Fergus said seconds later, but even quieter now, almost whispering down the line. 'Should I come over later, have our peedie catch-up then?'

Freya was about to agree when she remembered she had already made plans to go out with Tom and his friends from work. She'd been out with them once or twice before, they were nice people, but the temptation to say yes to Fergus and get out of it was strong.

'I can't tonight,' she conceded in the end. 'I could do tomorrow morning though, before work.'

'Perfect. Let's say Finstown at eight.'

'Okay.'

He hung up without a goodbye and Freya was left sitting with her phone to her ear for a few more seconds before she put it back in her coat pocket. She was sitting for a while, letting everything she had just heard settle in her mind, when a white Transit van, rust at the edges of its doors, rattled into the car park in front of her.

An invisible hand grabbed her throat.

For the briefest of seconds, she was back on the clifftops in Yesnaby, the light leaking from the sky, the sea roaring beneath her feet, watching the whites of a masked man's eyes as he fell backwards into the abyss.

The van door banged, bringing her back. A middle-aged man in grease-covered overalls with the logo of Northlink Ferries on the back got out and started jogging across the road to the ferry terminal. Freya pressed hard on the studs in her ear, counted them in order, forwards and backwards, and took a moment to breathe.

One, two, three, four, five. Five, four, three…

She needed to get out of this stuffy vehicle.

Time to stamp her foot on that nail.

7

The biggest criminal ever to operate in Orkney was the psychopath who had installed the hot drinks machine in Kirkwall police station. Fergus winced as he sipped the scalding liquid the machine had spewed out when he'd pressed for a black coffee. Ordinarily, he'd rather lick a stranger's armpit than drink this swill, but he needed caffeine, it had a been a long morning. And the afternoon was looking even longer.

Eilidh was leaning against the wall in the dull corridor outwith Magnus Robertson's office, scrolling through some quickly typed up notes on her phone. Once the scene had been secured and officers had been sent looking for the light-coloured Polestar, Fergus and Murray had been summoned back to Kirkwall to update the chief inspector and begin coordinating proceedings from base. She looked up when she heard Fergus approach.

'Didn't get me one?' she said, nodding at the plastic cup in his hand.

'Trust me, I'm doing you a favour.'

'Who were you on the phone to just now?'

'A good pal of mine called Myndja.'

Eilidh nodded. 'Aye. Myndja Own Business, by any chance?'

'You know her, then? You happy to lead on this?'

Eilidh raised an eyebrow. 'Isn't that your job?'

'It is, but if you're wanting to convince the boss there's something worth investigating here, you're going to have to do it yourself, because you haven't fully convinced me yet.'

'Are you serious? With the writing on his arm and everything?'

'We don't know what—'

The door opened beside them and a deep voice beckoned them inside, cutting Fergus off. The bright, late morning sunlight caught in Fergus' eyes the moment he stepped into the office. A large window behind the chief inspector's desk looked out across the glittering water of the Peedie Sea, the view stretching across the west of town to the green slopes of Wideford Hill in the distance. The sun was still climbing to its highest point and had yet to travel far enough west to be seen through the glass but, although Magnus had cracked a window to let in the breeze coming off Kirkwall Bay, it had still done enough already to make the air in the office close and stuffy. Fergus felt beads of sweat blossom beneath his shirt collar.

'Where are we up to?' Magnus asked as he took his seat at his desk. No time for niceties. He gestured for Fergus and Eilidh to take the two seats across from him. As he sat, Fergus noticed Magnus close the laptop on his desk. His Outlook calendar had been open, and Fergus had spotted the appointment scheduled to follow this one: a Teams call with the PSD investigation into historical corruption. That perhaps explained Magnus's sharp tone instead of the false, chummy demeanour he often went with.

As discussed, Eilidh took the lead. 'There's no name for our John Doe as yet, sir. His pockets are empty save for some cash and what looks like a burner phone. No ID on him, no keys. The body is at the morgue at The Balfour, ready to go off to Aberdeen, but we've tried to lift a print off him. We'll send that on ahead, see if we can get a match from it.'

'Cause of death: any early indications of what it might be?' Magnus had his head down as he spoke, scribbling on a pad of paper.

'Also unclear. There are no signs of injury or any kind of altercation having taken place. Doesn't look like he was using drugs. We won't know for certain until the autopsy, though.'

'Which will be when?'

'The pathologist said she'd see it was prioritised, but we're still looking at a couple of days.'

Magnus nodded, a stern knot between his brows and an intensity in his dark eyes suggesting he wasn't happy with that answer but he would accept it. He was a younger man than Fergus by almost a decade, only the slight flecks of grey in his neatly trimmed black hair giving away the fact he was in his mid-forties. His rise to the role of chief inspector had been rapid – one of his more polite nicknames around the station was Rocket Robertson for how quickly he'd shot up the ranks, partly because the man was a pure rocket. He scribbled something down and Fergus watched him, his mood darkening with every stroke of Magnus's expensive-looking pen. The chief obviously needed to take notes to brief the higher-ups in Inverness, but it still bugged Fergus. Everything about this man was as false as a glass eye. He had the aura not of a cop, but of an overly enthusiastic actor learning to play one.

'Okay, so, in the meantime, have we got anything to suggest the death might be suspicious?'

'A couple of things, nothing concrete. The location coupled with the timing. Early estimates put the time of death between midnight and 3 a.m. The rain started last night in Hoy just after one thirty, and the body's bone dry. Then we've got the couple who found the body – the Bothamleys. They spotted a car leaving the scene as they arrived last night.'

'Did they get a registration?'

'No, but they were able to give a fairly detailed description – a light-coloured Polestar. It's quite a distinctive EV. We've got a couple of uniforms out looking for it now. We've also got this.' Eilidh passed her work phone across the desk. On screen was a photo of the dead man's watch, still in place on his wrist. 'That's an Apple—'

'An Apple Watch, I'm aware.' Magnus pulled up a crisp white shirt sleeve. 'I've got one myself. They track absolutely everything. Bloody thing's forever pestering me to stand up and move around.'

Eilidh forced a subordinate smile for her boss. Fergus couldn't muster the same energy.

'Sorry, sir. I had to explain what it was to DI Muir this morning.'

'I knew what it was,' Fergus interjected. 'I just didn't see your point immediately.'

'I'm assuming the point is there should be an iPhone to go with it,' Magnus said. 'You mentioned a burner.'

'A cheap model, sir. Not an iPhone.'

'So, you think the watch means there's another device somewhere?'

'That, and the watch itself could tell us a few other things.'

'Such as?'

'Well, it all depends if we can get into it. Unfortunately, the battery's dead, but we've sent it away for digital forensics to take a look and, if we can get it open, it'll tell us exactly when his heart stopped beating. It'll tell us how he got there too – there were no other vehicles at the scene, and none was seen or heard by the Bothamleys all night. If the deceased walked up there, the activity app in the watch will have tracked it. If we're lucky, it could even give an indication of whether he may have had a heart attack. Plus, it'll give us the details of his iPhone so we can get on to the network and trace it.'

'Should we need to,' Magnus said. 'Don't get me wrong, we've got to treat this as a suspicious death until we know it isn't, but is there something I'm missing?'

'Tell him about your spider senses,' Fergus said.

'The what?' Magnus asked.

Eilidh ignored Fergus and asked Robertson to swipe to the next photo on her phone. An image of the dead man's right arm appeared on screen, his sleeve pulled back.

'There's this too,' she said.

Magnus squinted, moved the screen out of the glare of the sunlight. 'What am I looking at here?'

'Three words, but they're written backwards,' Eilidh explained. 'The deceased's watch is on his right wrist, so we're assuming he was left-handed. If that's the case, it's likely he wrote this himself.'

She reached across the desk to swipe the screen for Magnus. In the next shot, the words scribbled in what appeared to be biro on the inside of his forearm were clear enough to read: The Dying Light.

Magnus took a moment before saying anything. Fergus watched him closely. He noticed he hadn't written that down in his notebook.

'Any idea what this means?'

'None yet,' said Eilidh.

Magnus didn't take his eyes off the screen, and Fergus didn't take his eyes off him. He wasn't sure if the words meant something to Magnus or if this was yet more of his act of playing a cop.

'So, what are your suggested next steps?' Magnus eventually asked.

'Find out who he was and what he was doing there. But we're going to need more help from uniform for that.' She asked for her phone back and swiped the screen again to show. 'We're getting a sketch done of the deceased that we can use for house-to-house. It's merely a question of how much manpower you can spare.'

Magnus turned in his chair, looked out across the Peedie Sea with his fingers steepled beneath his chin. Another theatrical move.

Eventually, he said, 'I'll speak to the duty sergeant, but we're stretched thin. We need bodies out and about in cars as part of the Safer Roads campaign. It's important to the people of these islands that we're visible right now. I doubt he'll have more than two or three officers available, at best.

Getting your priorities in order, I see, Fergus thought. 'Two should be enough to cover most of Hoy today.'

'What about the press?' Magnus looked at Fergus. 'Have we shared any of this with the media yet?'

Fergus knew why that was directed at him. Magnus was well aware of his connection to Freya. He didn't think he knew they were investigating Neill Spence's old notebooks together, but he'd long held suspicions he was being closely watched.

'No, sir,' Fergus lied. 'We planned on doing that once we had the sketch.'

'Good, get it done through the formal channels before word gets out and it looks like it leaked. I want us to be seen to be open and to be doing all we can in the event that it does turn out to be something more sinister. Especially with the bad press we've been getting of late.'

Magnus turned to his laptop, his point made. The meeting was over. Fergus and Eilidh stood to leave.

'And, the pair of you, make sure we do everything completely by the book on this one,' Magnus said as they did, eyes on the screen. 'The last thing we need is another stick for anyone to beat us with.'

'Of course, sir,' Eilidh said.

Fergus sipped his piss-poor coffee and winced.

8

Angus was already waiting inside the cafe when Freya arrived. They had agreed to meet at a small place on Victoria Street, the main cobbled lane that snaked through the oldest part of Stromness, drawing both tourists and locals. As Freya had expected, this morning it was proving extremely popular with both, and, although a door was open to a small outdoor area with a stunning view out onto the harbour, it was ridiculously hot. It had been Angus's choice. Freya wouldn't have picked it. Not for something like this.

He stood as she approached the table, her stomach falling in tandem with his rise. She had wanted to get here before him, have some time to settle in, prepare. Too late now. She was going to have to do this on the fly and she didn't really know where to begin.

There must've been a look on her face that he misread. 'I'm not here looking for a fight. You've no need to fret.'

Freya tried a tight-lipped smile and shook his outstretched hand. It was large and calloused, and although he didn't grip her hand hard she could feel the strength in it. For a man in his sixties, he was still well built and clearly took care of himself. The grey hair he had left at the sides of his head was trimmed short almost to the point of being shaved, and he had the slightly tanned skin of a man who had spent a lot of time outdoors. Most people were tall compared to Freya, but he was especially so, yet he didn't come across as intimidating. She had heard the words he'd said, but their meaning eluded her until they were both sitting down. Even then, she didn't know how to respond.

'Thanks for agreeing to meet with me,' she said as she slipped her coat over the back of the chair, relinquishing her grip on it like a nervous swimmer letting go of the side of the pool.

'Trevor needs someone to tell his side of the story, seeing as he's not around to tell it himself. And someone needs to correct the awful things folk are saying about him.'

'None of the rumours came from us.' Freya noted her tone, thought she might've sounded defensive again, when really she was just stating a fact. She added: 'I hope you don't think that they did.'

'No, not from anything you printed. But one of your lot hasn't been backwards in coming forwards. I've seen comments online.'

Freya knew what Angus meant. Despite claiming she 'didn't do the Internet and refusing to put any of her stories on *The Orcadian's* social channels, Gill Irvine had been pretty prolific in posting from her personal account on Facebook in groups that had been discussing the circumstances of Trevor's death.

A waitress came and took their order, breaking the tension momentarily. Angus ordered a bowl of tomato soup, which seemed a poor choice in this heat. Freya didn't feel comfortable enough to eat, and was too hot to order her usual oat milk latte, so she opted for a cherry Coke instead. She asked Angus if it was okay to record their conversation and she put her phone on the red and white checked tablecloth between them, switched to airplane mode so no messages would interrupt them.

'First thing I want to make clear is my brother was no bent cop,' Angus said. There was no anger in his voice as he spoke, simply a conviction that offered no invite to argue. 'If Trevor had been up to something he shouldn't have, I would've known about it. And I would never defend it.'

'Were the two of you close?'

'Once. Not so much in recent years, but when we were younger we talked a lot. Over the phone mostly. I moved away from the islands, coming back years later, like most of us seem to.'

Freya wondered if that was simply another statement of fact or if he'd done his research on her. Maybe this was his subtle way of letting her know.

'When you do the jobs we did, the only people who really get it are the other people in it with you. Other cops.'

Freya nodded. She had done her research on him too, though information about Angus had been scarce online. She hadn't found any social media profiles for him, but clearly he had one if he'd seen Gill's comments. He must've set one up under an alias, or changed the way he spelled his name, like she knew some cops did.

'You were in the police?' she asked. 'Did you ever work here?'

Angus shook his head. 'Back in the day, when I was starting out, it was Northern Constabulary here, not Police Scotland. There was none of this degree entry or any of that malarky. Didn't matter that our dad was a policeman too, the force wanted boys with life experience. Our Trevor had held a job down since he was in his peedie breeks. He knew people, how they ticked. And he had a work ethic. None of that was for me.' He smiled, looked through the window to the sea. 'Trevor was the Golden Boy, you see. And I was the rotten apple. I tried to join a year or two after Trev, but they wouldn't have me. So, I went away to sea.'

Freya frowned. She thought he'd said he was a cop.

Angus must've seen the confusion on her face. 'I went off to the Royal Navy. I was sitting around at home one morning, watching the telly, and our dad came in and threw the newspaper at me. Your paper. Folded open to a page with an advert on it for signing up. He marched me down to town that afternoon to join.'

There was a pause while the waitress returned with their order.

'I went away to Portsmouth a few weeks later,' he continued when she'd gone. 'Best thing that happened to me. Who knows what would've become of me if I'd stayed here. Nothing good, is my guess. You see, everybody thinks these islands are idyllic, that there's no bad men here like there are down south, but the difference is they simply know how to hide themselves better. You have to here. If someone wants to make a life for themselves by nefarious means, you can do it. Drugs, trafficking, stolen goods, it's all here. It just hides better in plain sight.'

Freya took a sip of her drink. It was icy cold and precisely what she needed. She tried to decide how to phrase her question. She really wished she'd had time to plan this.

'So, how exactly do you know Trevor wasn't involved in something that's going to show up in the Professional Standards report?' she asked. 'Just because you talked and he never told you?'

That wasn't the way to phrase it.

Angus visibly bristled, but he soon seemed to settle. His eyes scanned her face. He took a breath, collected his thoughts before he spoke. 'I can see why you'd be sceptical of anything I told you. Nobody wants to think badly of a member of their family. Especially after they're gone. We turn them into plaster-cast saints. But I promise you, if my brother was bent, I'd be the first to call him out. That's what I did.'

Freya frowned again. She really wasn't following where Angus was going with what he was telling her. And because she'd arrived feeling on the back foot, she wasn't in control of the flow of conversation either. She needed to get on top of it.

'How do you mean, that's what you did? I thought you said you were in the navy.'

'At first. A few years in, I decided to join the RNP. The naval police. I guess the calling was in my blood. I was always going to end up being a cop one way or another.' He chuckled, stirred his soup. 'When my time in the navy was up, I decided to move back to Scotland. I joined what was essentially the PSD for the Northern Constabulary. I policed the police.'

'You mean you joined Professional Standards up here after leaving the navy?'

'I was based in Inverness, not Orkney. But aye.'

'And you did the full twenty years military service before retiring?'

'I left a week before my thirty-ninth birthday.'

Freya did the maths in her head. That likely would have meant Angus had joined PSD about twenty-five years ago. The late nineties, early two-thousands at the latest.

'So, what Allan Tait did, it happened on your watch?'

Again, she caught her tone too late. Shit, this is what happened when she didn't have a clear plan. She shouldn't have been so direct, but Angus didn't clam up like she had feared.

He grimaced but nodded. 'I know how that looks – if we didn't spot Tait, then there's every chance I wouldn't know what my brother was up to either.'

That was exactly what Freya was thinking.

Angus poked at his soup again. He'd yet to take a mouthful. 'It's the obvious conclusion to draw. But here's the thing, we did suspect Tait back then.' His gaze flicked back and forth between Freya's eyes, trying to gauge her reaction. 'Or at least, we suspected things weren't as they should be in Orkney. That people were bending the rules and letting things slide. Clearly, we never knew the degree of it, but there were rumours circling that things weren't right up here.'

'Then why didn't you investigate?'

'Because to investigate you need actual evidence, not hearsay. We had a whistleblower. They came forward after a case about a teenage boy going missing who nobody seemed too interested in going to find. They said they thought Allan Tait was deliberately trying to influence the investigation, but they had nothing concrete for us to go on, so there was nothing we could do.'

That invisible hand reached inside Freya's chest this time, wrapped its fingers around her heart.

A whistleblower. It couldn't have been…

Her mind went to her dad's notebooks. Fergus had said it himself when he had given them to her, on their own they weren't evidence of anything. They suggested her dad had been watching Tait and his cronies, but there was no indication he'd caught them doing anything illegal. At least, nothing that he'd documented. But maybe he had seen something, or knew something, and was trying to take it further.

She studied the face of the man sitting across from her. His expression was a foreign language to her. It meant nothing. Though he was sitting patiently enough, like he was aware she was toying with some thought. He seemed to be waiting for her to speak next.

She almost didn't dare ask. 'When was this?'

'The late nineties,' Angus said.

'And the whistleblower, were they anonymous or did you know who it was?'

'Oh, I knew them.'

'Was it my Neill Spence?'

Her heart sank when an expression flashed across Angus's face that was far too easy to read: surprise.

'Now, what would make you think it might've been your him?'

Freya couldn't answer. Not only because the disappointment had sapped all life from her, but because Fergus had made it abundantly clear that nobody else could know about the notebooks. There was still the possibility that corruption lingered in the Orkney police, maybe as high as the chief inspector himself. Magnus Robertson's name had cropped up multiple times during the grooming ring case, and she knew Fergus had major doubts about the man and just how closely linked he had been to Tait. If word somehow got back to him, Freya's investigation would never get anywhere.

Angus had started poking at his soup again. He set the spoon down now, stroked his chin. 'I don't suppose you remember me, do you?'

Now it was Freya's turn to look surprised.

When she didn't respond, Angus continued, 'One of my investigations at PSD did bring me to Orkney. We had to look into the death of a detective during active duty. A car accident.'

Freya felt those fingers squeeze her heart again.

'Neill was your dad, wasn't he? How old were you when he died?'

'Ten,' she said. 'Almost eleven.'

'I came to your house, spoke to your mum. The poor woman was in pieces, understandably. I remember you being there.'

Because her dad's death had occurred in the line of duty, an internal investigation had to be launched. She remembered officers from the Northern Constabulary coming from Inverness to visit. They had spoken to her mother but not to her. Even if they had, she doubted she would've remembered Angus after all these years.

'The whistleblower was my brother,' Angus said. 'Trevor was working with me to get information on the chief inspector and anyone connected with him. And that's how I know my brother wasn't bent, and there'll be nothing in that report to suggest he was. What happened to Trevor, what he did…'

His voice trailed off. He momentarily looked away, to the blue water outside with silver sunlight reflecting off it, before composing himself. He looked Freya directly in the eye and she had to force herself not to look away.

'Trevor died because he couldn't live with the things he didn't do, not the things he did,' he said. 'He grew to hate Allan Tait. When we spoke privately, he told me he was convinced the man was being controlled by someone else. Either an individual or a group who had something on him, or he was in their pay. He told me about orders Tait gave that didn't make sense, people who were cut loose or never lifted in the first place on his say so. He'd started to gather evidence on him, but then one day he just stopped. Told me he couldn't do it anymore and that was that. No explanation, no nothing. And I believe he regretted that decision until the day he died.' Angus swallowed hard. His glance flicked between Freya's eyes again. 'When your story came out, when you uncovered for certain who Allan Tait was, it confirmed my brother had been right all along. He knew something wasn't right, but he chose to give up. Then, when he found out what that monster had done to those poor girls, Trevor couldn't live with the guilt. That's what he meant by his note, I think. He knew he could've done something if he hadn't walked away.'

'Why did he stop?'

'I don't know, but I can guess. Somebody got to him. And whoever it was, they did a proper job. Scared the living shite out of him. He dropped the whole thing immediately, hardly spoke to me again after that.'

That cold hand around her heart squeezed again. Thoughts spun through her mind like symbols on a slot machine, never stopping. Never landing on the prize. But within it all, there was a feeling – a feeling that all of this was connected. Someone stopped Trevor Scott from speaking up about Tait. She knew in her bones that same someone had stopped her dad too.

Angus was watching her again. Freya felt like he was begging for her to tell him about the notebooks. It was almost like he knew, and that had been the reason he'd wanted this interview. And she wanted to tell him. The words rose onto her tongue like bile, difficult to swallow back down.

In the end, she didn't have to say anything.

'Why did you ask about Neill being the whistleblower, Freya? Do you think he knew about Tait too?'

She simply nodded.

Angus stroked his chin. He finally pushed the bowl of soup away. 'Your father's death, it was determined that he suffered the degree of injury he did when the tyre blew out because he wasn't wearing his seatbelt. Did you know that?'

Another nod. She did. She had never understood it.

'Did you ever know your dad to get in a vehicle without wearing his seatbelt?'

A shake of the head.

'I always thought that was odd, and I always wondered…' Angus's voice tailed away. 'Someone scared my brother half to death. I always wondered what they would've done to him if he hadn't given up, if he'd kept going after Tait.' He lowered his head to look Freya in the eye. 'You don't believe your dad's death was an accident, do you?'

'No.'

'No,' Angus echoed. 'Neither do I.'

9

THE HULL OF THE roll-on-roll-off ferry lowered agonisingly slowly, hitting the concrete pier with a metallic clunk.

Fergus squinted through the glare of the sun off his car's bonnet and watched as vehicles slowly began to file off the boat. The first one was a marked police car. It was followed by a sleek, white sedan that Fergus assumed must be a Polestar.

'Get your coat,' Eilidh had said to him when he'd walked back into the CID office after having been to the bathroom. His third trip since they'd been back at the station.

'Have I pulled?'

Eilidh had glowered at him. 'Just get your jacket before I have you up on a sexual harassment charge, you dirty old man. We're away to Houton. Jake's found our light-coloured EV.'

Now, sitting in the passenger seat of Fergus's Volkswagen Passat, Eilidh said, 'I think I'll let you take the lead on this one.'

'That's awfully kind of you.'

'Well, it's your turn.' She popped a Soor Ploom into her mouth. She offered the bag to Fergus, but he shook his head.

'What are you expecting they'll tell us?'

'Not much. I'm guessing they won't have seen anything. My gut tells me the deceased turned up some time during the night, after they'd been and gone.'

Fergus glanced at his colleague. Her lips were pursed, her cheeks sucked in as she rolled the sweet around her teeth. 'You're dying for this to be something, aren't you?'

Eilidh shrugged. 'I'm dying for something bloody interesting to do. It's been three months and the most serious things I've dealt with have been two nasty RTAs and those farm vandals.' She looked at him. 'Don't you get sick of it?'

'It's all I've known. And besides, if this turns into something bigger, it'll get passed to MIT. You know that. We'll be pushed to the sidelines.'

'Doesn't matter. Being on the sidelines of something is better than being neck deep in fuck all.' She nodded towards the front of the car. 'Here we go.'

Fergus observed his colleague a moment longer. He still didn't know what had prompted her transfer from Perth to Kirkwall, but he got the distinct impression the move hadn't been her choice.

At the sound of tyres crunching gravel, he turned back to look through the windscreen. They were parked at the side of the road down to the pier, on a strip of land in front of a row of old garages and shipping containers. The police car pulled in ahead of them, the Polestar following behind.

The two detectives got out of Fergus's car, the breeze off the Hoy Sound ruffling the older detective's hair and giving some welcome relief after sitting in the stuffy vehicle. A uniformed male officer got out of the police car – PC Jake Drever. He was tall, dark complexion, early forties. He strode across the short distance between the vehicles in a few long steps and held out his hand for Fergus and Eilidh to shake. Fergus and Jake were on first name terms, but they had never socialised out with work, or spoken much during it for that matter. Drever kept himself to himself, was a man of few words, and Fergus was more than okay with that. He knew he had a wife and a young family, but that was about it.

Jake had been assigned the task of contacting the ferry company to find out if any cars that matched the description the Bothamleys had given were booked on any crossings from Lyness back to Mainland in the near future. Unsurprisingly, the search had only turned up the one: a white Polestar 2, due to cross later that morning. He took off his police cap, wiped the sweat from his brow as he explained how he had gone to the harbour to wait for them to show up.

'They say they didn't see anything on the Rackwick road last night,' he added, 'but I figured you'd still like to speak to them.'

'You figured right,' said Fergus. 'Who are they?'

'Couple of tourists.' He checked his notebook. 'Callum Parks and Dylan McCoy, up from Lanarkshire. They told me a similar tale to the English couple who found the body.'

'I take it you've got the details of where they stay down south, where they're stopping here?'

'I have.' Jake chewed the inside of his cheek. Fergus figured the PC was annoyed by the question; he had been on the force a good long while, he knew what he was doing. Still, Fergus had needed to ask.

'Okay, thanks, Jake. Where are you headed now?'

PC Drever nodded towards the RO-RO bobbing in the calm water at the end of the jetty. 'Back over to Hoy, chapping on doors. Heard just now on the radio that the sketch will be coming through on email any minute. We're going to get started with the house-to-house.'

'Right you are. Good luck. And thanks again for this, it's good work.'

Jake nodded. His dark brown eyes flicked between Fergus and Eilidh. 'No bother at all.'

Callum and Dylan were standing by their vehicle, waiting. They were wearing sunglasses and smart summer clothes, looked like they were in their mid-to-late twenties. One of them had longer hair, the other wore his closely shaved, but they both had neat beards. Fergus thought they looked more like the type of tourist you'd get in Milan or Dubrovnik than Orkney, but he guessed he didn't know what young folk liked to get up to these days. Maybe he should've let Eilidh handle this one.

He shook hands with them both as he introduced himself. He showed them his warrant card and Eilidh did the same.

'My colleague PC Drever tells me you didn't see anything last night at the Dwarfie Stane but, if you could tell me a bit about what you did yesterday evening, that would be helpful.'

'Are we under suspicion?' Callum asked. He seemed genuinely worried Fergus was about to throw the pair of them in jail. 'The other guy said there'd been an incident, but he didn't say—'

'You're not going to prison just yet, Mr Parks, don't worry,' Fergus said with a smile, but it only seemed to make things worse. He changed tack. 'There's nothing to worry about, we're simply trying to get a picture of what happened last night on the Rackwick road. This morning, two tourists found a body at the Dwarfie—'

'A body?'

'Please, it's nothing to be alarmed about. We're merely trying to get an understanding of how he got there and what might have happened.'

Fergus explained that a car matching the description of their own was seen driving away from the area last night around eleven PM.

'It's not ours,' Callum said. 'It's a rental.'

'Aye, but we were in it last night on that road, that's what they're meaning,' Dylan said.

'We simply want to know what you saw while you were there,' Fergus said.

'Nothing I can think of,' Dylan said. He seemed less phased to be talking to a detective than his partner was. 'I mean, we visited the tomb. There was nobody else there, which is what we wanted. That's why we were there so late. We walked back to the car…' Something dawned on him. He looked at Callum. 'There was that vehicle on the road behind us though as we drove away. I saw the headlights. But they'd vanished by the time we got to the junction at the end of the road.'

'They would be the other people we've already spoken to, Mr McCoy,' Fergus said. 'After you reached the junction, where did you go from there?'

'Back to our hotel for the night. Cal was done in so…' Something occurred to him. 'Actually, no. We didn't go straight back. Cal was falling asleep, but I took a wee detour down to that churchyard. I wanted to see the sunset.'

'Aye, you did,' Callum concurred. 'And the road was all bumpy and it woke me up. And there were those men down there.'

'Men?'

'Aye, three of them on the beach.'

Fergus shared a quick glance with Eilidh before turning back to the two witnesses. 'So, where did you stay last night?'

'It's a hotel in a lighthouse. Cantick Head,' Dylan said.

Fergus knew it. It was at the far eastern tip of Hoy. The wrong direction for watching the sunset. 'And, after you left the Dwarfie Stane, you didn't drive to your hotel, you went to a church instead? Where was that? On the way back to Cantick Head?'

'No, it was … just a sec, here.'

Dylan took a mobile phone out of the pocket of his jeans and, after a few taps of the screen, held it out for Fergus to see.

'It was here.'

Fergus leaned in to look. Dylan was pointing at a satellite image on Google Maps. A little symbol marked the location of the Hoy Old Parish churchyard, not far from the start of the Rackwick road. A narrow strip of yellow sand backed right up to the tarmac beside it.

'And there were three men there?'

'Not at the church, on this beach there. They had a boat up on the sand. I couldn't tell if they were coming in or about to go out.'

'What were they doing?'

Dylan shrugged. 'Just talking by the looks of things.'

'Could you describe them?'

'I dunno. Old. Fifties, at least.'

Fergus ignored that. 'All three of them?'

'Aye, I'd say so. Though the light was beginning to fade and they were down by the water. And we were there for the sunset, so I wasn't really looking, sorry.'

'No need for sorrys. Anything you can tell us is a great help. I don't suppose you remember anything about what they were wearing?'

'Aye, it was random,' Callum cut in, seemingly more excited than nervous now. 'Two of them looked like you'd expect proper fishermen to look, you know? In overalls and all that. Covered in grease. But this one guy looked like he'd come straight from the office.'

'How do you mean?'

'White shirt, smart trousers. Looked like he was carrying a jacket. Remember I said, Dylan, "Where's he off to dressed like that?"'

Fergus glanced at Eilidh. She understood, took out her phone.

'Did the man with the jacket look like this?' she asked.

She held up her screen for the couple to see. On it, she'd opened the attachment of the artist's sketch which had been sent out to all officers moments ago on email.

'Is that him?' Callum asked. 'Is that the man who died?'

'Is this who you saw?' Eilidh pushed again.

'Like I said, it was getting dark, and they were down by the sea, but...' Dylan looked between the two detectives. 'Going off the clothes, the hair, the age of the guy, then aye, I'd say that's him.'

Saturday, 21st June, 1997 - 12.46 a.m.

'MIKE, WAIT!'

Michael was already at the foot of the stairs when Alice called after him, as loud as she could while still technically whispering. He stopped and looked back up through the darkness at her, standing in the gloom on the landing. Barely visible in the low light, she looked like an apparition in her white summer dress and pale denim jacket.

'What?'

'Where are you going?'

'Where do you think?'

'For Christ's sake, just…'

She gestured with her hand for him to come back upstairs, but he ignored her.

'Mike!!'

Michael could hear Alice hiss his name through gritted teeth as he set off for the living room. Slowly. The others needed to know, but he was well aware of the rocket that would go up the minute he told them they weren't alone on the island. He needed a second to think. Fingers of red and yellow light flicked into the dark hallway from beneath the door; the others had clearly lit a fire with all the furniture they'd broken. He could hear Rabbie's hyena laugh as he neared, the trying-too-hard howls coming from Isla.

And footsteps, soft but hurried, coming down the stairs behind him.

'Mike, stop a minute!'

He turned. Alice joined him in the shadows in the hallway. She put a hand on his elbow and guided him back towards the stairs.

'Let's think this through,' she whispered.

'We've got to say something. There's someone else out there. What the fuck are we supposed to do, let them kill us all in our sleep?'

'And what do you think Rabbie's going to want to do when you tell him? You've seen what he's like. And you've heard the same stories as me.'

'Nah, he'll…'

Michael stopped as soon as he'd started. As if on cue, another cackle of animalistic laughter came from behind the door at the end of the hallway. He had seen and heard enough about Rabbie now to know exactly what he'd want to do. There were rumours his dad could be violent, that he had been in prison for battering a man so badly he'd lost an eye, and the apple didn't fall far from the tree. Rabbie was homeschooled because neither of the secondary schools in the islands would take him. Or, at least, that's what Rabbie claimed. As soon as Michael told the others what he'd seen, Rabbie would want to find whoever was out there and kick fuck out of them. He wouldn't even do it under the guise of defending themselves, he'd simply do it for the craic.

He felt the touch of Alice's fingers on his chin, pulling his face towards her.

'Listen,' she whispered, her lips close to his. 'We don't really know what you saw. We should look into it ourselves before we bring Rabbie and the others into it, right?'

He could feel the breath of each word on his skin. He didn't at all relish the idea of stepping into that unsettling half-light, unsure of what exactly waited for them, but in that moment, he would've listened to anything she said.

The wind had picked up outside. It was darker now too, the time approaching 1 a.m. The surrounding scattered remains of dwellings were still visible, though. The shrieks of the seabirds nesting on the nearby sands had quietened, but the hush of the waves had grown to a low-level roar. Or maybe it was a trick of the mind, sounds seeming louder in the low light.

Alice held on to Michael's arm, pointed towards the beach with her free hand. 'The view from the window looks out that way. We should try over there first.'

The further they walked from the house, the stronger the wind grew, whipping strands of Alice's hair across Michael's face. It blew through their clothes, sending another shiver through him, and he felt Alice pull herself closer. This was madness, they had no idea what they would find and nothing to defend themselves with. They didn't even have a torch. And yet out here in the cold and dark, alone with Alice, her arm looped through his, Michael realised he somehow felt the most relaxed he had all night.

At the derelict steading, Michael stopped, but Alice kept going towards the old schoolhouse building further on. She turned back to look at him, the pale wash of light from the distant lighthouse on the clifftops sweeping across her body as she did.

'Isn't this where you saw them?' she said, her voice raised over the wind.

'What do you mean, where I saw them? You saw it too, right?'

'Mike, it's getting fully dark out here now. Who knows what we saw?'

The wind snaked between the bars over the broken windows of the building beyond her. It rattled the KEEP OUT signs and sent whispers through the holes in the glass from inside. Michael thought they spoke of nothing good. How was she so unafraid? He couldn't be the one to be the coward in this situation.

He looked around. There were broken beams of wood on the ground, debris blown here at some point during the four decades the island had lain abandoned. He picked one up, felt the heft of it in his hand.

Alice laughed. 'What the hell are you doing?'

'We don't know who's in there. We'll need to protect ourselves.'

'So, you're going to stand up for me this time, then?'

She was smiling as she said it, but it still landed a blow as heavy as any of these wooden planks could.

The old door didn't take much forcing. There were no bars across it, and the lock that had been secured to it had been broken by someone else. What little light that crept in showed a narrow room with stone floors. A few of the old desks remained, as did the giant frame where the chalkboard would've been. Michael's imagination threatened to run riot. He saw little children in cloth caps still sitting at the desks and had to shake the image away. There was a smell – damp and decay and something else. The acrid smell of urine and faeces. It could've been from an animal. Could've been from whoever had forced that door. Could've been someone living here. The person he'd seen—

'Mike.'

Alice's voice came from somewhere further inside the building. He hadn't moved from the doorway.

'Alice, where did you go?'

'Over here,' her disembodied voice replied. 'This place is incredible. You coming, or what?'

He wedged the door as best he could with a pile of bricks he found lying nearby and went after her. After only a few steps inside, the darkness grew as thick as death and Michael willed his eyes to grow accustomed to it, but they wouldn't, at least not quickly enough for his liking. Instead, the blackness filled with interference, like the white spots on the TV screen late at night when all the programmes had finished for the day. He remembered reading once about how the human brain didn't like the unknown and so it filled in the gaps, such as trying to convince you there were things your eyes could see when it was too dark to make out anything at all. That was happening now. He imagined a whole class of young children and their teacher, unseen but there, watching from somewhere out in the black, growing angry at the interruption.

He bit back a scream as a human outline appeared out of the black.

'Alice! This is daft, we can't see a thing.'

This close, he could just about make out the features of her face, her eyes searching for something in his.

His heart clamped to a standstill when Alice shattered the silence with a sudden, almost-deafening: 'Hello?'

They waited. Michael could barely hear anything over the sound of his own rapid pulse beating in his ears, but he was certain there was no reply.

Alice drew breath to shout again. 'Hel—'

'Alice, for fuck's sake.'

'Ah relax, there's nobody here.' He could hear the grin in her voice. 'We've got the place to ourselves.'

She kissed him then, that same jolt of energy rushing through him as before, only this one was short-lived. He couldn't possibly relax here, couldn't lower his guard.

Alice must've felt the tension in his body. She pulled away. 'Jesus Christ, Wishy, I don't know why I bother with you.'

He saw her silhouette quickly vanishing towards the dim glow of the doorway.

He went after her. 'Alice, wait.'

She spun on her heels. 'You know your problem? You've never had anything in your life to be truly afraid of, and it's making you shit-scared of everything.'

'Are you for real? How are you not shit-scared of this? We're on an abandoned island, standing in the pitch-black dark of some creepy bastard classroom with someone out here—'

'Argh, will you drop it? There's nobody here! It's your mind playing tricks on you because you were shiteing it about coming here. I could see it on your face, back at Rabbie's.'

'I wasn't—'

'You fucking were, Wishy,' she carried on, yelling now. 'This was our first chance to spend a night together. Did you even have any intention of trying to fuck me tonight? It's not as though I've not given you enough signals.'

'Well, yeah, I—'

'What's your problem? Are you gay or something?'

The question hit him like a knife to the stomach. 'No, of course not!'

'Why "of course not"? People are.'

'Aye, well, I'm fucking not.'

'And you should've stood up for me before. You should've stepped in when Rabbie and Jake were trashing the place. You should've said something. You should've… You should…'

Her voice tailed away into the breeze that whispered in the walls and made the old building creak. Michael hoped the shadows hid the impotent look on his face.

'You're right,' he said finally. 'I was a pussy, I'm sorry.'

'I wanted one night, you know? One fucking solitary night where I could be me and I didn't have to worry about anyone else. Where I could just relax for once and do what I wanted. And now…'

He saw the outline of her face as she turned away, looked towards the door. They'd only been official now for a couple of weeks, but even before they'd got together, he'd been aware that her home life wasn't great. Everyone knew she had a twin brother called Ryan, who she was highly protective of, but who didn't go to their school. He was disabled, the story was that something had happened to him when they were both born, but Alice hadn't told him exactly what, and he had never asked. It seemed like prying. He also knew Alice and Ryan lived with their dad, who she seemed to despise, but he wasn't sure why, or what had happened to their mother. She could have been dead or she could've left, Alice had never said.

Alice sniffed and wiped her face on her sleeve. 'I'm going back to the house.'

'No, wait.'

Fuck this, he was sick of being scared. Sick of being confused. He dropped the wooden plank to the ground and reached out and grabbed Alice by the arm. When they kissed, it was clumsy and awkward and their teeth clattered together, but he didn't care. He couldn't let her walk away.

Alice began to fumble with his belt buckle.

'Hold on a second.'

'Mike, Jesus, you can't—'

'No, we're going to do this, it's just…' He tried to catch his breath. 'Not here, okay? It's bloody creepy. And I'm not going back to the house either.'

'Then where?'

'The boat,' he breathed, his lips still pressed against hers. 'There's a cabin below—'

A scraping sound made him fall silent.

They were plunged into perfect darkness as the schoolhouse door slammed shut.

FRIDAY, 6TH JUNE. PRESENT DAY.

10

Strands of yellow sunlight slipped through the blind in the kitchen window, casting stripes across the table where Freya was sitting, mug of steaming coffee in her hand. The sun had been streaming in for hours, and Freya had been at least semi-awake for most of them. Already the room was beginning to heat up, even with the back door wide open, letting in the breeze. Their black Labrador, Luna, lay in the shade by the doorway, nipping at the occasional insect that dared enter her airspace, while beyond her, Thorfinn, the German Shepherd they'd adopted in the winter, pottered around the garden, his long, pink tongue lolling out the side of his mouth as he moved from flower to flower, gently poking his wet nose into all the petals. Freya tried to take it all in, to be in the moment, in spite of the hundreds of other thoughts racing around her head.

'Did you wet the bed or something?'

She looked up. Tom came into the kitchen, fastening the last two buttons on his shirt, grinning. His sandy hair had turned dark where it was still wet from the shower.

'What?'

'You're up,' Tom clarified. 'And it's barely after seven. Do I need to call someone?'

Freya put her hand in the pocket of her yellow dressing gown, rummaged around, then pulled it out again with her middle finger extended. 'No, I just wanted to make sure you didn't leave for work without this.'

He gave Freya one of those smiles that made her forget the rest of the world existed, and leaned over to kiss his wife on the forehead. 'And here I was thinking you'd got up to make me breakfast.'

He patted Luna's head on his way past the door to the coffee machine on the counter, then called to Thorfinn too, but the elderly gentleman was too busy sniffing everything there was to be sniffed to pay his new dad any attention.

'Want a top up?' he asked, lifting the pot. It was filled with a dark roast from the Orkney Roastery, the smell alone of which was doing a fantastic job of dragging Freya out of her slumber.

'No thanks,' Freya replied with a smile. 'This is my second cup already.'

'Seriously though, how come you're out of bed this early?'

'I'm meeting Fergus before work.'

Tom nodded as he took a sip of coffee, no doubt remembering the conversation they'd had last night. Freya had told him how Fergus hadn't turned up to their catch-up due to the discovery of the body on Hoy. When Fergus had first asked Freya to help him decipher her dad's notebooks, he'd told her that nobody else could know, and that included Tom.

'Take your time,' Fergus had said. 'Give it some thought.'

She hadn't needed to.

'I'm in,' she'd replied after barely a few seconds. Then, with her next breath, she'd said, 'But I'm telling Tom. I want to know what happened to my dad, but I'm not losing my husband to do it.'

Having to hold anything back from Tom would've been a deal-breaker. She'd almost destroyed her marriage by keeping secrets; she wasn't about to do it again.

Tom leaned against the kitchen counter as he waited for the bread he'd put in the toaster to pop. He sipped his coffee and looked out through the back door. 'He's pure loving it out there, isn't he?'

'Thorfinn? He's been out on the grass since I opened the door, sun-pigging.'

'Are you coming back for them today, or will you be busy? I can probably get away around midday, if you need me to.'

'No, I'll nip back. I'll have time.'

'Will you not be working on whatever it is that's going on in Hoy?'

Freya sipped her coffee, shook her head. The press release that Fergus had told her about yesterday, the one with the sketch of the man they had found in the Dwarfie Stane, had come in while Freya was interviewing Angus Scott.

'Kristin's asked Gill to cover it,' she said.

'You feeling all right?'

When Freya looked at him, Tom was grinning again. 'What, now?'

'A big story like this and you're going to let Gill Irvine take it?'

She shrugged. 'She can have it. I've got other things I need to work on.'

'Are you not even the slightest bit interested, though? Like, it's so weird, don't you think? A guy showing up there, dead.'

'I guess. But like I said, I've got other stories that need writing up. And I've got to leave the self-proclaimed most senior reporter in Orkney something to do.'

Tom nodded slowly, watching her as he did.

'It's got nothing to do with what I'm doing with Fergus.'

'I didn't say it did,' he said, holding up his hands.

'Good, because it hasn't. I'm keeping that separate. I'm not letting it get in the way of my work.'

The toaster popped. Tom put the warm slices on a plate and started to cover them in butter. 'It just feels like this would've been exactly the type of story you would've killed for a few months ago,' he said over his shoulder. 'And certainly not the kind of thing you'd leave to Gill.'

'It's the type of story you would've freaked out about me taking a few months ago.'

She didn't say that with any malice, she was simply stating a fact, but when Tom didn't reply, didn't even turn around to face her, she knew she'd prodded a wound that hadn't yet healed. She had a habit of doing that when she really didn't mean to.

'I'm sorry. I didn't intend for that to come out the way it did.'

Tom brought his plate of toast to the kitchen table and sat down. He waved away her apology. 'It's fine. It's a fair hit, I would have. Though an off-the-books investigation into the potential murder of your own father is hardly any less dangerous. I think I'm doing well to keep it all together.'

He grinned, and Freya smiled back. She leaned across the table to kiss him. 'You are, you're being a very brave soldier.'

She didn't tell him that she'd rattled James Cooper's cage, that he had put in a complaint about her at work and threatened police action. It was all bluff, but it might panic Tom, if she mentioned it. It was okay to keep some secrets.

'I get it, you know,' Tom said. 'If I was in your position, I wouldn't stop until I knew the truth. It doesn't mean I don't worry about you though.'

Freya smiled. 'I know.'

'And I don't worry because I don't think you're capable. It's just … I don't know what I'd do if anything happened to you.'

Freya reached across the table and took his hand. She knew she sometimes got so involved in an obsession that it was easy for her to forget about everything else, including her own husband. It wasn't that she didn't love him, it was that, when she was focused on something to that level, everything else vanished. Not just Tom, she even forgot about herself. About her own needs, her own safety. It was a difficult thing for people to understand. She wasn't even sure she understood it herself.

Tom downed the rest of his coffee, then he picked up his last slice of toast and stood up. 'I'd better go. If I head in now, I'll get the place to myself for an hour. I do my best thinking when I'm there on my own.'

Freya smiled. She might not be a morning person, but she definitely understood that.

'There's a good chance you'll have the place to yourself for most of the morning,' she said. 'Judging by the state of your pals last night.'

Tom laughed at the memory. They'd gone to the quiz night at Helgi's in town, had finished second, but they probably would've won if Tom's work colleagues had focused on the questions more than the drink. They'd all left a little worse for wear.

'Yeah, it was a good night, wasn't it?'

Freya smiled and nodded. And she was being genuine, she'd had fun, but it had been a lot of effort. She wished it wasn't, that she could do the simple things other people took for granted. Since moving to Orkney, Tom seemed to have made a raft of new friends – because she was from islands, he used to make jokes that she would know everybody here, but when they bumped into someone in town, it was more likely to be someone he knew than she did. He was an engineer at the European Marine Energy Centre in Stromness and seemed to be on first name terms with everyone there, while after six months she still barely knew a thing about the people she worked with. He'd joined a bunch of social groups who did all sorts of things, from building Viking-style boats to picking litter off beaches. He'd even joined a choir, and the man couldn't sing for toffee.

'That's why being in a choir's so much fun,' he'd said. 'I get to sing away at the top of my lungs, and nobody can hear me over the sound of everybody else.'

He'd truly embraced life here in a way Freya sometimes wished she could. For people like Tom, these things seemed effortless. Whereas for her, every conversation had to be planned in advance, every interaction meant constantly monitoring the position of your eyebrows and the tone of your voice, and whether or not you were staring into the other person's eyeballs enough, while trying to hear whoever you were talking to over the sound of music and laughter and a million other conversations in the room. And when life was like that every single moment of the day, then socialising wasn't only unenjoyable, it was bloody exhausting.

But apparently, while all of that was consistent with being autistic, some stranger in a natty waistcoat who'd read about autism in a textbook and spoken to Freya for all of two hours had decided none of it caused her enough day-to-day difficulty for her to be diagnosed. And so, she was trying not to let these things bother her, because who knows, maybe the clinical psychologist had been right. Last night, she had gone with Tom and his work colleagues to the pub and attempted to join in. But she'd been worried she was answering too many of the questions and was looking like a smart arse, so she'd kept her mouth shut on a couple of occasions and was furious with herself when they had narrowly lost.

'It's a shame not everyone could make it,' Tom said before taking a final swig of coffee. He stood to leave. 'I reckon we could've won it if Alice had been there.'

Freya raised an eyebrow.

'What?'

'She's smart is she, this Alice?'

Tom shrugged. 'Smart enough.'

'I suppose she's pretty too?'

Tom grinned again, and Freya felt her heart race in her chest. When he gave her that mischievous look, his whole face lit up. It made her feel alive. She loved that things were like that between them again.

'She's all right, I guess.' He bent down and kissed her, slow and lingering. A kiss that made her wish he didn't have to rush out to work. 'Trouble is, she's a brunette. Lucky for you, I only have a thing for redheads.'

'Get out,' Freya said. 'I'm changing the bloody locks while you're gone.'

11

THE SHRILL SOUND OF Fergus's phone shattered the early morning silence.

He was sitting at one of the picnic benches overlooking the Bay of Firth, breathing in the sea air and watching the sun dance on the water's surface. It had put him in mind of the peace of the Trowie Glen yesterday morning, and how beautiful these islands were, especially on days like these, and how rare it was that he ever stopped and simply enjoyed being here.

Then his phone had started to ring, and he remembered why.

It was a number he didn't know. 'DI Muir.'

'Hello DI Muir, it's Gill Irvine here, from *The Orcadian*.'

He glanced again at the screen. He thought he had Gill Irvine's number blocked. She must've got herself a new one to get around it.

'I've told you a thousand times, Gill Irvine from *The Orcadian*, there's no need to say where you work. I know who you are, you're quite unmistakable.'

'I need a line from you about the dead body found in the Dwarfie Stane yesterday morning. Have you got a name yet? Any idea of the cause of death?'

Fergus pinched the bridge of his nose, shut his eyes. He'd given Freya the heads-up on this case before they'd sent out the official press release yesterday afternoon precisely so he wouldn't have to deal with Gill bloody Irvine. What was she playing at? He was going to have to have words with her when she showed up.

'I'll give you something better than a line,' Fergus said. 'Have you got a pen and paper handy?'

He gave her Eilidh Murray's mobile number.

'She's the OIC, she'll be able to tell you everything you want to know.'

'But—'

He hung up, the beast in his belly beginning to twitch. He didn't want to awaken it by talking to that woman for a second longer than he had to.

No sooner had he hung up, his phone rang again.

'Where are you?'

He could hear the excitement in Eilidh's voice. 'Trying to enjoy my bloody breakfast, like you should be.'

'I enjoyed mine three hours ago when the sodding dawn woke me up. I thought you said breakfast didn't agree with you.'

'Why are you calling me before eight, Murray?'

'Because you're not here. Why aren't you here? The most interesting case we've had since I got to this rock and you're missing it for a fry up, are you kidding?'

Things had not developed as quickly as they would have liked yesterday afternoon. The couple in the Polestar hadn't been able to provide a clear description of the two men they'd seen on the beach with the John Doe, or of the boat the three of them appeared to have arrived in. The sketch of the dead man had been sent to media outlets, transportation hubs, taxi firms, tour guides, tourist accommodation, restaurants, bars, cafes … anywhere Eilidh and Fergus could think of. So far nobody had come back to say they recognised the man. The house-to-house on Hoy had thrown nothing up either. There was still every chance the deceased was a tourist who'd hired a private crew to take him over to Hoy and had suffered a heart attack after making the trek up from the beach to the tomb, but there were too many little pieces that didn't quite fit the puzzle for them to rule out something more sinister. Trouble was, the little pieces didn't add up to much either – Major Investigations had been informed of the case but didn't feel it met the threshold for their involvement. For now, Fergus and Eilidh were on their own. And Eilidh couldn't have been more delighted.

'We've got something.'

'You've found out who our John Doe is?'

'Pretty much.'

Fergus sat up straight. He'd been joking. 'Don't muck about.'

'Would I ever? Check your work email for once. We've got a list of potential matches off the partial print. And it's not long, only four people. And only two of them are male.'

Fergus felt a grip in his chest. A kick of adrenaline. He then winced as pain shot through his stomach again. He hoped he hadn't made a sound Eilidh would hear. 'And you've checked them both out and found our guy, that's why you're calling me?'

'Not yet.'

'Then you know what to do.'

'Are you not going to come over right away?'

Fergus turned his head at the sound of a vehicle pulling off the main road into the car park behind him. He recognised the small turquoise Hyundai Getz. 'I'll be there at nine. I've got something to do first.'

'What?'

'I told you, I'm having breakfast. Run the two names down. Get photos if you can. Dates of birth. Anything we can use to ID our man this morning. Then we can start to find out who's missing him, if anyone.'

'I know what I need to do.'

'Then hop to it, Murray.'

'But—'

The car parked up in the spaces opposite Leigh's burger van and Freya got out. She waved to Fergus and started walking over.

'I've got to go,' Fergus said. 'I'll see you at nine.'

12

'DOESN'T LOOK LIKE LEIGH's opening up the day.' Fergus nodded to the burger van on the other side of the car park as Freya walked over to meet him. 'Shame, she does a good breakfast.'

'She doesn't open until nine.'

'Got the opening times memorised now, have you?'

'Well, aye, after that first Smoke Stack, you've got me hooked,' Freya said. 'And Tom loves the Rossini.'

'Glad to see I've had a positive influence on you both.'

He was the only person sitting on the picnic benches by the shore, the breakfast rush that would come when the van opened having yet to arrive. The sound of children's voices carried across sparkling blue water from Firth Primary School across the bay, where the first pupils were beginning to roll in, their laughter and cries competing with the usual background thrum of the quarry work on the hillside for space in Freya's brain. Fergus stood as she neared, shielding his eyes from the sun, but made no attempt to hug her. She knew he found it slightly odd only greeting each other verbally, and she felt bad, like she should make the effort and put up with the intense proximity for a few seconds, but it had become the norm now and it somehow seemed weirder to change it.

She took a seat across from him. 'Simon Cooper's son has threatened to report me to the police.'

Fergus burst out laughing.

'What?'

'Nothing. I've always enjoyed your no-nonsense approach to conversation, Red. Get the small talk out of the way quickly and dive straight into business.'

Freya felt her cheeks turning the same colour as her hair. 'Sorry.'

'Don't be. As I said, I've got no problem with it. And your dad was just the same. You're maybe too young to mind, but the number of times that man used to start a conversation mid-way through…'

A memory of her dad tweaked Freya's lips into a smile. He was forever getting into trouble off her mother for saying something that seemingly made no sense, the first part of whatever it was he was talking about having already happened in his head.

'No,' she said. 'I remember.'

'So, old Slippery Simon's son, that would be James Cooper, correct?' Fergus asked. 'The man widely tipped to become the next chief exec of the health board?'

Freya nodded.

'You certainly know how to make friends with the right people. What's he reporting you for?'

'Stalking.'

That earned her another chuckle. 'What did you do?'

'Nothing. Much.'

Freya explained how James had made a complaint to Kristin about her turning up at the hospital after an executives' meeting and asking to speak to him about his late father. She didn't mention she had also followed him in his car on a couple of occasions, and might have sat and watched his home once or twice too.

Fergus took a deep breath of the sea breeze, ran a hand through his hair. 'So, he's still your favourite for being the elusive SC, I take it?'

Fergus had given Freya a couple of names who might fit the bill, but as she'd started looking into them more deeply over the past couple of months, Simon Cooper had particularly caught her eye. One of the men Fergus had mentioned was a farmer from South Ronaldsay with a bad temper, the other a drug dealer from Manchester who'd spent some time hiding out in Eday, thinking he'd never be found, because of course there were no people, let alone police, in far flung Scottish islands. But Simon Cooper ticked a lot of boxes. He was a local councilman who'd been caught taking bribes. He'd been jailed shortly before her dad died, and his initials disappeared from the notebooks just before he'd been arrested.

'You know what Simon Cooper was lifted for, right?'

'Of course I do. Your dad led the investigation, but I was involved. I'd not long since made detective.'

'So, you know he was taking kickbacks to push through planning permission. But did you know that all the properties he granted permission for were built by a company called Kingfisher Construction?'

'It was a long time ago,' said Fergus. 'I don't recall the precise details.'

Freya took out her phone, touched the internet browser icon. One of the many tabs she had open was for the Scottish Land Registry, showing the details of a large house on a plot of land near the shore at Gorseness.

'You need to get that screen fixed,' Fergus said, nodding at the giant spider-web-shaped crack in the top corner from where she'd broken it six months ago and still hadn't got around to getting it repaired.

'This place was named in the court documents in Simon Cooper's case as one of the Kingfisher houses. But guess who bought it once it was built?'

'Enjoying yourself now, aren't you? Who?'

'Sigurd Holdings.'

Fergus nodded slowly. He'd know the connection. Sigurd Holdings was a property portfolio previously owned by Graham Linklater. The GL from the notebooks. All of the houses known to have been used by the grooming ring were in the same portfolio.

'So, who owns Kingfisher?' Fergus asked.

'That's where the trail runs cold. It's just some shell company.'

Fergus sat upright, took in a deep breath of the sea air. Freya could see he was thinking through what this all meant. He didn't appear to be as impressed as she had hoped.

'I know it doesn't prove Cooper was our SC,' she said, 'But it does at least show he was connected to what Linklater and Tait were doing.'

'It connects him to Linklater, not necessarily to Tait and what they were doing.' When he looked at her, he must've seen something on her face, because he said, 'But it's awfully good work, Red. And I know you're only one person – with the PSD lot poking around, I can't help you out as much as I'd like to. It's only going to get harder now we've got this Dwarfie Stane debacle to get to the bottom of too. So, we need to keep Cooper on our radar, but now James' cage is rattled, you're going to need to back off. Unless you want to get yourself sacked. Again.'

He smiled, and Freya tried to as well. But she couldn't help but feel stung by his lack of excitement at what she'd found.

He must've seen that too. 'Look, in any investigation, you follow all possible leads. And, if I can be honest with you, you have a habit of becoming fixated on one thing and ignoring everything else. Go back to the list I gave you, take a look at the other names too, give James some time to cool off. And you never know what it might throw up.'

He glanced at his watch.

'Are you really that keen for breakfast?' Freya asked.

'No. Sadly, duty calls. I'll have to set off in a bit.'

Freya nodded. She glanced behind her, saw the car park was filling up. She would have to leave soon too: she didn't want Gill making an example of her in front of everyone again.

'By the way, I've got a bone to pick with you,' Fergus said. 'What are you doing letting Gill Irvine get the Dwarfie Stane case? I gave you the heads-up specifically so I wouldn't have to deal with her.'

'I was out doing an interview when the press release came in. Kristin gave the story to Gill.' That jogged her memory; there was something else she wanted to ask Fergus about. 'That reminds me: yesterday I spoke to Angus Scott.'

Fergus thought for a second. 'Trevor's brother?'

'Aye, do you know him?'

'I met Angus once, but I knew Trevor. Quite well, in fact. It was tragic what happened, and sick what people are saying about him. He was a good man. I don't imagine that was an easy conversation.'

'Not really.'

'Did he tell you he was up here after Neill died?'

'He did. He told me a lot of things.' Freya glanced over her shoulder again, this time checking nobody had come to sit within ear shot. 'He said Trevor had tried to blow the whistle on Tait but didn't have any concrete evidence against him. Something to do with a case involving a missing boy.'

'Did he give any more details than that?'

He hadn't, and being unprepared for the interview and thrown by Angus talking about her dad, Freya hadn't asked. She could have kicked herself. She'd have to come up with a reason to approach him again.

'He only told me it was a case in the late nineties.'

Fergus looked out across the water, his brown eyes searching for something in the waves. 'Folk go missing all the time, it would be hard to narrow it down. And none stick out in my memory.'

'But it happened round about the same time my dad started the notebooks.'

'You didn't tell him about that, did you?' Fergus's eyes were now firmly back on Freya. 'Because if anyone finds out—'

'I didn't tell him.'

Fergus exhaled a sigh of relief. He checked his watch again. 'I'll have a think. Now, as much as I'd love to stay, I'm going to have to shoot off.'

'Angus said something else.'

'Tell me as we walk to the car.'

They both stood. 'He said Trevor took his own life because he couldn't stand the guilt of never following through on raising the alarm. Once the truth about Tait came out, it was too much for him.'

'Well, then that begs the question, why didn't he follow through on it? He was a young man back then. He had plenty of time to keep gathering intelligence on Tait.'

They stopped at the edge of the grass next to Freya's vehicle and waited a moment for the driver of a small grey van to get out and jog towards the public toilets.

'Angus claims he was stopped,' Freya said. 'He reckons he was terrified for his life.'

Fergus scanned the ground as he considered this. 'So, somebody knew what he was doing and put the wind up him?' He looked up. 'And you're thinking whoever it was…'

'Was the same person who got to my dad, aye. Only he didn't scare as easy.'

A shadow seemed to cross Fergus's face. 'That sounds about right.'

'How well do you know Angus Scott?' Freya asked.

'Not too well.'

'But you knew Trevor?'

'I did. We were quite good pals. He always seemed close to your dad too. They spoke a lot.'

'What do you think? Does this stack up, or do you think Angus is just creating a story to quash the rumours about his brother being bent?'

'If I had to bet, I'd be putting my money on Angus telling the truth. Those things they're saying about Trevor can't be true. If they are, then I'll be very sorry indeed. He was a good man.'

'Angus also said he doesn't think my dad's death was an accident anymore.'

'Aye, well, then that makes three of us.' Fergus's gaze searched for something in Freya's eyes. 'If it wasn't, we'll find out, you know. We'll get him the justice he deserves. That you all deserve.'

Slowly, he reached out a large hand and placed it on her shoulder, gave it the lightest squeeze.

'I know you don't do hugs, but…'

Freya put her hand on his, even though the intensity of the moment felt almost unbearable. 'Thank you.'

He nodded, waited a moment more. Then he walked towards his car.

'You know,' he called back as he opened the driver's side door, 'I always used to wind your dad up, tell him you must be the milkman's daughter on account of your red hair.'

Freya smiled. 'I think I get it from my grandma on my mum's side.'

'I'm sure that's what it was.'

Fergus stood by his open car door, didn't get in. Freya got the sense he was hesitating, thinking about saying something else.

'They were trying for a while before you came along. Your parents,' he said, eventually. 'They were so desperate for a little baby. Then when you showed up, he changed completely. I'd never known him so happy.' He looked away, drummed his fingers on the roof of his car. 'There's not a day that passes I don't wish he was still here.'

Fergus must have known the impact his words would have, because he didn't wait around long after saying them.

Freya got in her car, sat in the driver's seat a moment, her hand on the key in the ignition. Away to the north, a few small white clouds had gathered over the glistening sea.

She wiped her cheek with the back of her hand, started her engine.

She said to no one, 'I wish he was still here too.'

13

'I've bloody found him.'

Eilidh called Fergus over to her desk as soon as he walked into the CID office, waving at him like a drowning woman trying to attract a passing ship. It was actually quite nice; it had been a while since anyone had been this excited to see him. He was about to make that exact comment when he spotted the image on her computer screen over her shoulder and all jokes went out of his mind. It was a photograph of the man from the Dwarfie Stane, alive and well.

And in police uniform.

'Is that him?' Fergus asked as he came to stand beside Eilidh's chair, though he knew full well it was. The man was younger in the photograph, of course, but there was no denying the resemblance. The same hair, the same eyes. This was their guy. 'He's a cop?'

'Yep. That's how I tracked him down,' Eilidh said. 'Forensic services gave us four possible hits, two men, like I told you. I ran both names through all the usual places and this one popped up on the clearance database.'

All police officers were required to submit their fingerprints and DNA to a clearance database which could be used to rule out any traces they left at a crime scene during an investigation.

Fergus leaned in, squinted slightly against the glare of the screen as he read. 'Peter Moss.'

'Inspector Peter Moss,' Eilidh corrected him. 'Or he used to be. Retired due to health reasons four years ago.'

'Health reasons?'

'Doesn't go into specifics about what they were but, now we've got a name and date of birth, we can get his medical records.'

'So have you?'

'Have I what?'

'Asked for his medical records yet?'

Eilidh nodded at the coffee cup in Fergus's hand. He'd stopped at Beiting and Brew on the way into the station. He wasn't drinking that pish from the vending machine two days in a row. 'No, sorry, boss. All I've done is identify our unknown dead man while you've been swanning round getting a nice breakfast for yourself. I must try harder.'

'We'll address it at your next one-to-one.'

He only half caught the shitty look Eilidh gave him out of the corner of his eye. He was focused on the profile on the computer screen. Peter Moss had been an inspector for Lancashire Police in England. His date of birth put him at fifty-nine years old. The address on his profile was a place called Carnforth near Lancaster. They would have to check if that was up to date.

'Is he a mis-per?'

'Now that I have checked, and no.'

'So, nobody's reported him missing. He's got known, historical health issues…'

Eilidh knew what he was getting at. 'I know it's looking like natural causes, but it's still shady as fuck. Why was he out there, dressed like that, in the middle of the night? He'd left his phone behind somewhere and had a burner and all that cash on him. Plus, that message written on his forearm. The Dying Light. What the hell is that?'

'I know what it isn't: a crime. None of it is. And the thing about his phone is conjecture. He could've lost his iPhone and that was a cheap replacement.'

Eilidh shook her head. 'You've got to admit there's enough for us to continue to treat this as suspicious until the autopsy says it's not.'

Against his better judgement, something about this case made him agree. 'We'll have next-of-kin on here, I take it?'

Eilidh scrolled down the screen to show the details for a Mrs Linda Moss, born the same year as Peter, also based in Lancashire, though her address wasn't in Carnforth. The relationship box had been left blank.

'What are we thinking? Ex-wife?'

'Different address. Birthdays too close together to be siblings. Looks that way,' Eilidh said.

'Let's give her a call, shall we?'

'Be my guest. I thought I ought to leave you something to do.'

Fergus took out his mobile, started keying in the number. 'While I do this, how about you see about those medical records. We should get that name and photo out to all the hotels too, find out where he was staying. Is Jake or Kate or anyone else around today?'

'I'm not sure about Jake. I've seen Kate in.'

'Okay, get her to help out. We need someone to trawl his social media too. If we're going to keep this active for now – and it is solely for now – I want to know why he's up here and where he's been.'

Eilidh smirked, gave a mock salute. 'Yes, sir.'

Fergus pressed the green call button and put his phone to his ear. 'Hop to it, Murray.'

The phone rang four or five times before a woman answered. 'Yes?'

Fergus stepped away from Eilidh's desk, walked over to the window. It was a similar view to the one from Magnus's office, looking out over the Peedie Sea.

'Am I speaking to Linda Moss?' he asked.

'No.'

Fergus stumbled, surprised. He was about to ask who he was talking to when the voice on the other end said, 'Used to be. Who is this?'

'This is DI Fergus Muir from the Orkney Police. I'm calling in relation to Peter Moss. You're listed as his next-of-kin.'

Fergus heard a long exhale on the other end of the line. 'I can't believe he's got me down as his next-of-kin, the daft bugger. We haven't spoken in five years.'

'So, you're Peter's ex-wife?'

'You're a DI, you said? That's a detective?'

'Yes.'

'Aye, you're a good one, aren't you? Yes, I'm his ex-wife. I've remarried. I'm Linda Hall now.'

And I'm sure Mr Hall is a very lucky man, Fergus thought. 'Mrs Hall, are you somewhere we can talk? Are you with anyone?'

'Am I with ... What's this about?'

Fergus ran a hand through his hair. 'I'm sorry to have to inform you that Peter Moss was found dead yesterday on the island of Hoy in Orkney.'

Silence now. He hated doing this.

'Mrs Hall, are you—'

'I'm fine.' Another long pause, then, 'Is this a joke? Are you a mate of his?'

'I'm afraid not.'

'Bloody hell.'

Fergus glanced over his shoulder. Eilidh had found Kate and was explaining what she needed her to do. The young PC looked keen to help. Fergus had known she would be.

He waited a moment longer before speaking again. 'Mrs Hall, I know this—'

'Call me, Linda.'

'Linda, I know this is a lot to take in, and I know you said you'd not spoken to Peter in a while, but can you think of any reason why your ex-husband would be in Orkney? Does he know anyone here? Is it somewhere he's regularly visited?'

Linda laughed. Or at least Fergus thought that's what it was. A short, sharp explosion of breath that caused static down the line. 'I'm surprised he even knows where it is. I don't. He's never mentioned the place to me, not got no connections there as far as I'm aware. But like I say, we've not spoken in a while now. Last I heard, he was living somewhere up in Scotland.'

'Orkney is in Scotland, Mrs Hall.'

'Well then, maybe he's been living there. I wouldn't know.'

Fergus wedged his mobile between his ear and his shoulder as he took out a small notebook from the inside pocket of his jacket and wrote down: *Could be local.*

'How did he die?' Linda asked, her voice softer than before, like the news might have only just been sinking in.

'We're yet to establish that. But he doesn't appear to have suffered.'

'Shame.'

The tenderness left her voice as quickly as it had arrived.

Fergus bit his lip, passed his phone to his other hand. 'How about his health? Did he have any problems with his heart? Any long-term conditions? Anything like that?'

'If cheating, drinking and gambling count, he had those. And the bastard was incurable.'

He added drinking and gambling to his notes. The latter might explain the cash he had on him.

He was about to thank her and end the call when he thought of something else. 'One last thing, as you're down as his next-of-kin, would you be able to formally identify the body for us?'

'So, hold on a minute, you don't even know it's him?'

'We know from his fingerprints, and we'll know soon enough from his DNA, but it would help us massively if you could confirm it for us visually.'

'So, I'd have to come to Orkney. Where the hell is it?'

'No, Peter's body has been moved to Aberdeen for—'

'Aberdeen? That's bloody miles away. Are you paying for me to come up there?'

Fergus shut his eyes, tried not to sigh. 'It's not something we'd usually offer.'

'And do I have to?'

'Well, like I said, it would help us massively if—'

'Nah,' Linda said. 'That bastard bled me dry when he was alive, he's not doing it again now he's dead. Best of luck.'

And she hung up.

'How did it go?' Eilidh asked as Fergus walked back over to join her and Kate.

'I've changed my mind, this is a murder case. And I reckon we've got our prime suspect.'

'That well, eh?'

Fergus nodded. 'Where are we up to?'

'Kate's getting an email out to all accommodation providers, then she said she'll get started on the search of social media, but it's going to take a while. There are a lot of Peter Mosses.'

'Aye, and if he's an ex-cop he probably won't be using his own name online.'

'Yeah, I wondered that too.'

Fergus turned to Kate, who was sitting at a computer next to Eilidh's. 'Give it an hour tops on the social media search. Any longer will be a waste of your time.'

'I really don't mind,' Kate said.

'Give it two then, if you can spare it.'

Kate nodded and turned back to her screen.

'Before you ask, yes, his medical records have now been requested,' Eilidh said.

'Better late than never.'

She ignored that. 'I've emailed his details and this photo to the ferry terminals and the airports too, see if we can find out when he came in and how long he's been here.'

'And if he ever planned to leave. Could be a suicide we're looking at here. Also, the ex-wife mentioned he'd moved to Scotland. And that he liked a drink and a flutter.'

'Orkney's hardly the place for the latter. I don't think I've seen a bookie's here.'

'You haven't,' said Fergus. 'Might not have been the legal sort he was into.'

'Do you think that's what the cash was for?'

'Possibly.'

'So, if it wasn't the legal sort of gambling he was interested in…'

Fergus rubbed his eyes. If they were going to keep treating this death as suspicious, then a gambling debt was a possible line of enquiry they should chase up. He pointed to Eilidh's jacket on the back of her chair. 'Grab that. There's someone we need a peedie blether with.'

14

It wasn't yet nine by the time she got to Hatston, so Freya sat in her spot in the car park again and took a minute, before going up to the newsroom, to return to Fergus's list of names.

Sean Cotterill.

Seamus Cleat.

Steven Campbell.

Sandra Coyle, the solitary woman in the rogues' gallery.

Freya had looked over these names time and again, had dug into their backgrounds, tried to find anything that would identify them as SC. None of them stood out like Simon Cooper.

Upstairs, the door to Kristin's office was closed and there was only one other person in the newsroom.

'...once again, it's Gill Irvine, senior reporter for *The Orcadian*. Call me back on 01856 854555 as soon as you get this, okay?'

This was why Freya never liked getting to work early.

Gill was always the first into the office and the last to leave. She didn't acknowledge Freya's arrival as she hung up the phone, didn't even make a quip about her being at work before 9 a.m. It was unsettling.

Freya sat at her computer across the desk from Gill. 'Morning.'

No reply. Gill began hammering her keyboard with a single nicotine-stained finger on each hand, her intense gaze fixed on her screen. That was fine with Freya. She needed to finish off typing up her interview with Angus as quickly as she could so she'd have time to look into the missing person case he'd mentioned without Kristin becoming even more incensed with her. She wasn't happy about being told to drop the Simon Cooper angle, but she had to admit Fergus was right that it made no sense to piss his son off any more than she already had. If Cooper had been involved with Tait and Linklater, and if James knew, going after him would only make him more defensive. That didn't leave her with much else to go off. If Angus was telling the truth, then the missing boy case was the one that had tipped his brother off about Allan Tait being corrupt. In a lot of ways, it might even have been a better lead than anything she was likely to get from James Cooper.

'For pity's sake!'

She looked up as Gill slammed the handset on her phone down again.

'Your Uncle Fergus is a lazy wee bugger, do you know that, hen?'

'How's that?' Freya asked.

'I'm trying to get a line out of him about this Dwarfie Stane story, but he's gone and given me the number of that new detective they've got over there, and the bloody woman never answers.'

'Are you needing something to move the story on?'

Gill bristled at the suggestion. 'I'm well on top of this story, sweetheart, don't you worry. I've got my contacts in Hoy keeping me up to date. I just need a line from those corrupt bastards as well. For balance, as Kris keeps telling us.'

Freya forced herself not to grin.

She turned her attention back to her computer. She had a list of jobs as long as her arm to do and couldn't bring herself to focus on a single one of them. There was time to get her Angus Scott interview written up before it needed to go to print, but there was also a piece about a proposed council tax hike that she'd been tasked with at yesterday's meeting, another about disruption to inter-island ferry services while one of the boats was in dry dock. Neither got her pulse racing. She rubbed her eyes, tried to force herself to get some words down, but her mind kept drifting back to the case Angus had mentioned.

She looked up. Gill had given up with the phone and was staring intently at her computer screen again, brow suitably furrowed, her yellow fingers hammering her keyboard in a steady rhythm. Freya hid behind her computer monitor, pressed on the studs in her ears and counted them to herself, tried to decide if and how she should ask the question.

'You were here in the late nineties, right, Gill?'

Gill's eyes never left the screen as she replied. 'I started here straight out of school.'

Was that a yes? She was going to assume it was.

'Do you remember any stories about a boy going missing around that time?'

Now she had her colleague's attention. 'Why do you ask?'

'It came up in my interview with Angus Scott yesterday.'

Gill scoffed. 'Did it now? Let me guess, did it have something to do with how his beloved brother had no idea what was going on in that police force back in the day and was in no way at all as corrupt as the rest of them?' She rolled her eyes before pointing them back at her screen. 'Every single one of those buggers over at that station back then was as bent as that rotter Tait, you mark my words. They were all up to their necks in it, if you ask me.'

'Nobody's—'

She stopped herself short of saying Nobody's bloody asking you. She said instead, 'Nobody's going to know how far it went until the investigation's done.'

Gill said nothing.

'I take it you don't remember the story I'm on about then?'

'You'd have to refresh my memory, hen, it was a long time ago. When exactly are we talking?'

'Late nineties.'

'You can't be more specific than that?'

'Ninety-seven, maybe.' Freya had no idea if it was, but that was the year her dad's notebooks started.

Gill gave it a moment's thought. 'Well, there's nothing that immediately springs to mind. Folk go missing in these islands all the time, or they wind up here from somewhere else with the intention of vanishing.' She said it like Freya wasn't from Orkney herself and wouldn't know. 'I can't say I'm surprised Angus hasn't been more specific, though. I'll bet you anything you like he was making the whole thing up.'

Freya pressed hard on her studs again, felt the reassuring pinch in her fingertips. What angered her most was, part of her worried Gill was right.

She was about to turn back to her to-do list when Gill said: 'Shame you don't have something more specific to go off, sweetheart. You could've looked it up in the archives.'

* * *

The archives were on the ground floor; an oak-panelled room housing wooden cabinets containing a copy of every edition of the newspaper going right back to its inception in 1854. Freya covered her nose and mouth with her sleeve to block out the heavy odours of varnish and ink, pinched her ear piercings with her free hand again, as she walked along the rows of cabinets, looking for the year she was after.

She took out the January issues of 1997. There was nothing else for it but to go through the whole year week by week from beginning to end. She didn't even know if the case that had raised Trevor Scott's suspicions was the same one that had caused her dad to begin keeping those notebooks. Trevor could've known about Tait for years before her dad became involved. He might even have asked her dad to start keeping an eye on things once he'd been scared off and knew people were watching him. But in the absence of anything better to go off, picking the same year as the notebooks started seemed the only choice.

By the time she'd got as far as March she was beginning to see print in front of her eyes. The smell was really beginning to work its way into the back of her throat now, and the hum and throb of the presses from the printing business that shared the premises was pulsing through her brain. She decided to head back upstairs for a break, grab a coffee, when the door to the archives opened and Sophie came in carrying two mugs.

'Whatever it is you're doing down here, please say I can help.'

Freya smiled. 'How did you know I was down here?'

'Gill made some comment about you "swanning off to hide",' Sophie said. 'Jesus, between her girning about your uncle, and Kristin's arsey mood, I couldn't stand it up there any longer. So, I pretended you'd texted me and asked me to bring you a brew.'

Fergus wasn't Freya's uncle, he was her godfather and a very close friend of her mum and dad, so as a kid she'd always called him Uncle Fergus. She had once let the name slip in front of Gill, and the bloody woman had referred to him as that ever since, to the point that everyone else at the paper believed they were related. She had explained the truth of the matter to Kristin once, but much like the Fiona situation with Keith, she couldn't be bothered to keep repeating it to everyone else.

Sophie put Freya's mug down beside her and glanced at the old newspaper spread out in front of her. She swept a strand of brown hair from her eyes. 'What exactly are you doing?'

'I need to find an old story.'

'March 1997,' Sophie read. 'I wasn't even born then.'

'Thanks for making me feel ancient.'

Sophie giggled. 'You're welcome. Do you need a hand? I'm worried about your old eyes.'

Freya grinned too. She had a lot of time for Sophie. Despite her job, Freya had never found it easy to talk to folk – with an interview, there were defined roles and a structure to the conversation, questions and answers, but social interaction was so much more chaotic. As a result, she usually kept quiet around people, and had been told in the past she came across as aloof and uncaring, which of course she never meant to. It had always made it tough for her to make friends, and she often assumed people didn't really like her. But Sophie seemed to take to her from day one. There was something about her that made her very easy to talk to. If anyone else had come down here while she was working, Freya's heart would've sunk, but she was actually quite glad to have Sophie's help. nodded at the cabinets. 'Aye, start at December 1997 and work backwards. I'm looking for any mention of a missing teenage boy.'

'What was his name?'

'I don't know.'

Sophie frowned. 'So, you don't know who he was or when this happened? Why are you looking for this?'

'I interviewed Angus Scott yesterday. The brother of the cop who took his own life recently.'

Sophie nodded, rolled her eyes. 'Another of Gill's favourite topics.'

'Angus told me his brother suspected Allan Tait was corrupt, and it was this case that tipped him off. He said it happened in the late nineties.'

'Fair enough. It beats listening to Gill. Or writing up the shite I've been given to do.'

Freya smiled at her colleague. She hoped she was conveying sympathy. She knew Sophie was desperate to get her teeth into some meatier stories but, with Gill around, it was hard. Plus, Freya's connection to Fergus and her involvement in anything related to the PSD investigation must've made it harder for her too. Freya had tried to involve her in some of the stories around the grooming ring, where Kristin would allow it. Any time she had, Sophie had spent a lot of it asking Freya about her previous job in Glasgow, and what it was like to be a 'real' reporter in a big city. She clearly had her heart set on a move away at some point.

After almost an hour spent working in silence, Sophie stood up to stretch. Freya glanced up as she swapped out June's editions for July's. 'Anything yet?'

'Nothing. There was a story in the November about a girl who ran away from home, but they found her a week later. I've made a note of it just in case.'

They both turned back to the pages in front of them.

'This is nice this, isn't it?'

Freya looked up. 'What is?'

'This.' Sophie held her hand to her ear, like she was listening for something.

All Freya could hear was the ever-present thrum of the printing presses. She wasn't sure what she was supposed to be hearing. 'I can't hear anything.'

'Exactly,' said Sophie. 'No sweetheart this and hen that. It's bloody bliss.'

Freya smiled. 'You know, I've always found that weird. When I lived in Glasgow, people called each other hen all the time, but you don't hear it much here.'

Sophie's eyes lit up. 'Didn't you know?'

'Know what?'

'She's not bloody from here.'

Freya was genuinely stunned. From the way Gill spoke, anyone would believe she was descended directly from the first Jarl of Orkney. 'Seriously?'

'Aye, she was born in East Kilbride. Somewhere down there anyway. Her parents are both from down that way too. She only moved here when she was about six or seven.'

Freya raised her eyebrows, glanced back down at the pile of papers.

'Oh yeah, that woman's full of it. She lives in a fantasy land,' Sophie was saying. 'I mean, the fact she still wears her wedding ring is just tragic.'

Freya nodded, but she wasn't fully listening. She'd spotted a headline on the front page of one of the July issues: Tragedy Strikes Twice, over a photograph of a burnt-out house. But it was the subheading that really caught her eye: Parents of missing teenager tragically killed in house fire.

'Found something?' Sophie asked.

'Maybe.'

She read on, quickly.

A tragic turn of events has resulted in the death of a married couple mere weeks after the disappearance of their son. David and Mary Wishart, both 42, perished in the blaze that consumed their Burray home in the early hours of Tuesday morning after firefighters were unable to reach them in time. The alarm was raised when…

Freya skimmed on ahead, looking for mention of the missing boy.

… This terrible tragedy comes less than a month after the Wisharts' son was reported missing and has yet to be found. Michael, 17, was last seen on the night of Friday, 20th June, as he left his parents' home to stay with a friend in Kirkwall, but the parents of the friend in question say Michael never arrived. The investigation into Michael's disappearance indicates he may have run away from home. Chief Inspector Allan Tait told The Orcadian his officers were pursuing multiple leads that

suggest he may have been trying to reach relatives in Ullapool. The police do not believe there is any connection between the fire and Michael's disappearance …

'Oh my God, it says their daughter was at her grandparents' house. That's bloody lucky.'

Sophie was reading the article over Freya's shoulder. She'd clearly skimmed on ahead. Freya ran her eyes down the columns of ink too, looking for the section Sophie had seen. Sure enough, the Wisharts' thirteen-year-old daughter, Emma, had been out of the house at the time.

'Could you imagine?' Sophie was saying. 'How do you even cope with something like that, losing your whole family so young?'

Freya said nothing, but she could imagine. She hadn't lost her whole family, but at times it felt like it.

The paper she'd been reading was published on 17th July. She flicked back through the pile, looking for the issues from late June, early July. There was no mention of a missing boy on the front pages. Instead, she found a small article inside the last issue in June, simply detailing that Michael Wishart, a seventeen-year-old from Burray, had gone out to stay with a friend and had never come home, and that police were actively seeking leads as to his whereabouts.

Freya felt her pulse quicken. The timeline fit, and the mention of Allan Tait set alarm bells ringing. Could this be the case that had put Tait on Trevor Scott's radar?

And if so, why?

Freya looked at the byline. Gill had worked at the paper then, but it wasn't her article, which maybe explained why she didn't remember it. But the man who had written this story was still a reporter for *The Orcadian*. Just about.

15

The air was cooler in the shade of the trees outwith the Earl's Palace.

Freya marched straight through the crowd queuing to enter the crumbling sandstone towers and those of the Bishop's Palace across the street. She had seen the huge cruise ship docked at Hatston this morning as she'd driven into work, like a floating skyscraper, ready to deposit somewhere in the region of two thousand tourists onto the streets of Kirkwall before being packed into buses and ferried to every site of interest Orkney had to offer. Luckily, Freya didn't need to wait in line with them. The place she was heading for was behind them, and on no day-tripper's itinerary.

Keith Clouston was standing in front of the Sheriff's Court, smoking, looking like the human version of an unmade bed. His shirt was untucked on his right-hand side. On his left, his wispy white hair was standing on end like someone had rubbed it with a balloon. He stubbed out his cigarette as he saw Freya approach.

'Fiona, what are you doing here?'

Freya bit her tongue. Keith had been on sick leave when she'd started at *The Orcadian*, had returned while Freya herself had been off, recovering from her ordeal back in the winter. He was one of the auld guard, had been around at the paper for longer than even Gill Irvine had. He'd served his apprenticeship in the newsrooms of the 1980s, all cigarette smoke and rampant sexism. Freya guessed that, as he hadn't retired yet, he must be somewhere in his early sixties, but she wasn't sure; with his frail frame and white hair he looked closer to eighty, and he acted like it too. The first time they'd met, he'd misheard Freya's name, she hadn't corrected him, and he'd been calling her Fiona ever since. It seemed silly to point out the error now.

She delivered her rehearsed line. 'I need a favour. I was hoping you could help me with a story.'

'Well, you know me, always happy to help.'

Freya didn't know him, she knew next to nothing about the man. Keith very much kept himself to himself. It was one of the reasons Freya liked him enough to let him keep calling her Fiona.

'But I've got to get away back inside just now,' he said, glancing over his shoulder. 'Court's starting up again, and I'm the one who's drawn the short straw this morning.'

His smile made his already small eyes narrow even further. All the reporters at the paper took it in turns to report from Sheriff's Court, which was in session a few times each month. It could either be a treasure trove of interesting little titbits, or the most boring day of your life. Freya never really minded it, but everyone else seemed to despise it.

'About that,' she said. 'How about I swap you and take the rest of your morning in court if you can help me out?'

Keith straightened his back. That caught his attention. 'Must be some story.'

'It's related to a piece you wrote back in the nineties.'

Keith laughed. 'The nineties. Fiona, love, I don't know what I was doing last week, I cannot remember a thing from the nineties, bloody hell.'

She'd had a feeling he was going to say that. 'It was about a house fire. A couple died. The Wisharts.'

The laughing stopped. She hadn't been expecting that.

'Keith?'

'The Wisharts, you say? Aye, sorry, it's not ringing any bells.'

He took a packet of cigarettes out of his suit jacket pocket, lit up. A crow cawed in the high trees and he jumped, burned his fingers with his lighter. Freya saw a flash of anger in his eyes as he swore with the pain.

'Sorry, I really do need to get back in there,' he said.

'Before you've finished that?'

She pointed at the cigarette between his fingers. Keith looked at it like someone else had put it there. He dropped it to the floor, stamped it out. 'Look, I don't remember anything about the Wishart boy, okay? I can't help you.'

'I never said anything about their son.'

Keith glanced back at Freya as he walked away, realised his mistake, but said nothing. Freya watched him go, swore under her breath as he disappeared inside the entrance. Suddenly, the space under the trees between the ruined buildings felt cramped and she didn't want to be here anymore. There were too many people. The noise of the crowd, the cries of the crows in the trees, too loud. She needed to think about what Keith's reaction meant, and what she should do next, and she needed space to do that.

She was about to leave when her phone vibrated. A text from Kristin: 'Where are you now???'

Three question marks. That wasn't a good sign.

She knew she had stories she needed to be working on, but she couldn't deal with her boss being mad at her right now. Nobody was going to be refreshing *The Orcadian* website waiting to hear about bloody council tax hikes. She put her phone in her pocket, looked back at the entrance to Sheriff's Court just in time to spot Keith popping his head around the door, like a tortoise poking out of his shell. He immediately ducked back inside when he saw Freya was still out there. It would almost be funny if it hadn't been so pathetic. She walked over, found Keith lurking in the lobby. The door to the courtroom was closed, a security guard standing in front of it. The court must already have been in session and Keith would now be stuck outside until the next case started.

'Looks like you're in for a bit of a wait,' Freya said.

'It won't be too long.'

'Let me buy you a coffee before the next hearing. And I'm serious, if you can help me in any way at all, I'll take the rest of the day for you.'

They went to Cafelolz on the other side of the cathedral, but it was packed. Everywhere was. Freya got two coffees and two bacon rolls to carry out and they went and sat in the gardens off Tankerness Lane. The cruise ship crowd mustn't have had this place in their guidebooks, because apart from a couple of pigeons interested in their hot rolls, they had the tranquil space to themselves.

Freya wasn't sure how to play this. She didn't want to spook Keith any more than he already was, but her instinct was to ask him what the hell was wrong with him and what exactly had happened with the Wishart story to have him this spooked all these years later. As she often did, she decided it was best to say nothing, wait for him to speak first.

'I really don't remember all that much,' Keith protested again.

'But you remember Michael?'

Keith nodded, ketchup dripping from his chin. 'Some things, but it's hazy. It was a long time ago, you know. You probably weren't even born.'

Freya was seven by the time he went missing, but she didn't correct him. That was deflection and she didn't want to give him a chance to change the subject.

'The bit I can recall is the parents were in pieces after their boy ran away, as anyone would be,' Keith went on. 'But the rumour was the mum had taken to drinking. Some people said she'd fallen asleep while smoking, others said she started the fire on purpose.'

'So, Michael ran away?'

Keith took another bite of his sandwich, shrugged. 'That's what people said.'

Freya wanted to grab this man by the throat and shake him. Did he only ever report hearsay? Had he not tried to find anything out for himself? She fought with the urge to reach for her ear piercings and instead asked calmly, 'Who said?'

'People. The police.'

'The police concluded Michael had run away?'

'I think so,' Keith said. 'I told you, I don't remember.'

'How?'

'How what?'

'How did he run away? There's nowhere to go without getting on a ferry or a plane.'

'You know what it's like here. Folk talk. Everyone knew he'd run away. It wasn't a happy family, that one, for one reason or another. Rumour had it he knew how to sail. He stole a boat.'

'So, were any boats reported stolen? Was a boat ever found?'

'For Christ's sake, Fiona, I told you—' Keith stopped when Freya jumped at how angry he'd turned. He seemed to realise his surroundings, took a nervous glance around at a couple of middle-aged women who'd wandered into the gardens heading for the ornamental Groatie Hoose, before shrinking back into himself. 'Why do you want to know about all this anyway?'

This was the longest conversation Freya had ever had with Keith, the longest time she'd ever really spent in his company. Since he had come back to work, he'd disappeared into the background, like an old ornament that had been there for years, finally put back in its place on the mantelpiece. He had been more notable by his absence than his presence. She didn't know if these flashes of anger were normal or a result of this topic of conversation. She decided to test the water. 'It's for the piece I'm doing about Trevor Scott.'

The lines in Keith's forehead deepened. 'The cop who killed himself on his boat?'

'Yeah.'

'And how on earth would that be connected to this?'

She watched closely for his reaction. 'I spoke to Trevor's brother. He told me Trevor knew Allan Tait was corrupt years ago. He said this was the case that tipped him off.'

Keith looked for a moment like he might bring his bacon roll back up.

'What did Michael's parents think?' Freya asked next. 'Did they buy the story that he'd run away?'

'No, but then they wouldn't, would they? They didn't want to admit that their darling boy had abandoned them.'

'So, were they putting pressure on the police to find him?'

'Aye, but as I said, any parent would.'

This was starting to make sense to Freya now. Michael Wishart had gone missing and, for some reason, Allan Tait didn't particularly want to go looking for him. The Wisharts had pushed the police, called them out for not doing enough. Then a week or so later their house had gone up in flames.

This had to be the case that had made Scott see Tait for who he was.

But why wouldn't Tait want Wishart found?

'I think I should be getting back. The next session will be starting soon,' Keith said. 'I won't hold you to your offer. Thanks for the roll, though.'

'Allan Tait's dead, so who are you so scared of?'

She saw that flash of anger again, but he controlled it this time. It was unnerving how quickly this meek little man seemed to transform into something much more spiteful.

His thin lips parted, he was about to say something, but then he thought better of it. Instead, he wiped the corners of his mouth with a paper napkin and stood to leave. 'The past is the past, there's no point dragging it all back up again.'

Freya stood too. 'What happened to Michael Wishart, Keith?'

He glanced quickly at the middle-aged couple, then leaned closer to Freya. 'You have a family, don't you? People you care about?' he whispered.

This close, Freya could smell the bacon on his breath as he spoke. She forced herself to look him in the eye, could see the fear there. She nodded, and he nodded back.

'Aye, well then, for your sake and theirs,' he said softly, 'pray you never find out.'

16

They stepped out of the tiny twin-prop airplane, blinking into the sunlight. On the other side of an airport terminal no bigger than a small bungalow, a police car was waiting in the car park. It was busy this morning; five of the eight parking spaces were taken.

PC Dave Heddle lowered the driver's side window. 'You pair are lucky I was up here today or you'd be catching the bus.'

'Is there one?' Eilidh asked.

Dave checked his watch. 'Oh aye, of course there is. And you'd only have another ninety minutes to wait for it too.'

PC Heddle had Orkney's North Isles as his beat, and thankfully had already been on the island of Westray this morning when Fergus had got in touch. There was no police station here, no permanent police presence, so Dave rotated his days between the various islands in the north of the county. He was in his fifties with a round face that always seemed to be at least slightly flushed red, like he'd been standing outside too long in the wind. Given his beat, chances were he had been. He had grey hair now, kind blue eyes, and Fergus was pretty certain he had never seen him without a smile. He was another officer with whom Fergus went back years, the pair of them being a similar age and having joined the police around the same time. Fergus imagined he would have spent his career in community policing like Dave, and still been a PC now, if it hadn't been for Neill Spence talking him into taking the detectives exams. He wasn't sure if he wouldn't have preferred it.

Dave set off along the single-track road towards the island's main settlement of Pierowall. Eilidh sat up front, having called shotgun the second they'd landed. Fergus watched her from the back seat.

'Feeling any better?' he asked her.

'I was gonna say, you're looking a bit peelie-wallie, there,' PC Heddle added, glancing sideways at her as he drove. 'I'd rather you didn't get speweens all over my nice clean car, if you can help it.'

Eilidh stared straight through the windscreen. 'I'm fine.'

'That wasn't even a bad flight, you know.'

She shot Fergus a look over her shoulder. 'That plane was smaller than your car. I'd have felt safer if we'd been catapulted here.'

'Don't fret, we'll take the ferry back.'

Eilidh groaned.

'Boats aren't your thing either?'

'Not that.' She held up her phone, which she had just turned back on after the flight. 'Fifteen minutes we were in the air, and I've got eight missed calls, none of them about Peter Moss. Every single one is from that bloody reporter. How the hell did she get my number?'

'She's highly resourceful,' said Fergus.

'Meaning you gave it to her. Why aren't we dealing with your pal on this? I thought she was the star around here.'

'I think Freya's busy with something else.'

'Something bigger than an unexplained death in some ancient tomb? That happens a lot a round here, does it?'

Dave chuckled. 'Oh aye, in these parts we call that "Thursday".'

The road didn't widen out until they were on the edge of Pierowall, which wasn't much more than a scattering of houses, a small shop, and the ruins of an ancient church overlooking the most gorgeous turquoise bay. There was a stiff breeze coming off the sea, but the weather was really putting on a show now, with barely a cloud in the cobalt sky and the late morning sun blinking back off the water. Fergus almost forgot why they were out here. On the other side of the village, the road rose up as they headed south towards the centre of the small island. They would cross from one side of it to the other in less than twenty minutes if they were to keep driving this way, but Dave took a right, heading west past Loch Saintear into rolling green and yellow fields that rose and fell like waves. The land mirroring the sea. There were few vehicles out, but the people in the handful that did drive past all waved as they headed in the opposite direction.

'Everyone knows you here, then,' Eilidh said.

'Aye, they do,' Dave replied. 'But they'd be waving just the same if you were driving by yourself.'

'A place where people like the police? Never thought I'd see it. Back where I'm from, we got waved at a lot, but usually with one finger.'

'It's nothing to do with the police. That's what folk do out here in these smaller islands, give a peedie wave when they see someone go by.'

Eilidh looked back at Fergus. 'Is he winding me up?'

Fergus laughed. 'No.'

She narrowed her eyes. 'Where have you brought me?'

'It's nice, Murray. Folk are friendly up here.'

'That's why we're out here to see a guy who organises dog fights, is it?'

'Most folk. He's an exception, not the rule.'

The road rose further still and the rolling North Atlantic came into view ahead of them, twinkling in the sunlight. Tarmac turned to uncovered track as they approached the point where the island tumbled into the ocean. Before then, there was one final steading – a dilapidated farmhouse that to the unsuspecting eye would look abandoned, but Fergus knew better than that. He had grown up on this island, and the farm had been in the same family even back then.

'I have to say,' Dave said, glancing in the rearview mirror at Fergus, 'when you told me you were coming up here, I had a feeling this was where you'd be heading.'

'Have you had much bother with him of late?'

'Not since the winter, since it's been Gary on his own. Things have gone quiet. And I mean that quite literally.'

They came to a stop in the yard outwith the house and the first thing Fergus noticed was the silence. The Seator farm was infamous in these parts for the incessant sound of barking dogs.

Wild, demented beasts the Seators had always kept in cages behind the barn, that never shut up day or night. Now, all Fergus could hear was the sigh of the wind, the odd curlew cry, and the distant crash of the ocean.

'I'll wait with the car,' Dave said.

Fergus nodded. 'We shouldn't be long.'

He covered his nose and mouth as he stepped out. An almighty stench of urine struck his nostrils, but was mercifully carried away by the breeze. He could tell from Eilidh's face that she had smelled it too. There was the usual collection of dismantled vehicles piled between the farm buildings, tyres and various other parts scattered around, and several large metal barrels stacked near the barn where the dogs used to be. A quad bike was parked up by the farmhouse door; Fergus hoped that meant someone was home.

'I think you can take the lead on this one,' Eilidh said as they walked towards the house, her nose still wrinkled. 'I'll keep an eye out for banjo-wielding hillbillies.'

'Too late, one's already spotted us.'

In the doorway ahead of them stood a tall man in grey overalls and a black trucker cap that just about stayed in place on the shaggy brown locks falling out from under it. The shade cast by the peak wasn't enough to hide one of the ugliest faces Fergus had ever had the misfortune to clap eyes on, with a nose and cheekbones that had found themselves on the end of a fist or the bottom of a boot too many times to count. A thick beard couldn't mask a prominent scar along his jawline. In his right hand, Gary Seator was wielding an iron crowbar. He looked ready to use it.

'Not much of a welcome, Gary,' Fergus said.

'I heard the car. Thought it was tourists trying to get down to the shore again.'

'And you came out with a bloody crowbar?' Eilidh asked.

He glanced at her, ran his gaze from her head to her heels and back again, then turned to Fergus. 'She new?'

'Ish.'

'What do you want?'

'I heard you were on your own out here now. Where's your brother?'

Gary blinked twice, the kind of blinks that scrunched his wonky nose. It was a tick of his Fergus knew well. 'Away.'

'He's been away since December, I hear.'

No reply.

'In fact,' Fergus continued, 'a peedie bird tells me nobody's seen or heard from Darren since there was a spot of bother with someone firing a gun up at Yesnaby before Christmas.'

'It's been six months and you're only asking after him now?'

'Well, you never reported him missing.'

'He's not missing, he's—'

'Away,' Fergus finished for him. 'Aye, you said. He take the dogs with him, did he?'

Again, no answer, two more scrunchy-nosed blinks.

'Well, in any case, I'm sure he'll be back any day now.'

'What do you want?' Gary asked a second time.

Fergus took a folded printout of the photograph of Peter Moss from his pocket and held it up for Gary to see. 'We were hoping you might have seen this man. Does he look familiar?'

'No.'

'You haven't even looked,' Eilidh said.

Gary gave her the stare again, making Fergus grin. He was even more of a daft bugger than Fergus had him pegged for if he thought that was going to work.

Gary turned his attention back to the photograph, and stepped forward for a closer look. 'I don't know him. Who is he?'

'Someone who likes to gamble.'

'So, why would you think I'd seen him?'

'Because people have been coming to this farm since even I was a bairn to place bets on the dog fights your family have always held here.'

When Gary grinned, Fergus got a whiff of his breath. He prayed for the stench of piss again.

Gary cupped a hand to his car. 'I canna hear any dugs, can you?'

'Why did you get rid of them?'

'Just did.'

'I'd like to believe they all went to loving, caring homes, Gary.'

That grin again. Gary rubbed the side of his head with the crowbar.

'So where do folk who like a flutter go now?'

'I wouldn't know.' Nor would I care.'

'Someone will have taken over from you. One door closes, another opens.'

'Like I said, I wouldn't know.'

Fergus took a deep breath, regretted it. 'Gary, you know I'm a tolerant man, but I can tell you're starting to anger my colleague. If you're not running the dogs anymore, point us in the direction of the person we need to talk to.'

Gary raised the crowbar, held it out towards the track they'd driven in on. 'They'll be back the way you came.'

'Those barrels,' Eilidh said. 'I couldn't help but notice they bloody reek of piss.'

Gary eyed her again. 'So?'

'So, they obviously contain urea, which is a very useful ingredient in a number of things. Explosives and drugs being two of them. You wouldn't happen to have had a change of career, would you? Maybe we should come back with a warrant and take a closer look around.'

That got another yellow-toothed grin. 'In case you hadn't noticed, detective, this is a farm. I use it to make my own fertiliser. The pigs are pissing all the time, it keeps costs at a minimum.'

'I did notice,' Eilidh said, grinning too. 'I also spotted you're very close here to the sea. And the steep angle at which your land tilts towards the clifftops makes me think you'll get a lot of run-off into the ocean. Which would mean, if you were using a nitrogen-based fertiliser – which a homemade one from urea most certainly would be – you'd be in breach of SEPA regulations.'

The grin vanished. Fergus had to put his hands in his pockets to stop himself from clapping.

'Would be a shame if your farm got a surprise inspection. What do you think, DI Muir?'

'I think, without his side hustle, such a turn up of events could prove very costly.'

'Extortionately so.'

Gary ground his teeth, gripped the crowbar tighter.

'We know you and your brother didn't work in isolation,' Fergus said. 'So, who else should we speak with?'

Gary's nostrils flared. He was never the most patient man, but he was getting angry quickly, even for him. But Fergus thought he saw more than that in his eyes. He wasn't just raging, he was scared.

'Look, I got rid of the dugs because they were too much fucking work without Darren here, okay? And their constant bloody barking did my head in. That's the truth – believe me or no, I dinna care. I've no clue who your man is, and I've no idea where he might have been gambling.' The double blink again. 'Now, unless you want to come back with that warrant, or that inspector, get the fuck off my land.'

'Well, that was a wasted trip,' Eilidh said as they walked back to the police car. 'I risked my life on that death-trap plane for nothing.'

Fergus stroked his chin, nodded. 'Aye, though it wasn't exactly nothing. SEPA regulations?'

Eilidh shrugged. 'I dated an Environmental Protection Officer once.'

'Bet he was an interesting chap.'

'He was a she.'

Fergus double took. He felt heat rush to his cheeks immediately.

Eilidh saw it and laughed. 'Get in the car, Grandad. Before you make an even bigger arse of yourself.'

'Where to now?' PC Heddle asked as they slowly bumped their way back along the uncovered track.

'We'll head back to Mainland,' Fergus said. 'But drop us off at Rapness, Dave. We'll get the boat back. I won't put Murray through that flight again.'

'Fruitful conversation, was it?'

'Not particularly. Has he really packed in the dog fighting?'

'There's not been a peep of trouble reported about this farm in six months.'

'So, what happened to the dogs?'

Dave's gaze flicked up to the rearview mirror. 'I don't know, I'd like to think he sold them. I've a feeling I don't want to find out the truth.'

'So, his brother disappears, and he immediately goes straight?'

'Not likely. I get the sense he's still mixed up in something,' Dave said as they rejoined the tarmac road. 'I don't know what though. Or with whom.'

'He seemed scared,' Fergus agreed. 'I've never seen him like that before.'

Dave's eyes met Fergus's in the rearview mirror again. He nodded. 'The Seator brothers were the nastiest pieces of excrement I've had the misfortune to come across in my time on this beat. To think there could be somebody out there who'd have one of them rattled…'

He whistled, left the rest of his sentence hanging. It didn't need to be finished.

17

A NEW HOUSE HAD been built on the plot of land where the Wishart residence had once stood. The flustered-looking woman with a baby in her arms who answered the door to Freya knew the history of the place though.

'You'll want to speak to Gerry Firth, down at the boatyard.'

Freya was about to ask who Gerry Firth was and how he was connected to the Wisharts, but the infant began to cry and the woman shut the door in her face before she had chance.

It started to rain as she walked through the village down to the Burray Boatyard. Where the drops were coming from, Freya had no idea; it was still bright sunshine, only a smattering of clouds overhead. The whole thing about four seasons in a day was a lie: you could get all four at the same time in Orkney.

She was glad Keith hadn't held her to her offer to cover Sheriff's Court for him – she'd learned nothing from their conversation but hearsay and the fact he had a short fuse.

Her phone buzzed in her pocket before she reached the road down to the shore: 'Don't ignore me, Freya. Where are you?????'

Shit, she'd forgotten to reply to Kristin. She decided to bite the bullet and call her back.

The second Kristin answered, she was on her. 'Why aren't you answering me?'

Freya held the phone to her left ear, pinched the piercings in her right. 'Sorry, I was … I was talking to someone. I meant to text you back.'

'Who were you talking to?'

'Someone for the Trevor Scott story.'

'Didn't you speak to his brother yesterday?' Kristin said. 'I still haven't seen the write-up from that, by the way. Or either of the two stories I gave you this morning. Any chance of you giving me an ETA on them?'

Freya almost cried out as she pressed too hard on one of her silver studs, breaking the skin of her fingertip. 'I'll get to them this afternoon, I promise. I'll not be out long.'

'Good to know,' Kristin said. And she hung up.

Freya sucked away the blood from her finger, focused on the metallic taste, tried to calm her breathing. She knew her editor was under pressure, but did she really need to be her case to this degree? Hadn't Freya proven herself already? Those stories would take seconds to write, and the threads she was picking at here were leading to something big, she could tell. Trevor Scott's death was the tip of a very deep iceberg. Why couldn't Kristin trust her? Why couldn't she just leave her the fuck alone?

She closed her eyes, could feel that familiar bright ball of energy begin to build in the pit of her stomach, pressed harder on the silver studs in her ear as she counted faster and faster. The raindrops on her skin were cool, the pain in her fingertip, blistering hot. The combination focused her mind, stopped everything from unravelling.

When she opened her eyes, a woman walking a cocker spaniel on the other side of the street was staring at her from under the rim of a purple baseball cap.

'What?' Freya barked, then immediately felt bad. She was only showing concern.

The woman looked away, hurried off up the road with her dog.

The boatyard was two giant corrugated metal sheds beside the pier. The massive doors were open, showing what looked like a RO-RO ferry lifted off the ground on iron girders and blocks. Water vapour hung in the air and there was a strong smell of oil and rust that Freya didn't find entirely unpleasant. She could hear what sounded like a powerful jet wash on the far side of the boat.

She walked around the vessel and saw two figures in what looked like white hazmat suits firing a high-power torrent of water at the ferry's hull, where a large patch of grime had been cleared away. She wasn't sure how to get their attention, or if she should even be in here. She glanced around, looking for some kind of reception desk, wasn't sure if a boatyard would have one.

She didn't see anything, and she wasn't going to wait around or come back.

'Hello!'

She yelled three more times before one of them heard and switched off the machine. The protective head gear came off to reveal a weather-worn face under a shock of red hair and a look of pure disgust and anger that was impossible to misinterpret.

'Whoa, what the hell are you doing walking in here, woman?'

'Sorry, I'm looking for Gerry Firth.'

She was hoping to God Gerry Firth was the other guy, but God let her down. 'You've found him, but you can't come walking in like that.'

Freya wasn't sure what she was meant to say. She'd already done it, she couldn't change it. She decided simply to continue. 'I need to speak to you about Michael Wishart. I was told to find you here.'

Gerry Firth frowned. Anger became confusion. He turned to the figure behind him who, now his head protection had come off too, Freya could see was a much younger man. 'Go get your lunch, Joe. Back in half an hour.'

Joe nodded, walked away.

Gerry turned back to Freya. 'Who are you? Police?'

'A reporter for *The Orcadian*.'

The anger was straight back. 'And you want to know about Michael? Why now? Nobody much cared back when it mattered.'

'That's why I want to talk to you. My name's Freya Sinclair, I broke the story that started the Professional Standards investigation into the Orkney Police.'

Confusion returned, like the man's face could only express two emotions.

'I don't think the police investigated Michael's case or his parents' death correctly,' she said.

His expression betrayed a third emotion finally, though Freya wasn't sure what it was. Sadness, perhaps. 'Aye,' he said. 'Well, that makes two of us.'

'Is there somewhere we can go? An office or something?'

Gerry took off his gloves, threw them on top of the machine they'd been using to wash the boat. 'No. No office. But we can go next door. I've a feeling that'll be the best place for this.'

'What's next door?'

'A pub.'

18

THE WOOD-PANELLED BAR OF the Sands Hotel was busy with the lunch rush, but there were still a few places for them to sit. The lad pulling pints looked up and nodded at Gerry as they walked in. He was clearly a regular.

'What are you having?'

'I'll get this,' Freya said.

'Right you are. Jack'll know my order.'

Sure enough, the barman placed a pint of Scapa Special down in front of Freya without her asking. She ordered a cherry Coke for herself, then joined Gerry at a table in the corner near one of the windows looking out onto the water. The nautical theme was being laid on thick, with model boats above the bar and a ship's helm hanging on the wall.

'So,' Gerry said. 'Why now?'

'I did an interview yesterday with the brother of Trevor Scott, the retired police officer who took his own life recently.'

Gerry nodded. 'Aye, I heard about that. Can't say I was surprised.'

'You knew him?'

'He was the one they sent out when Mary reported Mikey missing. Useless piece of shite he was, too. Didn't do a thing to find our Mary's boy. All these years, I had him pegged as incompetent, but I'd just as easily believe he was corrupt.'

'Are you related to Michael?'

'He was my nephew. Mary was my sister.' Gerry sipped his pint, wiped his mouth with the back of his hand. 'Is this, what do you call it? On the record. Are you not meant to be taking notes or something?'

Freya had completely forgotten to even pretend this was for a story, so desperate was she to know what had tipped off Trevor Scott about Tait. 'Do you mind if I record our conversation?'

'Be my guest.'

Freya placed her phone on the table, set it to record. She'd forgotten to charge it in the car and the battery was running low. She hoped it would last. 'Were you and Michael close?'

'We were, aye. He was like a son to me in many ways. Or I suppose I was like his dad. I probably had more of a go at it than his actual father did, anyway. Mikey used to help me out with the boats now and then. I taught him to sail.'

'I heard there was a rumour Michael had run away from Orkney and might've stolen a boat.'

'Aye, the police tried to make us believe that one as well.'

'You don't think he could have?'

'He could, but he wouldn't. As I say, his dad wasn't ever going to win any prizes for being Father of the Year, but Mikey wasn't an unhappy boy. Our Mary loved him dearly, and he knew that. He had friends, a pretty girlfriend. He had no reason to run away. And besides, if he had, where did he go?'

'I read a story that mentioned Ullapool.'

'His grandparents on Dave's side lived there. But Mikey never showed up with them. If he ran, he either fell off the face of the earth completely or…'

Gerry took another sip of his drink, didn't say what he was about to.

'What do think happened to him, Mr Firth?'

Gerry didn't hesitate. 'I think his best friend killed him.'

Freya was taken aback. 'Really?'

'Really. And you can quote me on that.'

'What makes you believe that?'

'Occam's Razor. The simplest answer is usually correct, and all that. Mikey went missing, the police didn't want to know, Mary and Dave kicked up a fuss and, the next thing you know, their house goes up in smoke with them in it.'

Freya's head filled with questions.

Gerry must've seen her confusion, because he explained, 'Mikey's best pal, the one he was meant to have been with that night, was a lad called Jake Drever. And his dad was a cop.' He shrugged. 'It makes perfect sense to me that the Drever boy did something to Mikey and his dad covered it up for him, got his police pals to make it go away. He's in the police too now, by the way.'

'Who, Jake?'

Gerry nodded. 'It wasn't only that Tait guy. The lot of them are as rotten as they come. Not that this so-called investigation will say that.'

Freya was glad she'd started recording this. She needed to remember that name. She'd have to ask Fergus about Jake Drever.

'So, you think someone from the police started the fire?'

'It sounds far-fetched, but no more far-fetched than the things they said about our Mary. She would've never started that fire, and she wasn't drinking nearly as much as folk tried to make out she was.'

'Was Trevor Scott involved in the investigation into the fire?'

'No, we actually got to speak to a detective that time. His name began with an S too, but it escapes me now.'

Freya felt her fingers tingle. 'Was it Spence?'

'That was the one. Have you spoken to him too?'

Freya couldn't answer. She could barely breathe. She pressed her fingernails hard into her legs beneath the table, tried to calm herself down. This was all beginning to make sense – she believed Trevor Scott had tried to investigate Michael's disappearance but had been stopped for some reason by Allan Tait, resulting in Trevor's suspicion that Tait was corrupt. Her dad had then taken on the investigation into the fire and had no doubt been hindered by Tait as well, raising his suspicions too. Is this what inspired him to start the notebooks? Everything started from this case.

But why?

What about Michael Wishart's disappearance made Allan Tait so desperate to make it go away? Could it really be as simple as a cover-up for another police officer's son?

'Are you okay?'

Freya realised she hadn't said anything for at least a minute. 'Sorry,' she said. 'I'm trying to think it all through.'

Gerry drained the last of his pint. 'You mull it over. But I can tell you now, Jake Drever killed my nephew, and his dad and his police pals killed my sister and her husband to cover it up.'

'You have a niece as well, don't you? Emma? She was out at the time of the fire.'

'That's right, thank God.'

'Do you think whoever set the fire knew?'

'I don't think they much cared. If they had to kill a thirteen-year-old girl to cover their tracks, I truly believe they would have.'

'Are you still in touch with her?'

Gerry ran his tongue over his teeth, watched Freya for a moment. He was weighing up whether or not to lie, which meant he knew where Emma was.

'I want to get to the bottom of this,' Freya said. 'If I give you my contact details, will you pass them on to her? Then she can decide if she wants to talk to me.'

'It's been a long time, and a long road for her,' Gerry said. 'I don't know if it's a good idea for her to be dragging it all back up.'

Freya took a card out of her coat pocket, handed it to Gerry. 'Pass on my number, then she gets to decide.'

Gerry looked at the card, tapped it against his thumbnail. He nodded. 'Will do.'

Outside it was raining again. Clouds had gathered overhead, though the sky was clear out over Scapa Flow, the June sunlight still glistening on the water's surface.

'So, this is going to be in the paper on Thursday, is it?'

'Probably not. It's part of a bigger investigation I'm doing into police corruption.'

Gerry nodded. 'You're not leaving it up to the professional standards folk, or whatever they call themselves, then? You're going to bring them down all by yourself.'

'Something like that.'

Gerry smiled. For the first time while they'd been talking, he didn't look like he despised her. 'Well, best of luck to you, Freya Sinclair,' he said. 'You're going to bloody need it.'

19

'Sir, come look at this.'

Suspicion dug trenches in his brow as Fergus went over to where Eilidh had stopped, near to the statue of Dr John Rae in all his Arctic clobber staring meaningfully out to sea. Eilidh, however, was looking in the opposite direction. He followed her line of sight to the object that had caught her eye.

His colleague smiled. 'Think I need to get that for you. What's your size?'

On the other side of the window of the souvenir shop was a t-shirt emblazoned with a photo of a road sign for the unfortunately named Orcadian village of Twatt.

He shook his head. 'Should've known you were taking the piss when you called me "sir".'

They had come to Stromness on a hunch. Fergus's hunch. On the ferry back from Westray, Kate had been in touch to say her social media search had found no trace of their Peter Moss. There had been no positive response from any accommodation providers either, while the ferry and airplane companies had replied to say they had records of multiple individuals with that same name arriving in Orkney over the last three months, but none in the last week. Kate had managed to rule a few out from their dates of birth, but there were still more to go through.

'I'm being called back out to go sit in a lay-by on the A965,' Kate had told Fergus. 'Part of the boss's traffic campaign. I'll try and keep searching on my phone while I'm out.'

'No problem, Kate,' Fergus had said, trying to hide his disappointment. 'Thanks for your help.'

It was going to be a case of finding a needle in several different very large haystacks.

'How are we doing this?' Eilidh asked as they walked across the square to the foot of the steps outwith the first pub.

'We can go together or split up.'

'Split up. It'll be quicker.'

'Right you are. You can start here. I'll walk to the other end of town and start there. We go in each of the bars we come across and meet in the middle.'

Eilidh looked up the steps, took in the grubby curtains and peeling paint on the window frames of the Hamnavoe Hotel and Bar. 'Nah, you can take this one. I'll walk across town.'

'Do you think you'll ever follow one of my commands?'

'When you give one worth following.'

She winked at him and walked off along the windy, cobbled lane of Victoria Street. Fergus's plan was to ask around in the pubs and bars for anyone who might've seen Peter Moss two nights ago. Two things had made him think the town's drinking holes would be a good place to check: one, Moss's ex-wife had said he was a drinker as well as a gambler; and two, the fact there were two other men seen with Moss also suggested it wasn't his boat, meaning he'd likely asked around for a lift.

'The way he was dressed in a shirt and what have you tells me he didn't sail himself out to Hoy,' Fergus had said while they were walking back across Kirkwall from the harbour to the police station. 'I'd say he went looking for someone to take him at short notice. And, if he was looking to cross the Sound, he'd ask in Stromness.'

'That's pretty good detective work,' Eilidh had said.

'I have my moments.'

Fergus scaled the steep steps to the austere old building across from the harbour, clutching his stomach as he did. He took a moment at the top to catch his breath, and cursed himself. There were barely ten steps to climb, he shouldn't be this out of puff. He decided he would give it another week, then go and see the doctor on Monday. If things hadn't improved. And if he could find the time.

He pushed open one of the wooden double doors and was immediately hit with the smell of stale beer. The Hamnavoe might have been a swanky place at one time. It wasn't now. The carpets were threadbare, the wallpaper dated and, in places, peeling. It hadn't been refurbished or even refreshed in a very long time and it showed. Fergus wondered if this might have been the place where Peter Moss had been staying. It might explain why he'd chosen to crawl into a damp hole in a rock to sleep instead.

There was nobody on the reception desk. The bar (or Saloon, as the wording on the frosted glass in the doors labelled it) was off to the right. It was a little after 1 p.m. now, still lunchtime, but the place was dead. There were one or two punters at the tables by the windows, looking out over the harbour, but Fergus could hear the sound of his own footsteps on the carpet as he walked over to the bored-looking young woman standing behind the bar. She had a brass name badge on her white blouse. It said she was called Steph. She was scrolling on her phone as he walked over, but she glanced up under her brunette fringe as he neared. He took out his warrant card and she seemed to spring to life.

'DI Muir,' he said. 'Any chance you were on shift in here on Wednesday night?'

'No, but Glenn was.'

'Glenn?'

As he asked, a thin lad in his early twenties came through the door at the back of the bar, carrying a crate full of bottles. He had on the same white shirt–black trousers uniform, and a head full of floppy black hair. He had the same brass name badge on too, confirming this was the aforementioned Glenn.

He put down the crate and came over to them when Steph beckoned him.

'This man's a detective. A DI,' she said, a jolt of excitement in her tone. 'He wants to speak to someone who was on shift on Wednesday night.'

'Were you working that night?' Fergus asked him.

Glenn glanced at Steph, like he might've said no if his colleague hadn't already thrown him under the bus. 'Aye, from six till closing.'

'What time's that?'

'Eleven for non-guests, but we stay open until about midnight for anyone who's got a room.'

Fergus took out his phone, got up the photo of Peter Moss from the clearance database. 'Any chance you spotted this guy in here?'

Glenn leaned in to look. Steph did too, despite not having been there on the night in question.

'He was in here,' Glenn said. 'Don't think he was staying here though. He was sat at the bar. I remember I served him a whisky. Highland Park.'

'Any idea what time?'

'It was later on when he came in. Probably about nine thirty-ish.'

'Did he talk to anyone?'

'Yeah, a few folk. I heard him asking about getting over to Hoy, but everyone was telling him the ferries had stopped for the day.'

'Did he find anyone who'd take him?'

There was a flicker in Glenn's eyes then. That seemed to spark a memory. 'No, but I did hear someone telling him to try in The George along—'

'I know where it is,' Fergus said, sighing. The George was an infamous pub on Alfred Street, named after a boat sailed by the Orcadian pirate John Gow in the eighteenth century. Fitting, if you knew the story – The George pub tried to pass itself off as a reputable establishment, but in truth it was anything but. It was the kind of place even Gow himself might've steered clear of.

Fergus thanked the bar staff and left, texting Eilidh as he made his way down Victoria Street in the direction of the pub. The George was at the southern end of town where Eilidh had started her route. She might even be there already.

There was no sign of her as he entered the dimly lit pub. He was glad of that. Eilidh could handle herself, but The George was hardly welcoming for cops, even in the middle of a sunny weekday. He half expected the jukebox to fall silent as he walked in. It didn't, but several of the clientele paused their conversations to glance at him. He recognised some as people he'd come across more than once in a work capacity.

The barman here was much older than the pair at the last place. His was a face Fergus also knew well. Barry Grieve was an amateur boxer in his youth who'd got his sports mixed up once or twice at the Ba' in Kirkwall and had spent a night in the cells to calm down. A short, middle-aged man with an even shorter temper. He narrowed his already tiny eyes and folded thick arms across his barrel chest as he leaned on the bar. He wore a grey t-shirt, showing the faded tattoos on his forearms.

'Dropping by for a spot of lunch, detective?'

'Didn't realise you served food here,' Fergus said. 'This place has gone up in the world. It'll be one of those gastropubs now, aye?'

Barry's scowl didn't crack. 'What do you want?'

'I'm looking for information about someone who was in here on Wednesday night.'

He took out his phone again, but kept a tight hold of it. Even with him being a detective, one of the regulars in here might still have chanced pinching it. They were that stupid.

He showed Barry the photograph.

Barry shrugged. 'Never seen the guy.'

'I've been told he was here.'

'By who?'

Fergus smiled, said nothing.

'He looks like he's one of your lot,' Barry said. 'We don't get many polis drinking in here. I think whoever you've been speaking to is mistaken.'

'He was retired. He was looking for someone with a boat to take him over to Hoy. And by all accounts, he found them.'

'Well, that's awfully lovely and all, but I don't know the beuy. Never seen him afore in my life.'

Fergus turned his head, looked around the pub. Most of the clientele were looking back at him. 'I know a few of the faces in here. I know they're men who know their way around a boat too. A fair few of them have their own craft. Maybe I'll start asking them a few questions.'

He said it loud enough to be heard. A man sitting over by the pool table stood up to leave.

'Let me see that picture again,' Barry said.

Fergus turned back to the bar, showed Barry the photo, keeping one eye on the man walking towards the exit. He was one of the boys Fergus was familiar with.

'Aye, I maybe do remember him. Can you zoom in on this?'

Barry started touching the screen, pressing the phone hard. Trying to draw Fergus's full attention. The man reached the door.

Fergus took his phone back, put it in his pocket. 'Excuse me,' he said to the man trying to leave.

He didn't turn, kept walking for the way out.

'Let me see that again,' Barry was saying. 'You know, I do have a vague recollection of someone like that being in here.'

'Oi, you,' Fergus said again.

The man at the door glanced back. His eyes met Fergus's.

Then he bolted.

Fergus gave chase. Another man to his left stood up, walked in Fergus's path, trying to make out like it was an accident. It was enough to make Fergus stumble to the side, fall into the wall and lose a second or two on the man making his escape. There was a roar of laughter from the other punters, but he ignored it. He pushed through the door and out into the street, bright daylight piercing his eyes.

Where the bloody hell had the man run?

He looked left, then right. Just caught sight of the lower legs and trainers of the man as he disappeared round a corner into one of the lanes that climbed the hill.

Fergus was away in pursuit, but after only a few feet he felt that tearing pain in his stomach again. He breath caught in his chest, he was wheezing before he'd even turned the corner.

But he kept going.

Up the hill, lungs burning, limbs aching, his stomach feeling like it was splitting in two.

The man was ahead of him. He wasn't a young man by any means, but he was getting away. Fergus saw spots in front of his eyes. There was no way he was going to…

There was a shriek of pain. For a moment, Fergus worried it was him. He looked up, and the man was on the ground, a woman standing over him.

Fergus slowed, tried to catch his breath. Spat a thick lump of phlegm into the pavement. He was sure he could taste blood. When he caught up to them, the man was lying face down, his arms up his back behind him. Eilidh was kneeling between his shoulder blades.

20

'GET THE FUCK OFF me.'

Eilidh hauled their runner to his feet. As he'd expected, Fergus knew him. Davie Leslie had been in and out of the custody suite at Kirkwall police station several times over the years, never for anything serious, but enough for Fergus to have been able to recognise him from the back of his head. It was also frequent enough for Fergus to know a few personal facts about him, such as he stayed here in Stromness in the houses up the brae, he was a regular drinker at The George, and he knew how to pilot a boat.

Eilidh pushed Davie up against the wall of a house, kept his hands in a locking hold behind his back. He yelled again as his cheek scraped against the abrasive pebble dash.

'Fuck's sake! This is police brutality.'

Eilidh pushed his hands further up his back and he squealed again. 'Not yet, it's not. Wait till I really get brutal with you, you'll not be able to scream.'

Fergus looked down the hill. A small crowd had formed at the junction at the end of the lane, watching them. Any minute now someone would start recording.

'Murray,' he said, calmly.

Eilidh looked at him out of the corner of her eye. She loosened her hold.

'Hello, Davie,' Fergus said to the man with his face pressed against the wall. His cheek was squeezing his right eye shut. 'I'm not going to ask my colleague here to let you go until we can be certain you're not going to run.'

Fergus stood against the wall as he spoke, hopefully blocking the view of the small crowd.

'Can we trust you not to bolt?'

'Aye.'

'Then why did you run in the first place?'

'Because…'

Davie howled again in pain. He wasn't really hurting, this was a show for the onlookers. They needed to move him, but Fergus's car was all the way back on Ferry Road. Walking him back through the throngs of tourists in the centre of Stromness was going to cause a scene.

'You bide not far from here, is that right, Davie?'

He nodded.

'Then DS Murray is going to restrain you in handcuffs while we walk back to yours for a cuppa. Kick up a fuss, we'll take you back to our place instead, understand? And the tea isn't nearly as nice.'

It wasn't far to walk, and thankfully free of onlookers. Eilidh unlocked the cuffs at the front door of Davie's bungalow so he could let them all in. He made a big show of rubbing his wrists. Eilidh rolled her eyes.

Inside, Fergus quickly determined he wouldn't be drinking tea or anything else this man offered. The house was a state. It smelled of sweat and stale cigarette smoke, and the heat was only making it worse. Piles of unopened mail and old newspapers cluttered a small table in the kitchen, while unwashed dishes sat in dirty water in the sink. A bluebottle was tapping against the glass, trying to get out. Fergus unlatched a window and put them all out of their misery.

Davie stood by the kitchen counter, still massaging his wrists. 'I don't think I have any milk.'

'We'll skip the tea,' said Fergus. 'Tell us why you ran.'

Davie shrugged. 'Because you chased me.'

'I chased you because you ran.'

'Well, aye, I didn't want to be seen talking to you in there. I'd never have lived it down.'

'Last time we spoke, you'd been lifted for using red diesel to fuel your van. Wouldn't be doing that again, would you?'

Davie straightened up. 'See, this is precisely why I ran. There's no talking to you people. You're always accusing folk of things.'

Fergus showed Davie the photograph of Peter Moss. 'I want to know what happened the other night when you spoke to this man.'

Davie glanced at the photo. 'Not sure I know him.'

Fergus nodded and he rubbed his chin. Without taking his eyes off Davie, he said: 'DS Murray, call through to dispatch, will you? Tell them to send a tow truck. We're impounding a vehicle.'

'On it, boss.'

'Now hold on a blink,' Davie protested.

Eilidh took out her mobile, started dialling.

'Let me take another look at the picture.'

'You don't need to look,' said Fergus. 'You bloody know who he is, so tell us what happened when you took him across to Hoy.'

'Dispatch, this is DS Murray,' Eilidh said into her phone.

'Okay, okay. He was looking for a way to get to Hoy. Said he'd pay three hundred quid. One fifty out, one fifty on the way back.'

Fergus nodded at Eilidh. She hung up the phone. Or at least pretended to. Her act was so good, even Fergus wasn't sure if she'd called them for real or not.

'Tell me how the conversation went.'

Davie picked up a packet of cigarettes off the counter, rattled it and smiled a nicotine-stained grin at the fact there was at least one left. He put it in his mouth and lit it. Eilidh plucked it from his lips and threw it in the sink with the dirty dishwater where it extinguished with a satisfying hiss.

'Talk,' she said.

Fergus saw the thought of protesting flash across Davie's face, but it quickly vanished.

Davie licked his lips. 'So, Wednesday night, this beuy comes into the pub, starts asking folk if they've got a boat and can take him over to Hoy. I was drinking in there with my pal, Dennis.'

'Dennis Mckenzie?' Fergus asked. Another name he knew.

'Aye. So, me and Dennis told him we had a boat, but you cannot just be crossing the Hoy Sound any time you like. The swell through there is something else, it needs to be at the right time. The man says he's happy to wait, and he'll pay us, like I said.' He stopped, rubbed his mouth, looked around the worktops. 'Can I at least get a glass of water?'

'Keep talking while you do,' Fergus said, quickly, before Eilidh had a chance to say no. He could see she was about to. 'Did he give you his name?'

Davie took a sip before answering. 'This is to do with whoever you found in the Dwarfie Stane the other morning, isn't it? Was it him, is he the man?'

Fergus nodded.

Davie paled. 'We had nothing to do with that, you know. Whatever happened to him, we weren't involved. We just took him to meet whoever he was going there for and waited for him, like he asked, but he never came back.'

'How do you know he was going to meet someone?' Eilidh asked.

'He told us that was why he needed to get over there that night, to see an old friend,' Davie said, looking at Fergus as he spoke, not Eilidh. 'We both thought it was funny, heading all the way out there, but we guessed it was something fishy, you know? Something they didn't want other folk to see, so we asked no questions. But I was hardly going to tell a polis I was caught up in it somehow, either, was I? That's why I ran.'

'What else did he tell you?' Fergus asked.

'Nothing, that was it. He was meeting an old pal and could we take him. We said he'd have to wait an hour for the tide, so then he texted someone and bought the three of us drinks while we waited. But he never said a thing. Although…'

'Although what?'

'He wrote something on his arm while we were sitting there. Looked like it said "dying light", but I didna try to look too hard.'

'Does that mean anything to you?'

Davie shook his head. 'Not a clue.'

Fergus watched Davie's eyes. He was a terrible liar, couldn't keep his gaze fixed on you when he was trying to pull the wool over you. This time he did. He was telling the truth.

'So, you get to Hoy, what then?'

'He said he was going to the Dwarfie Stane, so we dropped him off on the beach in the Creekland bay and waited. He said he'd be no more than a couple of hours. He'd bought us some cans from the bar, so me and Dennis sat on the boat, talked shite, and waited.'

'And when he didn't come back…?'

'When he didn't come back, we figured nothing good had happened. Like I said, we assumed whatever he was up to was hardly legit, we weren't going to walk up there at that time of night and wander into the middle of it. Either that or he'd conned us with talk of paying for the return trip when he had no intention of making one. We'd got half the money, so we decided fuck it, we'd leave the scamming bastard behind afore the tide changed again.'

'What time was that?'

'It was getting lighter. I'd say about three, three thirty.'

'And he didn't give you any names, any clue where he was staying, whether he was local?'

'He was English, and I don't think he was a ferry-louper,' Davie said, using the Orcadian term for someone who'd moved to the islands from elsewhere. 'He said he wanted to go to the dworfy stone, said it like that. I didna even ken where he meant at first, it was Dennis who guessed it.'

'When he paid you, did he hand you the money from a wallet?' Eilidh asked.

Davie looked at Fergus again. 'Why does that matter?'

'Just answer the question,' Fergus said.

'No, he took cash straight from his pockets. And we knew he had the other half there because he counted it out.'

'And the phone he used to text, did you get a look at it?'

That was Eilidh again. Davie looked at her this time as he answered. 'Aye, it was some old-looking thing, nothing bougie.'

'He didn't have an iPhone?'

'Not that I saw.'

She glanced at Fergus, he assumed looking for confirmation that Davie was showing no signs of lying. Fergus gave a slight nod.

'I think we'll be getting out of your hair now, Davie,' Fergus said. 'See that wasn't so painful, was it?'

'Easy for you to say,' Davie said, rubbing his wrists again.

They left Davie fishing his cigarette out of the sink. Outside, the sun was high overhead, and a slight breeze off the water cooled the air a little. Fergus took a deep lungful of it to swill the stench of Davie's house from his nostrils. He took off his jacket, threw it over his shoulder as they walked back across town to his car.

'What did you make of that?' Eilidh asked him.

'I've sat across a table in an interview room with Davie Leslie a few times. I know when he's lying. We got the truth out of him there.'

'So, where does that leave us?'

'Not much further on than where we were this morning. Though we know he was trying to meet someone.'

'And digital forensics should be able to get that text. I'll chase that up.'

Fergus nodded.

'He wasn't using his iPhone to text, and he only had enough cash on him to cover his trip,' Eilidh continued. 'That phone, a bank card to get cash out must be here somewhere, surely.'

'Aye, and if he was here doing the rounds of the pubs, there's either a vehicle parked up here somewhere that belongs to him or he's got a room in the town.'

'Kate said none of the accommodation providers had claimed him yet, didn't she?'

'She did.'

'Maybe he was stopping with someone? A friend or something,' Eilidh suggested.

'Aye, maybe.'

Eilidh sighed, puffed out her cheeks as they rejoined the cobbled streets snaking their way alongside the harbour back to Ferry Road. Overhead, fulmars circled, their cries echoing through the narrow lanes. 'What now, then?'

Fergus wasn't sure. It felt like the boost they'd got from this morning's discovery was petering out. 'We go back to the drawing board while we wait to hear about that text. Trawl through the Peter Mosses Kate got us from the ferry companies, see if any are our guy, and go back out to the press asking the public for more details.'

Eilidh grinned. 'You feel it too now, don't you?'

'Are you talking about my spidey senses again?'

'Hey, you said it right for once. But yes, you know this is more than a straightforward case of a natural death. Something's not right here.'

The pain stabbed in Fergus's stomach again. He winced, tried not to let it show, but his hand drifted to his midriff. 'Something's not right at all.'

Saturday, 21st June, 1997 - 1.04 a.m.

The decaying wood burst against his shoulder.

The doorframe of the old schoolhouse snapped as Michael threw himself against it. He stumbled outside, his hands slipping on the damp grass and he struggled to keep himself from falling face first into the ground. He steadied himself, drew himself upright and anxiously threw his gaze from side to side, scanning the surrounding buildings for his assailant. Long shadows swept across the space around him as the beam from the lighthouse on the clifftops sliced through the darkness.

Nothing.

He could see no one, hear nothing other than the unremitting rumble of the waves, the shriek of the seabirds on the wind.

'Mike?'

Alice came running out of the schoolhouse behind him, helped him to his feet.

'Jesus, you could've pulled it open, you know,' she said, smiling. 'It only blew shut in the wind.'

'It was jammed,' Mike replied through gasps, his heart still in his windpipe. 'It wouldn't open, there was…'

He fell quiet as his eyes adjusted to the low light. A plank of wood, like the one he'd picked up, was hanging from the handle of the broken door.

'See! That bastard was wedged shut. Someone tried to lock us in.'

Alice said nothing as she looked back towards the doorway. Her mouth opened, she was about to speak as they heard the footsteps.

He heard Alice yell 'Fuck' as a figure scurried out of the shadows and raced across the open ground towards them.

He saw no features, simply a short, silhouette shape. One arm raised, a fist the size of a football on the end of it. Everything happened so quickly Michael didn't have time to process the sight before he felt the blow. It was cold, heavy. Wet against his skin.

Then heat.

Burning, raging heat that raced through his skull and across the back of his eyes.

He heard shouting, couldn't tell from where. Couldn't tell who.

When he tried to peel open his eyes, he found only one would work. The left one was sealed with something sticky. In his limited range of view, he could just make out two people running away towards the shore. Then one stopped and came back.

'Fucking hell, Mike, are you okay? Can you see?'

Alice's hands were on his face. The sound of her voice was a soothing balm, enveloping him, keeping him safe.

'I'm … yeah, I think I'm fine.'

'Stay here, I'm going after them.'

'No, Alice, wait!'

It was too late. He watched her running away again.

He dragged himself to his feet and the island tipped sideways. The night air bit harder, the cold reaching his bones. He felt like he was going to throw up but he needed to chase after Alice. He couldn't leave her alone with whoever that was who had attacked him. Whoever it was that had somehow come to be on this abandoned island with them.

He stumbled forward, his feet eventually finding the right pattern to carry him in the direction he wanted to go. Grass became sand and up ahead he heard raised voices again. Alice's.

She was yelling, 'Stop!'

Screaming, 'Get the fuck away from there!'

There was a splash. Another followed soon after, louder than the last. The air around him burst with the cries of seabirds launching into the night sky. As he reached the water's edge, he could make out two figures thrashing around in the waves. His left eye was still swollen shut, and the throbbing in his head felt like a drumbeat. Incessant. All consuming. He waded into the sea and snatched a flailing limb, began to pull them towards land.

They shrieked and screamed words at him that he couldn't understand.

'Get her ankles,' he heard Alice yell.

He became aware that he was being kicked. Two more blows hit him before he grabbed hold of wet skin on the next one. He and Alice dragged their attacker from the waves like they were carrying a sack of potatoes between them, dumped them on the beach, and Alice threw her weight on top of them. Michael fell to the sand and felt like he was going to throw up. Everything was spinning. Alice was wrestling with the unknown assailant. She had their arms pinned down and was lying over the top of them while their legs thrashed in the air.

'Mike, grab her fucking feet!'

He rolled over and put his weight on the two bare legs as they tried to kick underneath him. Slowly, he was able to focus on their catch.

It was a girl.

About their age, he'd say. Maybe younger. Pale skin and dark hair. Her face creased in anger.

She spat in Alice's eyes. *'Kuce! Kuce!'*

Alice took her hand off one of the girl's wrists to wipe her eye and the girl slapped her hard. Alice screamed and hit her back, grabbed her arm again.

'Who are you?' she yelled.

But the girl didn't answer. She kept making the same sound, speaking a language they didn't understand. *'Kuce! Nokāp no manis! Kuce!'*

Alice howled in the girl's face, overcome with rage. Michael had never seen her like this.

'Fucking lie still,' she shrieked. 'Tell us who you are.'

Michael was struggling to hold on. To stay awake, even. His head felt like it was collapsing in on itself and he just wanted to curl up into a ball on the wet sand and go to sleep.

'Bāc tevi! Bad man.'

'I don't think she speaks English,' Michael heard himself say.

'Where the hell has she come from?'

'I don't know.'

'Bad man,' the girl cried again in what seemed to be heavily accented English. 'You, bad man. Deeing lickt.'

'The fuck is she saying?'

'I don't know that, either.'

Alice glanced back at him. 'Shit, don't you dare fall asleep on me, Wishy.'

He felt his eyes start to close as he heard her say, 'Oh God, she hit you really hard.'

Her voice sounded far away, but oh so comforting. He could just lie here, listening to the sound of the waves and the breeze and her voice and just let…

'Mike!!'

He snapped awake, the pain in his head roaring back like an engine starting. The girl under his torso was still writhing, still trying to wriggle free, but with less intensity now, growing tired.

'Bad. You,' she said again. 'Deeing lickt. Bad.'

'What are we doing?' Michael asked. 'We can't hold her down out here all night.'

He was beginning to get cold now, soaking wet, lying in the frigid night air. He'd thought it was the girl trying to shake herself free, but he realised he was shivering.

'We need to get you inside,' Alice said, glancing over her shoulder. 'But we can't let her go. She hit you with a bloody brick. And what if there's others? She's younger than us, she can't be here alone.'

Michael looked along the beach, still struggling to see out of his left eye. Hard to spot in the shadows if there was anyone else out there. A shiver rumbled through him. The cold was like icy fingers stroking his insides.

'Who are you?' he heard Alice yell again. 'Where have you come from?'

The girl started to laugh. It grew wilder. She said something impossible to decipher. She had her head turned towards the water.

Alice and Michael both looked the same way.

The boat they'd come in, Rabbie's dad's boat, was untethered and was drifting out to sea.

'Fuck!'

Without thinking, Michael leaped to his feet. That boat was their only way off the island. They had no means of calling anyone. If it floated away, they were screwed.

His legs tied themselves in knots beneath him and he crashed face first into the sand.

'Mike.'

Alice rushed over to him, helped him to his feet, but he stumbled again. There was no chance he was going to be able to swim out to the boat, even less chance he could climb aboard it if he did. And he was the only one other than Rabbie who could pilot it. By the time they'd got back to the house to fetch him, even if he came straight away without kicking off, the boat would be too far out.

In the half-light, the scene seemed almost unreal, like Michael was going to wake up any moment in his own bed and find it had all been a bad dream.

He felt fatigue smother him like a landslide.

A noise behind him made him turn.

Alice looked too. They watched together as the strange girl ran off along the beach and disappeared into the night.

SATURDAY, 7TH JUNE. PRESENT DAY.

21

THERE WAS A BLACKENING in the town.

Amused locals and bemused tourists stood side by side the pavement on Broad Street, looking on as a pickup with its horn blaring, lights flashing, came to a halt outwith St. Magnus Cathedral. A gang of screaming women, dressed in white veils and angel wings, jumped down from the flatbed, hauled a hogtied bride-to-be covered in what looked like treacle off the back of it, and dragged her towards the Mercat Cross.

Freya was glad she and Tom had sneaked off to Gretna Green when they had got married; she didn't see the attraction in being kidnapped by your friends and strapped to a stone cross with cling film in twenty-degree heat. But then she was weird like that.

'Oh, I haven't seen a good blackening in years,' Helen said beside her, her face beaming as they watched from across the street.

Freya decided to keep her thoughts to herself about the whole spectacle, knowing full well they would only be dismissed by her mother. 'It's just a bit of fun,' she would most likely say. 'You need to lighten up.' Being covered in treacle and cling film in this heat would be fun for Freya in the same way as skydiving would be 'just a bit of fun' for someone who was terrified of heights, but she knew from years of experience she would never get her mum to understand that.

Tom was out with his boat building group - or maybe it was wild swimming today, she wasn't sure – so Freya had decided to ask her mother if she fancied a day out in Kirkwall. It was something they had talked about doing since Freya had moved back to the islands six months ago, but had never got around to. Freya's relationship with her mother had always been strained, but it was another thing she was trying harder to work on.

However, it was proving to be the hardest thing of all.

'This town's gone to the dogs,' Helen had said as they walked through the centre of Kirkwall, looking for a place to get a coffee. 'It's so busy here now. It never used to be like this.'

Every place Freya had suggested was either 'too modern', 'too expensive', or had 'too many tourists'. Yet somehow, the cafe her mother had finally decided she liked the look of was at the back of a gift shop directly opposite the cathedral.

Now, they were sitting with a coffee and a slice of cake each – Orkney fudge cheesecake for Freya, an empire biscuit for Helen – the howls and whoops from the bridal party across the way filling the silence between them.

'It's warm again the day,' Helen said, eventually. 'They say it'll be hot again tomorrow.'

Freya nodded, unsure what to say. She readied herself for the follow up that always came.

'You'll finally have to take off that coat of yours. You always used to wear one all the time when you were a bairn too, do you remember?'

There it was. Although she was braced for it, Freya dug her nails into her palms under the table, and tried not to react.

When she was younger, she was convinced her mother hated her, but she wasn't sure why. No matter what Freya did, it always seemed to be the wrong thing. If she stayed silent, she was being rude. If she spoke, she'd be accused of getting carried away and not waiting her turn. And then, of course, there was her mother's favourite phrase of all: 'Why can't you just be normal?'

It got worse after her dad died. A lot worse. And so, on reflection as an adult, Freya wondered if it all was simply her mother's inability to cope with the loss of her husband. Kids never think of their parents as being human beings with their own feelings and emotions, she supposed, and while Freya was obviously fully focused on her own grief, her mother would have been struggling too. It was no excuse – her mother could most definitely have been kinder – but she did wonder now if that was what had caused the rift between them, and then they had simply fallen into a pattern of Freya always being braced for her mother to say something mean, and Helen never missing an opportunity to oblige. To be fair, before her dad died, she spent so much more time with him that if the rift had been there already, she wouldn't have noticed it. But again, that was because she had more in common with her dad than her mother. Being with him was easy, effortless, while when she was with Helen, Freya felt like she was constantly being judged. Her mother had always seemed so alien to her, that on more than one occasion, Freya had gone hunting through the house for adoption papers. But then didn't all teenagers do that?

'Do you remember the cheesecake your father tried to make you for your birthday one year?' Helen asked, nodding at the dessert on Freya's plate and breaking the silence again.

The question surprised Freya, and brought the memory flooding back. 'I do. It was when I was six.'

'It was. And a bloody mess he made of it too.'

Helen smiled at the memory. This didn't seem to be a putdown for once. To be fair, she was one hundred percent right – the topping hadn't set, and the base fell to pieces.

'God, I remember we ended up eating it with our hands,' Freya said, grinning too, her mind now cast back to the past.

'That's right, you and the one friend from school you had over.'

'Jessica. She was my best friend, and it was my party. Why would I have invited anyone I didn't really want to be there?'

'It was a bit sad, a birthday party with only one other bairn there.'

'But why does it matter if I was happy?'

Helen sipped her coffee, said nothing.

'I remember it tasted good though,' Freya said, determined not to let her mother ruin this happy memory.

'You would've eaten that cheesecake no matter what. Your dad could do no wrong in your eyes, nor you in his. You were his Peedie Red Rabbit, Peedie Red Cupcake, and a million other Peedie Red names besides. You were the apple of his eye.'

God, now *that* was a blast from the past. More often than not, her dad would simply call her Red, same as Fergus still did, but there were longer, rarer versions of the nickname too which sometimes made an appearance.

Freya prodded at the cheesecake on the plate in front of her. This was another reason she found it difficult to spend time with her mother, it always reminded her how much she missed her dad. People say time is a great healer, but it was a slow one too. Twenty-two years after his death, the hole he'd left in her life seemed as gaping as ever.

'Do you still think about him?' Freya asked.

'Your father?' Helen seemed surprised by the question. 'Every single day.'

Freya nodded, continued to poke at her plate. She supposed she shouldn't be shocked by her mother's response; Helen had never remarried, hadn't even dated anyone else in the twenty-two years since he'd died, as far as Freya knew.

There had been something Freya had wanted to broach with her mother since Fergus had handed her the notebooks. This was as conversational as they had been with each other in as long as she could remember, so maybe now was the time.

'You gave some notebooks of his away to Fergus last year,' she said, dipping her toe in, testing the water.

Helen took a bite of her biscuit, nodded. 'They were to do with his police work, what use would I have for them?'

'How did they were? Did you read them?'

'Of course. When I found them I had a glance through. I couldn't make head nor tail of them, so I gave them to Fergus to deal with. And from the sound of it, he's shown them to you.'

'Did Dad never talk to you about his work?'

Helen finished her biscuit, began to brush stray crumbs from the table onto the empty plate. 'Why would he? It was none of my business. I never brought schoolwork home and he never spoke about the police.'

'But weren't you interested?'

Helen sighed. 'No, Freya, I wasn't. I don't have the same sick fascination with death and violence as you seem to share with your father.'

Freya's nails dug in her palms again just as her phone started to vibrate in her pocket. A welcome distraction, given the mood was beginning to sour once again. The number on the screen was from an unknown mobile. She was about to answer, thinking it would be Fergus – she had got no answer when she had tried to call him yesterday to ask about Jake Drever, the man Gerry Firth had mentioned – but at the last moment she realised the final three digits were wrong.

'Aren't you going to answer that?' Helen asked.

'It's a withheld number, I don't know who it is.'

'Well you won't find out unless you answer.'

'But I already know it's not someone I want to talk to,' Freya said.

'How?'

'Because if I don't know them, why would I want to speak to them?'

The phone buzzed again, fell silent, the screen went black. Freya waited a moment to see if the caller would leave a voicemail. Instead, she got a text this time:

Hi, my uncle gave me your details. I'm trying to reach Freya Sinclair. If I've got the right person, please call me back on this number. Thanks. Emma Wishart.

Pins and needles coursed through Freya's fingers. Gerry Firth must have passed on her number right away. She'd never thought it might have been Michael Wishart's sister calling her.

'I actually do need to take this,' Freya said.

Helen sipped her coffee, gave her a look over the rim of her mug that could only mean *I told you so.*

Outside, the blackening party was still making a din. Freya jogged along the street and round the corner, back to the gardens on Tankerness Lane where she had spoken to Keith yesterday, and the noise diminished.

She pressed Emma's number. A woman answered on the second ring. 'Hello?'

'Hi, is this Emma Wishart?'

'It is.'

'Hi Emma, it's Freya Sinclair. You just tried to call me.'

'I did, aye.'

'Thanks for calling me back'

Silence then. Freya was expecting Emma to fill it, seeing as she had been the one to call first. In her hurry to return the call, Freya hadn't planned what to say.

'I'm really glad you called,' she said. 'When I spoke to your uncle yesterday I wasn't sure if he'd pass on my details or not.'

He spoke to me just after you'd seen him,' Emma said. 'He said you were a reporter investigating what happened to my family. He said you seemed trustworthy.'

'Really?' Freya hadn't meant to sound so shocked. 'Sorry, I got the impression he didn't like me.'

She heard a puff of air in her ear that might have been Emma letting out a weak laugh. 'He's like that with everyone at first. Don't take it personally.'

Silence again. Freya quickly needed to decide what she was going to ask, and how she was going to phrase it.

Before she could, Emma said: 'I'm actually surprised you pieced it together so quickly.

Freya didn't know what she meant. Was that sarcasm at her getting in touch a quarter of a century after Michael had vanished? 'I read about you in the old news stories. They mentioned Michael had a sister, so—'

'No, not Michael.' Another weak laugh. 'Obviously, I know how you knew he and I were connected. I meant me and Peter.'

Peter? She tried to think fast, but even at this distance she could hear women screaming at the Mercat Cross, the drone of traffic on Junction Road, even the birds in the trees of the gardens seem too loud. All of Freya's thoughts arrived in her head at once, like sentences written over the top of one another on a page.

'Do you know what happened to him?' Emma asked. 'And what the hell was he doing out there? I read the police think he'd walked out to the Dwarfie Stane in the middle of the night.'

And then it clicked. 'Peter? You mean the man who died in Hoy?'

'Is that not why you wanted to speak to me?'

Now it was Freya's turn to stay silent. She needed to say something. Anything. *Just lie, say yes*. 'You knew him?' She asked finally.

'Knew. Aye, I knew him,' Emma said, her voice cracking as she used the past tense. 'I'm the reason he's dead.'

SUNDAY, 8TH JUNE. PRESENT DAY.

22

The dream was the same as always.

The whites of the eyes through the balaclava, the figure falling backwards, never landing. Perpetually suspended in air, in a state of disbelief. The waves rolled in beneath him, almost in slow motion, but there was never any sound. Not to begin with.

Then came the scream.

She jumped awake as she felt her world tilt to the left.

'Sorry,' Tom said, glancing across from the driver's seat. 'Took that one a bit quickly.'

The road bent again, in the opposite direction, and the town appeared beside the water beneath them. It had been years since Freya had last been to Ullapool. The buildings had changed slightly, but the landscape hadn't. Giant, green-sloped mountains stretching away into the distance along the glittering shore of Loch Broom.

'I'd rather not do this over the phone,' Emma had said. Freya could relate. 'And I'm not ready to come back there. Could you meet me?'

It had been a long drive to get here – three hours since getting off the ferry in Scrabster, plus an hour on the boat before that – but Freya and Tom had split it between them. Tom looked over at his wife as they drove down the hill into town. 'You alright?'

'Fine, why?'

'You were talking in your sleep.'

Freya tensed. 'What did I say?'

'I couldn't tell, you were sort of mumbling. It was more the sound you were making. You sounded afraid.'

Freya swallowed, rubbed her eyes. She still hadn't told Tom exactly what had happened at Yesnaby. About the man she'd had to push off a cliff to save her own life. She was done keeping secrets, but this was something nobody could ever know.

'You know what I'm like, I hate sleeping in the car,' Freya said. 'I don't think I fully settled.'

'Funny that,' Tom said with a grin. 'For someone who hates it, you're pretty good at it.'

Freya smiled, punched him in the arm.

Tom pulled up outwith a house on West Terrace, on the edge of a housing estate that bordered the sea loch. The view across the water to the hills on the other side was breathtaking.

'I'm going to find the chippy, and the bookshop, then sit and watch the boats while the dogs play in the water,' he said. 'Call me when you're done?'

Freya leaned across to kiss him. 'Will do.'

Emma Wishart was waiting at the open front door. She was tall, dressed in jeans and a t-shirt that showed the tattoos on her arms. She was in her late thirties and, despite her dark red hair being cut short to give her face a pixie look, Freya might have guessed she was older. She supposed losing your entire family within the space of a few weeks would do that. Emma greeted Freya with a handshake and led her inside. Freya accepted the offer of a drink, simply because people seemed to think it was rude if you said no – there had been days when she had been busting for a pee but still had to say yes to another cup of tea, simply to get people to talk – and they went through to the living room where a West Highland White Terrier leaped from the sofa and jumped up Freya's legs. Freya couldn't hide her excitement.

'He's gorgeous, what's his name?' she asked.

'Wesley,' Emma said. 'Wesley the Westie. He'll pester you till you give him a treat.'

Freya didn't mind that.

They took seats on the sofa and Wesley joined them, sitting between the two of them, excitedly licking Freya's hand.

'It's a beautiful view.'

Emma glanced out of the window like she wasn't sure what Freya was referring to, as if it was the first time she had noticed it was there. 'It is. I suppose I've become blind to it by now.'

'Have you been in this house long?'

'This was my grandparents' house. They left it to me when they died, about ten years ago now. It's where I came when my parents were killed, and I've been living in or around Ullapool ever since.'

Her choice of words – 'my parents were killed' – wasn't lost on Freya.

'Thank you for coming down,' she went on. 'I wouldn't have felt comfortable discussing this over the phone. And I'm not ready to go back up there.'

Freya asked if she could record the conversation. She wasn't even sure if this counted as work, but she wanted to be able to recall all the details. And at least she was doing it in her own time, so Kristin couldn't be mad at her.

Emma didn't seem too bothered about small talk, so Freya decided to dive straight in. 'What made you say you're the reason Peter Moss is dead?'

On their phone call the yesterday, Freya had already admitted that she hadn't tracked Emma down because of Peter, that she was looking into Michael's disappearance instead.

Emma put her cup down on a coffee table at the side of the sofa, like she'd suddenly lost interest in drinking anything. She hugged herself tightly, thought for a second before speaking.

'I've known Peter for a couple of years now. Or knew him, I guess. Still seems strange that he's gone.'

She fell silent a moment, and Freya let her. She didn't want to push.

'He moved here a year or so after he'd retired from the police. I think he'd had a difficult divorce. He never really spoke about it, but I got the sense he was here to escape a few things. We had something in common in that respect.'

'Were you…?'

'A couple? No. No, it was nothing like that. Or at least, I never saw it that way. He was almost twice my age, but we had a bond – Peter had a brother who'd died when they were teenagers too. He told me about it, told me that's why he'd become a cop. And I suppose we were both here running from the past. When I told him about how my brother's disappearance was investigated, how quickly everyone seemed to accept he'd run away from home, and then what happened with the fire, it rang alarm bells in him. He offered to go there and look into it. He was keen to do it.'

'So, he was there to investigate Michael's disappearance?'

Emma nodded. She wiped a stray tear from her cheek with the back of her hand. 'That, and the fire. He was hoping to set up as a PI. He said this would be his first case.'

The finality of what had happened to her friend seemed to hit her then, the full weight of it juddering through her as she burst into fitful tears. Freya noticed a box of tissues on a table beside the fireplace. She stood and fetched them and passed them to Emma, sitting again beside her.

Emma took one. 'Thank you. I'm sorry.'

'Don't be,' Freya said. 'I'm sorry if I've upset you with these questions.'

Emma shook her head. 'It's just so fucked up, you know. From the things he'd told me, I knew he'd made a tonne of mistakes in his life. He had so many things that he regretted and he wanted to change, and he knew he never could. And he'd finally got to a point where he could look forward instead of back, where he'd found a way to balance out some of the shite by putting something good back into the world, and then...'

Her sobs carried her words away.

Freya swallowed the lump in her throat. She knew exactly what Emma meant, and yes, it was very fucked up.

Minutes passed in silence save for the tick of the clock, the odd car going past outside, and Emma's gentle crying. Freya wasn't sure what to do. She reached out a hand, like a child hoping to pet a large dog, and placed it on her knee. Hugging seemed too much, but she thought she should probably do something.

Emma smiled, put her hand over Freya's. She began to compose herself. 'I only saw the story by chance yesterday morning,' she said. 'It wasn't a big write-up. Barely a lines on the Highlands and Islands page on the BBC. I don't think it's really sunk in until now.'

Freya nodded, unsure what to say.

'The story didn't say how he died,' Emma added.

'I don't think they know yet.'

'Do you think someone knew what he was doing there? Someone who didn't want him finding anything out?'

Freya wished she'd asked Fergus more about the case now. 'I don't think it's been determined whether or not he died of natural causes.'

'Aye, but come on, he goes away north looking into a multiple murder that's been covered up by the police, and winds up dead within days of getting there? He wasn't in the best shape, by any means, but he was hardly at death's door.'

'Who would he have spoken to?' Freya asked. 'If you think someone killed Michael and your parents, after all these years you must have someone in mind.'

'Jake Drever,' Emma said without hesitation, same as her uncle had. Freya hadn't tried again to contact Fergus last night, hadn't trusted herself not to mention that she was coming here, and she wanted to give Emma a chance to go to the police herself. But now it was becoming clear she really needed to speak to him about Drever.

'Your uncle said he was Michael's best pal.'

Emma snorted a laugh. 'He had been. They were inseparable until they turned fifteen, then it all became a bit one-sided. It was embarrassing, to be honest. Kids these days would call it "cringe". Jake didn't seem as bothered about my brother anymore, he was more interested in getting laid, but Mike didn't seem to get the memo. It was almost like…'

'Like what?'

'Well, I was thirteen when Mike was killed. I didn't understand certain things. But looking back at it now, I'd say my brother was in love with Jake.'

'And you don't think the feeling was mutual?'

'I don't even think my brother knew. He had a girlfriend too. But I reckon Jake was aware Mike was a bit too attached to him, and I think it used to piss him off. Like I said, at the time I didn't really put it together, but if something happened that night, if Mike maybe said something or did something Jake didn't like, who knows what might've happened. You hear awful stories about people being killed with one punch, or he might've pushed him and he could've fallen, or...'

She stopped, reached for another tissue.

'But it wasn't only Mike and Jake that night. He said he was going to Jake's, but I'd heard him talking about meeting up with his girlfriend. He didn't get to see her much outside of school, something to do with her family. No doubt there would've been some other poor, unsuspecting girl that Jake had got his eye on with them too.'

Emma picked up her phone off the table next to her mug of tea. She tapped the screen a few times then turned it to Freya to show her a LinkedIn profile of a woman with auburn hair and a tired smile. But it was her eyes that Freya noticed the most, even on this small screen. There had been times when Freya had felt like she didn't want to be on this Earth anymore, and she'd tried to hide it, but the truth always breaks through the cracks. She saw that same truth in this woman's eyes.

'This is her,' Emma said. 'Alice Harcus. Doesn't look like she ever married. I looked her up years ago on social media, but this was the only app I could find her on. I had this mad idea that, if Mike was still alive, and if he didn't let me know for whatever reason, then this was who he might try and contact. It was stupid, really.'

It wasn't. Freya had wondered well into her twenties whether there had been some kind of huge mistake about her dad, that really he was somehow alive and well somewhere and would reappear one day. There were even times she thought she'd seen him, and for those fleeting milliseconds before she realised it was someone else, her heart always filled with hope. Grief was cruel like that.

'It's not stupid at all,' Freya said.

'Well, anyway, as far as I can tell, he never did. But according to this, she still stays in Orkney. She works in Stromness.'

Freya looked at the profile: Administration assistant, EMEC.

Her fingers curled into her palms, nails digging into flesh. It couldn't be...

'I told Peter about her too, of course,' Emma continued. 'I gave him as many names as I could remember.'

'Could you send me the link to that profile?' Freya asked.

'Of course.'

Freya took a breath, tried to calm herself. Wanted to count the piercings in her ear because that made her feel better and made everything slow down, but she couldn't in front of Emma. She also couldn't leave yet – she needed to ask more questions – but she desperately wanted to show that profile to Tom.

She sipped her tea, hoping that might help. It did. It was still too hot, but the stinging pain on her tongue and the roof of her mouth made her focus.

'Who else might Peter have spoken to?' she asked.

'Well, I told him about Kelly, who Jake seemed to mention a lot when he was at ours. She was probably the one with them that night. But I'm pretty sure there was an Isla who used to kick about with them as well. I was never clear on which one Jake was dating, if either. And I don't know their surnames, so I'm not sure if Peter will have been able to do anything with that.' She smiled. 'If anyone could, though, it would be him. I got the impression he was one of those cops that didn't always stick to the rules, you know. And he seemed to know a heap of folk who could help him find things out.' She turned to look out at the view. 'Fuck, I'm really going to miss him.'

'Did Michael have any other friends?' Freya asked, hoping to keep Emma on track.

Emma turned back to her. 'There was one other lad, but again I only had a first name and I'm not even sure that was right. Robbie.'

'Did they all go to the same school?'

Freya was wondering if speaking to one of their old teachers might be a way to track these people down. She'd done something similar before.

But Emma was shaking her head. 'The rest did, not Robbie. I don't even think he went to school. His family had a farm in South Ronald say; I think he was homeschooled there. I never met him, he never came over to ours, I only heard Mike and Jake talking about him. Mostly Jake, to be fair. He sounded like a bit of a fanny.'

Freya wrote his name down. 'So, you gave all these names to Peter?'

Emma nodded. 'He said it was enough to get started with. That he still had ways he could track people down, even with so little to go on. I didn't ask any more questions. I thought it was best not to know.'

'Why haven't you told the police any of this?'

Emma hugged herself tightly again. 'Have you had much involvement with the police, Freya? In your personal life, I mean?'

Freya's lips parted, about to answer the question truthfully, when her brain caught up with what her mouth was doing and put a stop to it. Given Emma's mistrust of the police in Orkney, it didn't seem wise to mention her dad used to work for them. She didn't see the point in mentioning her experience in Glasgow last year, either.

'Some.'

'You're told as a kid that the police are there to protect us. That when something goes wrong, they'll help,' Emma said. 'I thought my brother going missing was the worst thing that could happen to me. Then, within a month, my parents burned alive in our home and I realised it really fucking wasn't. And do you know what the police did?'

Emma fell silent, and Freya shifted on the sofa. Did she really want her to answer? After a few seconds, it became unbearable.

'Nothing?'

'Worse,' Emma replied. 'They blamed my mum and dad. They said they caused the fire themselves, probably by accident. But only probably. They actually investigated the possibility that my mum started the fire on purpose. They said … they said they might have even had a hand in Mike going missing. But here's the thing: my parents were convinced there was something more to Mike's disappearance, and they weren't going to shut up about it. Especially Mum.'

'You think the fire was started on purpose?'

'It's bloody unlucky if it was an accident, don't you think? To happen so soon after Mike. It was only a couple of weeks apart.'

'Who do you think started it?'

'My parents were saying there was a cover-up with Mike, that the police knew what had happened and were keeping it quiet for some reason. Mum and Dad were trying to get the reporter who'd written about Mike to look into it. I can't imagine that dirty pervert chief inspector would've been happy about that.'

'They asked Keith Clouston to investigate a possible cover-up?' Emma looked at her blankly, so Freya continued, 'He was the reporter who covered the Michael story.'

She winced, but caught herself too late. She hated referring to things as a 'story'. That wasn't what this was. People had died, lives had been destroyed. Reducing it to a tale to tell was something she never wanted to do.

But Emma didn't seem to notice. She reached for the box of tissues again. 'Then aye, that's who they asked. Fat lot of good it did. I don't remember him ever doing anything.'

'You'll need to tell the police about Peter, before they connect him to you. I know a detective in Orkney you can trust.'

Emma snorted a laugh as she dried her eyes.

Freya ignored her. She texted her Fergus's name and number. 'I've sent you his details. He'll listen to you.'

Emma said nothing this time, but she nodded.

Freya saw the time on her phone. She had been there almost an hour. She'd have to be going soon. It was a long drive back to Scrabster, and they needed to make it in time for the last ferry.

'Do you know where Peter was staying in Orkney?' she asked.

'I think he took his van. He had a small camper he used to go away in sometimes. It was a model with a strange name. Bongo, or something like that. I've got a photo of him with it. I'll send it to you.'

'But you don't know where he was stopping?'

'I'm guessing he'd move around as he needed to.'

Freya let out an involuntary sigh. 'Is there anything else you can tell me? I really want to find out what happened to Michael. And to your parents. I want to set the record straight.'

But Emma shook her head. 'Then be careful, because that's what Peter said too.'

As she left, it occurred to Freya to ask if Emma would leave calling the police until tomorrow night. 'I'd like to see if I can track down either Jake or Alice, speak to them before the police do and their guards go up.'

Emma agreed that she would.

Outside, the day had grown muggy. The air was close, felt almost thick to breathe. She found Tom where he'd said he would be, at the chippy across the road from the bookshop, feeding bits of fish to a very attentive Luna and Thorfinn.

'Hey, how did it go?'

'That Alice woman from your work, the one who couldn't make the quiz at Helgi's on Thursday night,' Freya said.

Tom grinned. 'That's random, even for you. What about her?'

Freya held up her phone with Alice Harcus's LinkedIn profile on it. 'Is that her?'

23

It was close to half past eight in the evening when they drove off the Northlink Ferry into Stromness, but despite the long drive, it didn't feel late. The sun was high in the sky, and there were plenty of people in the street, wandering along the harbour front down Ferry Road towards the pubs and restaurants.

'But it is too late to do that,' Tom was saying. 'Alice doesn't really give much away, but I know she's got a disabled twin brother she cares for. By the time I've found her address and we've driven over there, it's going to be well after nine.'

Freya knew Tom was right, but she also knew, if she didn't go and speak to Alice Harcus tonight, there was no way she was getting any sleep. This was all she'd be able to think about until morning.

'I'll go and get her address for you now, seeing as we're here,' Tom conceded. 'And I shouldn't really be doing this, so I'd rather not get caught at it tomorrow.'

Tom had explained there was a pot at work that everyone paid into, then whenever it was someone's birthday they could buy them a small gift. There was a spreadsheet with people's dates of birth on and addresses for the people who mostly worked from home.

'Honestly, you don't have to do this,' Freya said. 'I'll find another way.'

'Oh, I know, but I want to help.' He smiled. 'It's much more fun when you let me join in with all your mad shit.'

The European Marine and Energy Centre offices were based in the old academy building up on Back Road. Tom was in and out with the information he needed in a couple of minutes.

'She doesn't actually live far from here. She's over in Outertown.'

Freya gave him a look, a look that after almost fifteen years together he understood right away.

Five minutes later, they had left the town behind and were on a single-track road through fields that tumbled down to the

North Atlantic. The houses were becoming fewer and farther between, but some of them out here were impressive – gleaming, white-washed walls and bleached wood facades, and huge windows that blinked back the sun. The sky was beginning to turn pink, and the ocean threw mist into the cooling air where it collided with the rising shoreline of West Mainland. Across the water, the highest sea cliffs in the British Isles dropped dramatically in a near-vertical line into the water, Orkney coming to an abrupt end at its wildest edge. The road itself came to a stop soon too. An uncovered track led from here to a bungalow tucked into the landscape down towards the shore.

'That's it,' Tom said. He pulled into the turning space at the end of the road. 'I'll wait here. If she sees me, she'll know where you got her address from, and she won't be happy.'

Freya nodded. She'd been asking what Alice Harcus was like on the drive back up. Nice to a point, is how Tom had described her. She was by no means a loner, despite mostly working remotely, but Tom had told her how he felt that, with Alice, there was a definite limit at which point you knew you weren't going to get any more out of her.

There was a car parked in the gravel yard at the end of the track, but other than that, there were no signs of life. No windows open, no sound coming from inside. She could hear the waves crashing against the shore at Warebeth, the wind whistling over the undulating land. Net curtains hung at the windows, so it was impossible to see any movement on the other side. Freya went over her planned lines one final time and rang the doorbell.

She waited a minute, rang it again.

Still nothing. No sound. No movement.

She looked back up the track. She couldn't see Tom's car from here, which made her feel a little better. Something didn't add up though – Alice Harcus had been off sick since Thursday, the day Peter Moss had been found dead, but now she was well enough to be out?

She walked over to the car parked at the side of the house. It was dusty, but by no means a wreck. There were tracks in the ground where it had been driven over, but no signs of any other vehicle that was now missing. If Alice was out, she was on foot. Freya turned to go back to the front door and try again, when she saw the net curtain in one of the windows move. A face had been looking out at her.

She rang the doorbell a third time.

A shadow shifted on the other side of the glass. Someone was in the hallway.

'Alice?' Freya said gently. 'I'm sorry to trouble you. I was hoping we could talk.'

'I'm sick,' a croaky voice replied through the door. The same voice everyone uses to call in sick. 'I think it's Covid, I can't let you in.'

'Well, if you open the door a little, I'll stand back.'

'Who are you?'

'My name's F—' She stopped. If she gave her name, Alice might recognise it. She bloody hoped the women Tom worked with knew about her! 'My name's Gill Irvine. I work for *The Orcadian*.'

'Have you seen the time? What are you doing here?'

'I know, I'm sorry to bother you, but it's important.'

To her surprise, the door opened. Instinctively, Freya jumped back. She was sure Alice was lying about being unwell, but she didn't fancy gambling on it.

The door latched on the chain. To give be fair, the woman peering out through the narrow gap did look pale and tired, and a sweaty smell escaped the house. Freya took another step back.

'What could possibly be so important that you need to come out here at nine at night?'

Freya noticed the croak in her voice had vanished. 'I'd like to speak to you about Peter Moss.'

'I don't know who you're talking about,' Alice said.

'Peter Moss. The man who was found dead in the Dwarfie Stane last Thursday.'

A slight pause. 'And what makes you think that's got anything to do with me?'

'Because I've been talking to Emma Wishart.'

That got a definite reaction. The one eye Freya could see peering out widened. Quick, then any sign of a response was gone.

'I don't know anyone called Peter Moss,' Alice said. 'Now, please—'

'But you do know Emma,' Freya interrupted. 'And you knew her brother, Michael, didn't you? You were with him on the night he went missing.'

The gap closed, then Freya heard the chain come off. In the next moment, the door flew open and Alice came marching out onto the drive towards Freya.

Freya took several steps back, but Alice kept coming.

'How dare you? You know nothing about me, and you come here telling me you know who I've spoken to and where I was on some night a lifetime ago.'

She stopped and Freya did too, the gap between them shorter than Freya would've liked. Not because of the risk of catching anything, because Freya could see now there was nothing wrong with Alice. Nothing contagious, anyway. But even in Alice's dressing gown and with her hair tied up in a messy bun, the rage that burned in Alice's eyes was genuinely unnerving. Freya's gaze flicked instinctively up the hill to where Tom was waiting, but she still couldn't see the car, and she hoped Alice hadn't noticed. She wondered if he could hear them, because Alice was really shouting now.

'What kind of gutter reporter are you, anyway?'

'This isn't about a story. It's personal.'

Alice glanced Freya up and down. 'Aye, well, it's got fuck all to do with me.' She turned and walked back to the house.

'Emma told me you were Michael's girlfriend at the time he disappeared,' Freya said to Alice's retreating back.

'Emma lied.'

Alice stepped inside her house. Before she slammed the door, she turned back around. Freya could see the tears in her eyes.

'Michael was barely even a friend. Just someone I once knew. And I've never met anyone named Peter Moss,' Alice said. 'Now piss off and don't come back.'

* * *

'That was quick,' Tom said as Freya got in the car. He set away driving.

'She's hiding something. She claims Emma lied about her being Michael's girlfriend and that Peter Moss never came here.'

'Maybe he didn't.'

Freya looked at him. 'How well do you know her?'

'Not brilliantly well. She helps us with things like funding applications and reports, and she mostly works from home because of her brother, so it's not like we chat every day.'

'She's not sick. But she's been off since Thursday, right?'

'Aye. Or it might've been Wednesday afternoon.'

Freya looked out at the view, pressed the studs in her ear and counted under her breath as she tried to think. She needed to speak to Fergus, find out about Jake Drever, and maybe point him in the direction of Alice Harcus too. But all of that meant relinquishing control of this, handing it over to him. She knew they were supposed to be a team, but she didn't want to lose the momentum. There had to be something else she could do to keep this moving.

Tom took a sharp bend to the right, and as they rounded the corner, the universe provided Freya with an answer.

24

She was never going to be able to sleep.

Light crept through the curtains, filling the room with a grey half-light that somehow filtered through her eyelids too. Not that she'd had her eyes closed much. Freya lay on her back, listening to the sounds of the house in the night – her husband's gentle breathing, Luna's loud snores from her bed in the corner. Luna had always slept in the same room as them, but Thorfinn hadn't quite taken to it. She could hear him on the sofa in the living room, sounding like he was chasing something in a dream.

Freya turned to look at Tom lying asleep beside her. If he woke up while she was out, he'd worry. And she'd promised him she wouldn't do that kind of thing anymore. But what she planned on doing was illegal: did she really want to drag him into that? And if she woke him now and told him the truth, he'd definitely try to talk her out of it.

Slowly, she slid out of bed, grabbed her clothes off the chair, put her finger to her lips to keep Luna quiet while she tiptoed towards…

'Where are you going?' Tom moaned, his eyes still seemingly closed.

'I can't sleep.'

Tom breathed in deeply. 'What time is it?'

Freya checked the time on her phone. 'One in the morning. I'm going to go through to the living room to read.' She felt a weight in the pit of her stomach, hated herself. She leaned down, kissed him on the forehead. 'Go to sleep, I'll be back soon.'

The sound of his gentle breathing was his only reply.

* * *

She left her Hyundai at the car park at Warebeth. Bouncing down the uncovered road past the graveyard in the dead of night, the half-light playing tricks on her, had only reinforced the feeling that this was a really stupid idea, but it didn't stop her. From the beach, she took the path along the shore and back up over the fields to get to where she had seen the campervan as they had been driving away from Alice Harcus's house. It had been in a field behind a small concrete wall next to a farm track that ran down to the sea, but enough of it had been visible for Freya to recognise it from the photo Emma Wishart had sent her. This was Peter's van. Coming this way meant not having to go past any of the farms or houses, but it was completely exposed. It was as dark as the night would get, but still light enough to be seen, and if anyone else who had been unable to sleep was looking out of their windows, they would have seen Freya's silhouette making its way up the slope of the fields.

Somewhere close, a curlew whooped, despite the hour. There was an owl in the surrounding fields too. The ocean crashed against the nearby cliffs and Freya's heart pounded in her ears. The sky was mostly clear, but almost completely devoid of stars. It was too bright. She saw the van ahead of her and suddenly realised the true enormity of what she was doing. This wasn't just really stupid, this was illegal. Breaking and entering. Into the property of a man who had been found dead in suspicious circumstances. If she got caught doing this, she'd be going to prison. No fucking around. Not even Fergus could get her out of it.

And still she kept walking.

At the dark silver van, she stopped and listened. There were blinds over the windows, making it impossible to see inside. Had they been drawn earlier? She hadn't got out of the car to check, and she couldn't tell as they had driven past it. She saw the Mazda logo on the front grill, walked to the back and saw the model name: Bongo, like Emma had said. It was about the size of a VW Transporter but looked narrower and taller. She moved slowly between the van and the concrete wall to shelter from the wind and to listen for any movement inside.

Best she could tell, there was nothing.

She walked back to the driver's side door. She was exposed to the wind coming off the ocean here and to the open land, but shielded from the nearest house, which was less than a quarter of a mile away. She laid her backpack on the ground, took out the plunger she'd taken from under her kitchen sink, steadied her breathing, then planted it hard in the middle of the window. It landed with a thud, and she held her breath as she waited for the sound of an alarm, or for someone inside to wake from their slumber and ask her what the fuck she was playing at. Neither happened, so she took the duct tape from her bag, bit off a strip, stuck it over the cup of the plunger, bit off another and repeated this until the whole thing was taped solidly in place. When she had been working at The Herald, she had covered a story about a baby that had been left inside a parked car at Silverburn Shopping Centre on a hot day. A member of the staff from one of the stores had got into the car by taping a plunger to the window, pulling it down, and opening the door from the inside. She had no idea if it would work, but this was her first time breaking into a vehicle. It was the best idea she'd got.

She gripped the handle of the plunger and pulled.

The glass shifted.

She froze, waiting again for an alarm or an angry inhabitant to cry out, but still the only sound was the shriek of the wind, the call of the circling curlew. She pulled it again, and again, and slowly the window inched its way lower. She wished she was taller, or that she'd brought Tom with her, so she didn't have to pull the glass almost all the way down before she could reach inside. She found the button for the lock, struggled to get purchase on it with her gloved hands. Then the door clicked open with a satisfying pop.

She quickly wound the window closed, pulled off the plunger and stuffed it back in her bag, tried to rub the marks from the glass with her coat sleeve as best she could, then she jumped into the driver's seat. She slammed the door behind her, reattached the blind to the inside of the glass, and sank into darkness.

The stench hit her immediately. Stale sweat made worse by the heat of the last few days. Old alcohol breath. She gagged, wanted to open a window again, but couldn't without taking down the blinds, and it wasn't light enough outside for her to look around without her torch. It was a case of putting up with it or heightening the risk of being seen, but she was finding it hard to think straight, the smell flooding her thoughts. She opened the door again, only for a second, the meek light showing a dishevelled living space. Unmade bed covered in clothes. Dishes in the small sink. She gulped down as much of the damp night air as she could before shutting herself inside again.

Blackness returned. She held her breath. Coat collar over her nose and mouth. She took a moment to steady her heart rate, calm herself. Listened to the muffled sound of the wind and an occasional tapping, something knocking on the side of the van in the breeze. Turning on the torch on her phone revealed the same disordered scene in the cold, harsh glow. She climbed between the two front seats into the back and began picking through Peter Moss's belongings. She spotted the empty bottles along with the glasses in the sink. Three empty bottles of Highland Park whisky on the counter, probably more under the clothes on the bed. Small cabinets and wardrobes running the length of one side of the van stored clean dishes, cooking utensils, camping chairs and various bits of equipment in clear plastic boxes. She turned her attention to the bed, carefully lifting the clothes. At least nobody would be able to tell she'd been in here. At the top of the bed, beside a pillow, she found an iPhone. She tapped the screen with a gloved finger, tried to switch it on, but it was dead. There was a charger she'd seen plugged into a socket on the worktop, but she was sure it wouldn't work without the engine switched on, and even if she did get it charged, she had no doubt there would be a passcode. She dropped it back beside the pillow and heard it land on something hard. Pulling back the duvet slightly, she found a hardcover notebook – one of the Papier ones. Personalised. No doubt expensive. Someone had had it embossed with the words: Peter Moss, PI, on the case.

Freya swallowed, felt a tightness in her throat. She ran her finger over the gold-leaf lettering and wondered who had bought it for him. Emma, perhaps? It almost felt wrong opening it, but she had to. The first page had a list of ferry times for last Sunday, for both Scrabster and Gills Bay. The second page had what looked like a password written at the top of it. It had been scratched through with biro, but it was still legible: BlackDog09.

Beneath that, a list of names: Jake Drever, Alice Harcus, Isla Brown, Kelly Bain, Rabbie Cleat.

Freya held her finger over the last one. Cleat.

Next to each person, Peter had written down addresses and phone numbers. Emma had been right: he clearly did have ways and means of finding things out. There were notes next to initials too, not unlike her dad's notebooks. She couldn't help but see the similarities.

IB – No longer in Orkney, claims wasn't with Michael that night

KB – Hung up – follow up in person and claim IB said they were all there

JD – Stuck to original story. Need to be careful here – cop

AH – No answer. *Follow up in person. Tried home, no answer – try again. Answered door this time, says* 'Ask RC about The Dying Light'

RC – Will only talk in person. *Meet-up arranged @ ?? Dwarfy Stone*

The rest of the pages were blank. Freya snapped a photo of the two that had been written on and put the notebook back in its place.

She caught sight of the time – almost half two now. The sun would be rising in an hour or so and already she could see through the cracks in the blinds that it was getting lighter outside. She was picking her way through the mess back to the driver's side door when she heard a noise.

Footsteps.

She stopped dead, hoping she was wrong. Maybe it was the tapping sound again.

Bright light sliced through the gaps at the blinds' edges. A torch beam cut across the ceiling of the van. She was halfway between the two front seats. Didn't dare move for fear of rocking the vehicle and giving away there was someone inside. The footsteps came to a stop outwith the driver's side window. Freya glanced at the door. It was unlocked. If whoever was out there decided to open it, there'd be no time to hide.

A thud on the window.

She jumped as a heavy fist hit the glass. Her hand was clamped over her mouth, eyes fixed on the door.

The knocking on the glass came again.

Then she heard fingers gripping the handle.

She dived forward, slammed down the lock just as someone tried the door. They heard her, they couldn't not, and the fist pounded the glass again.

'Open this bloody door, I know you're in there!'

A man's voice. Older. Deep and enraged.

She realised she had her eyes scrunched closed, like a fucking infant. If she couldn't see them, they couldn't see her. She opened them again to see the torch beam flicking across the ceiling as the man outside circled the van, searching for a way in.

'I told you to get off my land. I've asked nicely. This is me no longer being nice.'

The handle on the tailgate rattled. She realised then that she'd come here so focused on her plan she'd never even tried any of the doors before forcing the window. Did this thing have central locking? It was ancient, so she doubted it. What if Peter Moss had left one of the other doors unlocked?

The van shook as the man tried the large sliding door on the side, then the passenger door. Both held firm. She was locked in, but she was trapped. No way out till this man went away.

Silence for a moment. In the lull between gusts of wind, she heard him panting.

'I saw your light through the blinds,' he said, more calmly now. 'I know you're in there. I'm not an unreasonable man, but you're trespassing, and I've asked you to leave twice already.'

Freya thought her heart might burst. Could feel it in her throat. What if he stayed out there all night? What if he sent someone else to keep watch?

'This is your final warning. I'm calling the police.'

Maybe she should give herself up. Maybe she could make up some story for the farmer, get him to go away. But, when the van was still there in the morning, he'd call the cops and he'd give them her description and then they'd come looking for her. Just like she was sure it was only a matter of time before they'd be after her for murdering a man at Yesnaby.

She only realised she had her eyes screwed shut again when she saw the balaclava. The whites of the eyes. The man tumbling backwards into the sea.

She snapped her eyes open. There was no sound outside the van now. No more shouting. No more banging on the windows or trying the doors. She waited for what felt like a lifetime before she dared peek between the blinds. On the road, there was a man in what looked like pyjamas, a dressing gown, and wellies, walking towards the nearby house. She slammed the blinds shut, waited another five minutes, checked again.

Nothing.

She bundled herself out of the driver's side door and ran.

MONDAY, 9TH JUNE. PRESENT DAY.

25

He watched the liquid in the glass turn cloudy, gave it a few more stirs just to be sure. He hated the chalky taste it left in his mouth – it was worse even than police station coffee – but the pain in his stomach was getting worse.

Fergus had risked preparing himself an Alka-Seltzer as he was the only one in the CID room. It was early still, nobody else was in. Not even Murray, who he'd expected to be here, excited to get back to it after Magnus had refused her overtime to work on the case over the weekend. He'd not slept well again, his stomach and the light through the curtains ganging up on him, keeping him awake. This powdery shite seemed to do a better job of taking the edge off than paracetamol had been doing, so he downed the glass in one, grimaced at the taste it left on his tongue, and bit into a Mars bar quickly to take it away.

Sun broke through the clouds and poured in through the window, warming the room already. It was still bright outside, but the wind had changed direction, you could tell, and the pleasant weather wouldn't last. They'd already been lucky to have it this long. Rain was coming. Fergus sat at his desk by the window and looked out at the morning joggers doing laps of the lakes at the Peedie Sea. Cars streamed along Pickaquoy Road, folk heading into town or nipping to the supermarkets before work. The laptop on his desk made one of its ringing sounds, but he ignored it. He was in no rush to start work, and besides, this was nice, sitting in silence, alone with his thoughts. He had that at home, of course, but this was different. At home, it felt oppressive. Things crept up on him that he would rather not think about, like why was the pain in his stomach getting worse? Why hadn't it gone away yet? It had been almost a month now. He knew he should probably get it looked at, but since when had doctors known what they were doing? They certainly hadn't when his father had got sick. Hid dad would've been around about the same age as Fergus was now when they'd diagnosed his cancer, in fact. He shook his head, took a deep breath, to keep that particular thought at bay and watched the joggers again. The cars. The comforting monotony of a Monday morning.

A phone buzzed in his jacket pocket on the back of his chair.

He fished it out, saw it wasn't his work phone. He'd been so tired, he'd forgotten to hide the burner. There was a text on the tiny screen: **We need to talk.**

His goddaughter was a woman of few words.

He glanced around. The office was still empty. He typed back, 'Are you free now?'

The reply came immediately. 'Yes.'

He hit dial and Freya answered on the first ring. 'Remember that case I asked you about? The missing boy that Angus Scott told me about?'

Fergus smiled to himself, decided against taking the piss. He'd come to recognise that tone in Freya's voice that meant she had her teeth into something. She'd been the same since she was a peedie girl. 'I do. I'm guessing you've found out who he was talking about?'

'Does the name Michael Wishart mean anything to you?'

'Not especially.'

He listened while Freya filled him in on the details. A teenage boy had gone missing in June 1997. A couple of weeks later, in July, his parents had both been killed in a house fire. That rang plenty of bells.

'I'd not long since made detective,' he said. 'I was involved, mostly shadowing your dad. So, this was the case that alerted Trevor to Tait, was it? How did you figure that out?'

The laptop made its annoying sound again. Two more emails. Both from digital forensics. He idly clicked on the first one.

'Trevor Scott was the PC called out when Michael went missing,' Freya said. 'Michael's parents felt like the police weren't doing enough to find him. Well, it was more than that – they thought the police were trying to sweep it under the rug.'

'Why?'

'I don't know, but I asked the reporter who covered the story about it too.'

'Bloody hell, would that be old Keith? Is he still going?'

'He basically tried to scare me off. He didn't, but what he did do was reveal that really basic things were never followed up. The police said Michael had taken a boat and sailed to Caithness, but Keith didn't know if anyone had ever reported a boat missing or if one had been found.'

'And you're thinking Trevor was told to bury the case by Tait and that's what made him suspicious?'

Fergus was skimming the email as he spoke. There were three files attached. The message explained that the boffins down in Fife had managed to unlock the basic handset and the Apple Watch. Text messages and the call log from the phone were detailed in the first attachment. The second was a list of who the numbers belonged to, retrieved from the various phone companies. The third one had an overview of the Apple Watch data.

The documents were password-protected. He opened the second email to get the codes.

'Aye, that's exactly what I'm thinking,' Freya was saying. 'And that, if my dad was involved in investigating the fire, that's what tipped him off to Tait too. The notebooks start a month later.'

Fergus held the phone to his ear in one hand, slowly typed the password for the first document in with one finger on his other. 'This is good stuff, Red. Maybe we should talk about this later, in person.'

The first file contained a report, the digital forensics team explaining what they had found. Often, they phrased it in such a way that assumed the person who was reading it was a time-traveller from 1985 and had never seen a mobile phone or a laptop before. Fergus welcomed that.

His eyes scanned quickly through the text. It explained how the phone was first switched on just over a week ago – Sunday the fourth – and that its position when it was switched on could be triangulated to a point not far from where Fergus was sitting right now. The phone didn't have GPS, it wasn't a precise location, but the cell towers it connected to placed it within an area that covered most of that side of Kirkwall. He glanced out of the window again towards Pickaquoy Road. He couldn't see it from where he was sitting, but there was a large Tesco supermarket there. If he had to guess, he'd say that's where the phone was bought, probably on the day Peter arrived in Orkney. Cheap, easy to keep charged, and – if it hadn't been found on his dead body – untraceable.

'I've found where Peter Moss was staying too.'

That brought Fergus's attention back to the conversation. 'What? How? I didn't think you were interested in that case.'

'He had a campervan. A grey Mazda Bongo. It's in a field in Outertown. You'll find it unlocked.'

Fergus rubbed his eyes. 'Jesus, Red. Please tell me you didn't go inside it.'

Silence.

'Freya.'

'The owner of the field it's in will probably tell you he thought he saw someone in there last night. I … I might need you to convince him he was mistaken.'

'Bloody hell.' Fergus sighed, but he couldn't pretend to be angry. She'd done him a favour. 'So, what am I going to find in there?'

'A notebook,' Freya said. 'There's not much in it, but you'll find a list of names and contact details. Do you know Jake Drever? Is he someone you work with?'

'He is.' Fergus switched the phone to his other hand, glanced around again to make sure he was still alone. 'Are you telling me Jake Drever's name is in that notebook?'

'What's he like?'

Fergus didn't answer. His stomach twitched again. He felt nauseated, couldn't decide if it was due to whatever was going on with his belly, or if this conversation was making his head spin. 'Let's back up a second. How did you find Moss's van? And why did you find it? I've had that bloody Irvine woman on my case all weekend.'

'Peter Moss was in Orkney to investigate Michael's disappearance.'

Fergus involuntarily let out a laugh. 'How the bloody hell did you get that before we did?'

'A source.'

'A source, aye? And do they have a name?'

'I've given them your contact details. They'll be in touch today.'

'Well, how about you give me their details and I'll save them the bother?'

Silence again.

Fergus sighed. 'Look, I know that's not how this works, but bloody hell, Freya, if anyone else but me finds out about this, you'll be in deep trouble for hindering an investigation into a suspicious death. You do understand that, don't you?'

'If they don't contact you today, I'll chase them up.'

'Be sure you do.' He rubbed his eyes. 'How positive can you be that Moss was here to investigate the missing boy?'

'One hundred per cent. Jake Drever was friends with Michael Wishart. He was the person Michael was meant to be with on the night he disappeared. That's in the news reports from the time. It'll be in the police reports too.'

Fergus leaned back in his chair, tried to process all of this. Peter Moss was here investigating an old case that Tait might've had a hand in covering up, and PC Drever was involved. He needed to decide how to play this – until Freya's anonymous source came forward, he didn't officially know any of this.

'Is Drever someone you trust?' Freya asked.

'I don't mistrust him. But he's never been someone I've had a whole heap to do with over the years. He tends to keep himself to himself.'

'There was another name in the notebook that stood out. Have you heard of Rabbie Cleat?'

Fergus's stomach churned again. 'I have, and he's exactly who you're thinking he is. He's the son of Seamus Cleat, one of the men I told you to keep in mind for our SC.' Fergus switched the phone back to his other hand. 'Red, I know you, and I know what you'll be planning on doing, so let me say this clearly – do not approach that man, do you hear me?'

More silence.

'Freya, I mean it. You'll not get anything useful out of Seamus these days, anyway. Last I heard, he wasn't doing so great. Parkinsons or dementia, something like that. Either way, you'll not be able to talk to him, and the Cleats are on another level of nasty altogether, every last one of them. Promise me you won't go near them.'

'Rabbie Cleat is the man Peter Moss was due to meet at the Dwarfie Stane,' Freya said. It wasn't lost on Fergus that she'd ignored his request. 'That's in the notebook too.'

Fergus let that final piece of information sink in. In the pause, he heard footsteps along the corridor.

'Look, I've got to go. We'll speak later. Do not go near the Cleats, do you understand?'

'I won't,' he heard Freya say with a sigh.

'Good. Don't.'

He hung up quickly, wishing to high heaven he believed her.

26

'This is an early start for you. If I didn't know you better, I'd say you were after a promotion.'

Fergus slipped the phone back into his jacket pocket as he turned to see Magnus Robertson standing in the doorway to the CID office. He looked as bad as Fergus felt. He hoped he hadn't heard any of that conversation.

'Couldn't sleep,' Fergus said. 'The light.'

Magnus nodded. 'Blackout blinds instead of curtains are the solution.'

They didn't look like they had solved anything for him.

Fergus smiled but said nothing. He'd never known his boss to be one for small talk. Magnus Robertson had got where he was by kissing the arses of those above him, not by being pleasant with those he regarded as being beneath him. That was the official version of Rocket Robertson's rise to the top, anyway. How much his ascent up the ranks had to do with him being in the pocket of Allan Tait, Fergus still hadn't decided.

He expected Magnus to carry on down the corridor to his office, but he didn't.

'Everything okay, sir?'

'How are we getting on with the Dwarfie Stane case?' Magnus asked, ignoring the question.

Fergus gestured to his laptop. 'Digital forensics has come back. I'm going through Moss's record of texts and calls.'

'Anything interesting?'

'I've only opened it just now. I've not been here long myself.'

Magnus nodded again. Fergus wasn't sure if his boss was aware he was lying, but he didn't want to give anything away about the connection to the Michael Wishart case and Jake Drever. No yet. He had decided, with Magnus, it was best to only let him know what he needed to, when he needed to.

'Get me an update later today,' Magnus said.

'Right you are, sir.'

'Morning, sir.' Eilidh appeared in the doorway behind Magnus, who stepped to one side.

'I'll leave you both to it,' he said.

'What's wrong with you?' Eilidh said when he'd gone. 'Getting here early, brown-nosing with the boss.'

'Thought I'd throw my hat into the ring to take over from him when he inevitably moves up a rank.'

'God help us all. What's this?' Eilidh asked, nodding at Fergus's computer.

'It's the report on Peter Moss's burner phone. Digital forensics have just sent it back.'

'And?' said Eilidh.

'You're not going to ask how my weekend was?'

'Piss off, you always tell me to mind my own business when I do.'

Fergus grinned. 'I've not got far with it. I'd only just opened it when the gaffer arrived. But it looks like the phone he had on him was bought from the Tesco when he got here last Sunday.'

'Is this the text log?' Eilidh asked, pulling up a chair beside him and leaning in to get a better look at the screen. The log barely took up half a page. 'Can you find the one he sent from the pub?'

It was one of the first on the list. A little before 10 p.m., which must have been the time Peter had arranged the boat trip with Davie, he'd written: I'll be there for midnight, but I have to say this seems excessive.

Ten minutes later, he'd got a reply. Two, in fact. The first said: When you hear what I've got to tell you, you'll realise why I want no fucker seeing me with you.

It was immediately followed by: And I told you not to text. Fuckin delete this.

Peter clearly hadn't. Nor had he replied right away. But there were still two more messages left in the list, sent by Peter to the same number.

At half past midnight: Where r u?

And at just after 1 a.m.: U got 10 mins, then I'm gone and tomorrow I'm going to the papers.

'Davie wasn't lying then,' Eilidh said. 'Moss was meeting someone.'

Fergus tried to keep his expression as blank as he could. He couldn't tell Eilidh he already knew these messages were from Rabbie Cleat. Not without giving away what Freya had been up to. 'Aye, and it looks like they didn't show.'

'Or they turned up in the ten minutes after that last text,' Eilidh said. 'Did the Digi lads get into the Apple Watch?'

'They did. Here.'

He used the same password to open the third attachment. While Eilidh was scanning it, Fergus was still trying to process everything Freya had just told him, trying to figure out how Jake Drever and Rabbie Cleat were connected, and how they were both linked to a boy who had gone missing over twenty-five years ago, and a man who had been found dead in a cold tomb just last week.

'Shit, look at this,' Eilidh said. She was pointing at what appeared to be a screenshot of a bar chart.

'What is it?'

'It's how many calories he was burning.' She pointed at the screen. 'Between midnight and 1 a.m., he burned nearly three hundred. That must've been him walking up from the beach to the Dwarfie Stane. Then look, after 1 a.m., nothing.' She reached over and spun the wheel on the mouse with her forefinger, searching for something else. 'There. His last recorded heartbeat was at 1.16 a.m. That's when he died.'

'So, about ten minutes after his last text,' Fergus said. 'Whatever killed him was quick.'

'Maybe whoever he was texting showed up.'

Fergus wondered if that could be true. 'Maybe. Though there's no sign of that at the scene. What else have we got on here?'

'Shift over and I'll take a look.'

'Gladly,' Fergus said, rolling his chair back to let Eilidh get to the trackpad. It was better for her to do this. It would give him more time to think.

Eilidh had a look through the rest of the report on the Apple Watch but didn't find anything that piqued her interest. She opened the list of numbers, searched for the one that Peter had been texting from Hoy.

'It's one burner contacting another,' she said, pointing to the last one in the list. All it said was: Unregistered. That wasn't a surprise.

Next, she reopened the list of text messages and looked at the earlier ones Peter Moss had sent. The first message was sent on the Sunday, almost immediately after the phone was first turned on: It's PM, i'll be on this number this week. Call when u get this.

The following two messages were replies from the same number, but they hadn't come until a day later, on the Monday evening: Check your email and BlackDog09.

Fergus looked at the second message. If he had to guess, he'd wager that was a password for whatever had been sent over email, just like he'd had two separate messages to open this. A follow up guess was that the aforementioned email probably contained the details of the people Peter Moss had come to Orkney to speak to. No doubt he had a contact inside Police Scotland, someone to access records and get him names and addresses, phone numbers, known associates, and so on. Rabbie was using a burner phone, but Moss had still been able to get hold of it, most likely from police intelligence on Rabbie's file on the PNC.

'Have we got the email?' Eilidh asked.

'If it's not on that phone, and it's not likely to be given how basic it is, then no.'

The call log was busier. Calls had gone back and forth to both numbers that Peter had been texting. There were several other phone numbers in there too, incoming calls and outgoing. Eilidh switched to the second document, the one that identified who the numbers were registered to. There were six numbers in total.

Unfortunately, the other one Peter had been texting – his source – turned out to be a burner too. Again, that wasn't a surprise either. But the other four numbers were registered. All of these had been called at least twice, and for all of them except one, someone had picked up and the call had lasted long enough for a conversation to have been had.

Eilidh took out her notepad from her inside jacket pocket and began to scribble them down. 'Okay, so what have we got? Unknown, Alice Harcus, Isla Brown, Kelly Bain, Jake…'

She stopped as she got to the last name before the final unknown number. She and Fergus had read it at the same time.

'Jake Drever?' she said. 'Surely that can't be…'

Fergus tried again to keep his reaction in check. He stood and headed for the door. Eilidh followed. Along the corridor, the duty sergeant, Kevin Fraser, was in the response room, sipping his morning coffee at his desk, chatting to a couple of uniforms who looked like they were about to head out.

Fergus glanced around, couldn't see Drever. 'Kev, is Jake on shift today?'

'He is, aye. What the devil's he done to have you two after him?'

'Where is he right now?'

'He's attending a domestic in Finstown. Left about twenty minutes ago. I'd say he'd be there by now.'

'What's the address?'

Kevin frowned. 'What's this about, Ferg?'

'I need the address, Kev.'

Kevin pulled up the details on his computer. 'He's on Parkside. Want me to let him know you're—'

'No, not a word to him,' Fergus said. He turned to Eilidh. 'I'll drive.'

27

Freya watched bands of sunbeams break through the clouds and shine a spotlight on the roiling sea. She counted, trying to settle her brain, trying to think clearly enough to plan what she needed to do next. After last night, she had so many questions, but she had no idea how she was going to get Alice Harcus to answer any of them.

She sat in her car at the end of the single-track road in Outertown, sipping her oat milk latte, and watched the clouds cast shifting shadows over the Hoy hills across the water. This was the third time she'd been here in the past twelve hours and each time the sky and the sea had been different. Fatigue was giving her a headache coffee was struggling to shift. She hadn't slept at all last night, partly because she was still wired after her brush with the owner of the field where Peter's van had been parked, but also because Tom had been awake when she had got home. He'd been sitting at the kitchen table with Luna at his feet, the day's first light illuminating the room just enough for her to see the sadness in his eyes. That alone would've been sufficient to break her heart, but there was more.

'Where have you been?' he'd asked.

'I couldn't sleep,' Freya had said. 'I went for a walk.'

His eyes flicked to the rucksack strap over her shoulder, and the disappointment was unmistakable. She'd promised there would be no more lies. It was a promise she had fully intended to keep. But this was the way she was, she couldn't help herself – there was a question she needed answered, and there was no way she was going to wait.

But she was determined to make it a one off, she didn't plan on restarting that habit. She prayed it hadn't undone all the good work they'd both done to repair their relationship over the past six months. She decided she would talk to him tonight when she got home, come clean. Then hope it wasn't too little, too late. A gust of wind rocked the car, and she looked up to see the first spots of rain on the windscreen.

* * *

Surprisingly, Alice came to the door after the first knock. Freya took a step back as she heard her unhooking the chain. Alice was dressed in jeans and a lilac hoodie, and looked a lot more alive than she had the night before. Her auburn hair was tied back in a ponytail, and she'd dabbed on a splash of makeup. The sickness act had gone.

'I had a feeling you'd be back,' she said.

'I'm sorry about last night. I shouldn't have come over here on a Sunday evening and disturbed you like that. But I do really need to talk to you.'

Alice took a step back and invited Freya inside.

She was ushered down a hallway towards the kitchen. She tried to keep her expression as neutral as possible in spite of the onslaught her nostrils were facing. That same stench of sweat, of a house shut up despite the heat, in desperate need of having a window open. But there was something more than that. A chemical, possibly even clinical smell, not unlike a hospital.

The door to the living room was open. She could hear Kaye Adams's voice coming from the radio inside. Good Morning Scotland. She glanced in as she passed and saw a man in a hospital bed set up by the window with the view looking out across the fields towards the ocean, the huge, tumbling cliffs of St John's Head in the distance.

'That's Ryan, my brother,' Alice said behind her.

'Hi, Ryan,' Freya said. He didn't move, but rolled his eyes in the direction of the sound of her voice. He was propped up on pillows, his arms folded across his chest. The lower half of his body seemed to be contorted beneath blankets.

'We'll talk in there,' Alice said, gesturing for her to keep moving.

The kitchen window gave a view onto the garden at the side of the house and the fields rising up to the clifftops that ran along the coast of West Mainland. Yesnaby wasn't far in that direction, and Freya had to look away to stop her mind from drifting there. Alice asked her to sit at the table, so she took a seat looking into the room rather than towards the window. It was a large, farmhouse-style kitchen with a huge Aga oven and copper pans hanging over the benches. Alice went to the kitchen counter, turned on the kettle. It didn't take long to boil: it mustn't have long since been used. There were two cups already set up on the worktop and Alice poured the water into them without even asking if Freya wanted a drink. Given the smell, she didn't particularly, but Alice seemed to have opened up this morning and she didn't want to offend her.

'Ryan and I are twins,' Alice said with her back to her.

'He's my little brother by five minutes. But he got stuck in the birth canal with the umbilical cord around his neck, was starved of oxygen that whole time. He was born with severe brain damage, my mother died, and my father hated Ryan from the second he came into this world. So, I've always been all he's got. The only one who'll look out for him properly.'

Alice came to the table with the two mugs, set one down in front of Freya.

She seemed to read Freya's mind, because she said, 'The reason I'm telling you this, is because I want to explain the way I was yesterday. I'm the only person who's given a shit about Ryan since the day he was born. I'm protective, I suppose. We've lived out here since father died and I could afford to buy us a place as far away from other people as we could get before dropping into the ocean. We don't often have guests. So when someone turns up at our house, demanding I answer the door, I can get a little worked up.'

'I'm sorry,' Freya said. 'It was the wrong time to come. I get carried away myself.'

'I'm guessing, if you've found where I live, you also know where I work?'

Freya wondered where she was going with this, thought about Tom. She nodded.

'I called in sick on Thursday because Ryan had a bad turn. I needed to look after him. And there's only so many times work will take that as a reason. They're understanding, but only to a point. It was just easier to say I didn't feel well enough to log on.' She caught Freya's gaze, held it. 'It had nothing to do with it being the same day that man was found.'

Freya fought hard not to look away. 'I wasn't accusing you of anything.' Though she had of course thought it was a strange coincidence.

'I didn't lie about not knowing anyone called Peter Moss, either. He gave me a different name.'

'He did come here, then?' Freya knew he had from the notebook she'd found, but she couldn't admit to that.

Alice nodded. 'The day before he was found dead. I don't really read the papers or watch TV. I'd rather read a book. The radio is only for Ryan, so he doesn't have to lie there in silence. There's enough awful things that happen in life, I don't particularly need to read or hear about everyone else's. So, I never realised that was him they'd found until you came here last night. After you left, I looked him up.'

'What did he want to know?'

'Like you, he was under the impression I used to be Michael Wishart's girlfriend.'

'So, you weren't?'

'I'm guessing you both got that from Emma, Michael's sister?' Alice said. 'She was a child when Michael died, no more than thirteen. At that age, she probably thought any girl he hung about with was his girlfriend. We were just friends. Michael was … sensitive, I suppose. I think he found it easier hanging out with me than with boys.'

Freya stored a question away in the back of her mind, asked a different one instead. 'Were there no boys he hung around with?'

Alice smiled, not an ounce of joy in it. 'Are you trying to catch me out?'

'No, why?'

'Because, if you've spoken to Emma, you'll know Michael was best friends with a boy called Jake Drever. Why are you asking me questions you already know the answer to?'

Freya shifted in her seat, sipped her tea, didn't like it. She tried not to wince, wondered if the smell in here was affecting the taste. She felt like the cup wasn't clean, like the house wasn't. It had put her on the back foot from the moment she'd stepped inside and this meant Alice had been controlling the conversation the whole time. She needed to do something to win it back.

'Okay, if you want me to ask questions I don't know the answer to, what's The Dying Light?'

Alice blinked. 'Sorry?'

'I know you told Peter Moss to ask Rabbie Cleat about the Dying Light, but I don't know what that is or why it's important to what happened to Michael. Or why the son of Seamus Cleat would have the answer.'

'How could you possibly know what I told that man unless … have you spoken to Rabbie?'

Freya said nothing. She twirled her mug between her hands, felt its warmth on her palms.

Alice studied her. 'You can't have, there's not a chance he'd talk to you. Do you know who he is?'

Freya ground her teeth. Alice's constant deflection was getting right on her tits. 'You started this conversation telling me about your brother and how he's the reason I shouldn't interpret your behaviour as suspicious. Are you somehow going to blame him for the fact that you've barely answered a single question I've asked you?'

That might've been a mistake, but she was past caring. This woman was hiding something, and she was going to get answers out of her one way or another.

Alice's nostrils flared as she released a slow breath, pulled herself up to her full height in her chair. 'It's a boat.'

Now it was Freya's turn to blink. 'What is?'

'The Dying Light. It was the name of Rabbie Cleat's dad's boat.'

'Why did Peter Moss need to ask Rabbie about that?'

'The night Michael went missing, I was with him. It was him, Jake, and me. Jake was pals with Rabbie, thought he was the big man because he got to hang around with this thug whose dad had spent time in prison. His own father was a cop, so I'm assuming it was his way of acting out. In any case, midway through the evening, Jake said we should go over to Rabbie's. I didn't want to. I only got to go out once in a blue moon. I never wanted to leave Ryan with Father for long. But I was a teenager, you know. I needed an escape every so often.' Alice paused to sip her tea. She glanced at Freya's. 'When Jake suggested we go to Rabbie's, I said I was going home. I didn't want to spend any time around that boy, he gave me the creeps. I knew his dad had a boat, and Rabbie and Jake used to go out on it. If anything bad happened to Michael that night, I think it'll have happened on that boat.'

'Did you tell the police that at the time?'

'I'm sure I did, yes.'

Freya made another mental note to ask Fergus to check that out when she saw him later. 'There was a rumour Michael had taken a boat and sailed to Caithness.'

'I know.'

'Do you think that was likely?'

'It's possible. If he stole a bloody boat from the Cleats, it won't have ended well for him. Who knows, maybe that's what happened.'

'But did he ever give you any indication he wanted to run away?'

'No, he was…'

Alice's gaze got lost somewhere in the surface of her drink. Freya saw her eyes swell with tears. For the first time since she'd sat down at this table, Freya felt like she was witnessing something genuine.

'He was happy,' Alice said finally. She looked up, blinked again, and the moment was gone. 'I honestly don't know what happened to him.' She sipped her tea, nodded to Freya's. 'That'll be cold. I'll make you a fresh one.'

'Thanks, but it's okay. I've taken up enough of your time.'

Alice looked offended, or maybe disappointed, but Freya needed to leave. She'd got as much as she could hope for. She couldn't stand a moment longer in this oppressive house.

Ryan was still lying in the same position as they passed the living room again. Freya stopped in the hallway as Alice opened the front door.

'There is one other thing,' she said. 'Before, when you were talking about Emma, you said she was only a child when Michael died.'

'She was. She was barely past twelve.'

'When he died?'

'Aye, he…'

Freya saw the penny drop.

The anger returned to Alice's eyes. 'So you were trying to catch me out?'

'No, I'm just wondering why you said "died" and not "disappeared" like you did all the other times.'

'Because he's not fucking here, is he?' Alice spat. 'People don't vanish for a quarter of a century and then simply reappear out of the blue. I don't know what happened to Michael, but if the Cleats were involved, I know it can't have been good.'

Freya stepped past Alice to leave. She flinched as she felt fingers gripping her arm.

Alice leaned in close to Freya's ear, making the hair on the back of her neck stand on end.

'You're not the police. I didn't have to answer a single one of your questions,' Alice said quietly. 'But I did, because you clearly want to know what happened to Michael. And nobody else ever seemed to care. But everything I've told you is off the record. If I see a word of it in print, I'll sue you for every penny you've ever earned. And if you ever accuse me of using my brother for anything…'

She pulled back slightly and her eyes bored into Freya's. She never finished her threat, simply left it hanging.

Freya tugged her arm away, had just stepped across the threshold before the door slammed hard behind her.

28

His tyres howled as he took the corner too quickly.

Fergus slammed on the brakes and his car came to a stop diagonally across the narrow residential street, blocking the road. They could hear the shouting as soon as they opened the doors.

Ahead of them was a U-shaped block of grey, roughcast houses around a yellowing patch of grass. Bungalows down one side where mostly old folks lived, two-storey semi-detached houses on the other two. At the end of the close, a woman in her twenties was leaning out of an upstairs window, yelling and screaming and throwing out what Fergus assumed were the clothes and belongings of the shaven-headed man standing on the green, who in turn was hollering obscenities back at her. There was no sign of Jake Drever.

Eilidh looked up and down the cars parked at the side of the road before the green. 'He's not here.'

'You see what you've done now, you stupid cow?' the man was yelling. 'The polis are back. Plain clothes now. That means you're buggered.'

The woman returned fire. 'You want to arrest him, officers. Breach of the peace. And a fucking lying bastard too.'

'Was there an officer here?' Fergus asked the man. Whatever this was, he wasn't getting in the middle of it. He needed to find Jake.

The guy with the buzzcut looked confused. 'What?'

'Has a police officer in uniform been here already?'

'Aye, and shite all use he was too. Didn't stop this criminal damage taking place, did he?' On cue, an acoustic guitar exploded on the pavement in front of the house. 'Aw, babe, come on! Stop this now.'

'Where did he go?' Fergus asked.

'Are you not going to put an end to this?'

'Where did he go?'

The man must've seen the look on Fergus's face. 'I dinna ken. He got a message on his radio and hopped in his car and bolted.'

Fergus turned to Eilidh. 'Someone's bloody tipped him off.'

'Who? Kevin?'

Fergus didn't know. He didn't think so, he'd known Kev for years. But he had no clue who he could trust at that station anymore. 'Get these two to shut up, will you?'

He stepped away from the rowing couple, walked back towards his car. A woman in a red Ford Fiesta was beeping her horn at him, wanting him to move his vehicle that was blocking the road. He held up a finger to tell her to wait as he called Kevin's radio from his phone.

'Sergeant Fraser.'

'Kev, it's Fergus. Drever's not here.'

'He's not responded to any other callouts. What the bloody hell's that I can hear?'

'That's the domestic he was supposed to be dealing with.'

'What's going on, Ferg?'

Fergus explained how Jake Drever's name had come up on Peter Moss's phone records. He couldn't tell him the rest, about how all of this connected to Michael Wishart, and possibly all the way back to Allan Tait. 'We need him found.'

'I'll check his GPS, see where his vehicle is,' Kevin said.

The woman in the Fiesta sounded her horn again. Fergus ignored her. A group of onlookers had gathered by the garages, watching Eilidh deal with the domestic. Some of them had started to film it on their phones. Eilidh, in turn, was glancing back at Fergus, willing her boss with her eyes to get a move on.

'He's on the Germiston Road,' Kevin said. 'But he's not moving.'

'Whereabouts is he?'

'About three quarters of the way down, near the loch.'

Fergus thanked him and hung up. 'Let's go,' he shouted to Eilidh, then turned to the woman in the Fiesta. 'You, move.'

She looked like she was about to argue, but she changed her mind.

The gears on Fergus's Passat made a horrible crunch as he threw it into reverse. One of the group by the garages had a mobile phone out, filming as Fergus performed a handbrake turn and shot away towards the main road.

'There's something we're missing,' Eilidh said as they flew past the speed trap on the edge of the village, the digital sign with the green smiley face turning to a harsh red SLOW DOWN.

'What's that?'

'Well, why now?'

'Like I said, someone must've tipped him off.'

'That we wanted to talk to him, aye,' Eilidh said. 'But, if he had anything to do with Peter Moss being in the Dwarfie Stane, he had some balls showing up there Thursday morning. Christ, he even tracked down the Polestar with the two witnesses.'

'I suppose, if he'd disappeared that morning, we would've soon been on to him. What choice did he have?'

They lurched forward in their seats, Murray grabbing the dash, as Fergus hit the brakes, swung the car to the left and joined the single-track road heading into the heather-clad hills.

'But still, why would Peter Moss be talking to Jake Drever?'

Fergus quickly glanced across at her before the road began to bend. 'Moss was in Orkney to investigate the disappearance over twenty-six years ago of a boy named Michael Wishart. Jake was Michael's pal. He was one of the last folk to see him.'

'How the hell do you know…' She stopped as it dawned on her. 'Your reporter pal. The redhead. When were you going to tell me this?'

'As soon as I knew it officially.'

'And how long have you known it unofficially?'

'An hour, no more. This is it.'

The road straightened out as it sloped away from the hills down towards Scapa Flow in the distance. Before it got that far, it skirted the shores of a triangular-shaped loch in the lonely valley floor. There were a handful of farms scattered across the landscape, no traffic, except for a single white car, with the sun blinking back off its reflective blue-and-yellow-checked pattern, abandoned in a passing place.

Fergus hit the brakes again, pulled in behind it. The driver's side door was open. Fergus knew long before he reached it what he'd find.

The car was empty, engine running, police radio on the driver's seat.

He thumped the roof of the car with the fleshy pad of his fist. 'Shit.'

Pain bit down hard in the base of his stomach, almost bending him double. He groaned.

'Christ, are you all right?'

He waved away Eilidh's concerns. 'I'm fine.' He hit redial on his phone, calling Kevin at the station. 'He's gone. Car's abandoned. He's nowhere to be seen.'

'Bloody hell, has he seriously done a runner?' Kev asked.

Fergus glanced up into the hills, then shielded his eyes from the sun as he looked back across the loch. There was no sign of anyone.

'Call every officer we've got,' Fergus told the sergeant. 'I want everyone out looking for Jake Drever.'

29

She took a left after passing the Hope.

This hadn't been the plan, but once she'd crossed the last of the Churchill Barriers, something had struck her. A memory that had been stuck there at the back of her mind all this time and had suddenly come dislodged.

Freya's original intention had been to go into the newsroom following her visit to Alice, but after leaving Stromness she had found herself turning off onto the Orphir road, her subconscious pointing her car in the direction of South Ronaldsay. She was well aware she should've shown her face at work first, especially as she hadn't finished either of the two stories she'd been assigned on Thursday, nor written up the interview with Angus Scott. But she also knew there was no way she would be able to focus on any of those tasks until she had been to Burwick.

But before that, there was time for a small detour.

The road she took was single track. It crested the hill and the North Sea unravelled before her, sparkling in the sunlight, the band of rain that had fallen on her car earlier staying in the west. The waves capped with white horses where the wind was picking up, and large cotton-ball clouds rolled across the seemingly endless Sky. Oystercatchers circled above the rolling fields on either side of the road: it was far less intimidating this morning than the last time she had been out here. She took a turn onto an uncovered track and stopped halfway along it. She didn't want to get too close. Ten minutes on foot later, she saw the fork where the route split in two. Through rising heat waves, she made out the wooden gate to the left with the large wooden sign on it. PRIVATE, KEEP OUT painted in thick capital letters. Even from this distance, she could see people had added their own words to it, daubed in thick paint.

Paedos

Scum

It was the first time Freya had been back to Eastwynd Farm since that night six months ago. But this wasn't the house she had come to see.

To the right, the track led away to a farm house near the clifftops. Freya could hear dogs barking, but saw no other signs of life. The fields here were open – like many places in Orkney, there were no trees or bushes at the side of the road to shield her from view. The sign by the gatepost was much smaller than the one on the other side of the track. She had to get a lot closer to it than she would've liked, but she needed to see it. She needed to be sure.

She'd remembered right. As she expected, there was a single word painted on it:

Cleat

Five minutes later, she was back on the main road, heading south again to ever-broadening views across the Pentland Firth to Scotland. She felt cold, despite the sun breaking through the clouds, beginning to warm the day and the inside of her car again. Six months ago, Freya had been spotted leaving Eastwynd by a woman and two men from the neighbouring farm. Without knowing it, she had come into contact with the Cleats. The thought made her skin crawl. She'd done her research on all the names Fergus had given her as possibilities for SC, and Seamus Cleat had been memorable. He'd done time in Peterhead for assault and attempted murder in the nineties, having lost his temper in a bar in Kirkwall and got into a fight with three men. One had gone through a window, another had had his head cracked against a wall, and the third had been beaten so badly he'd lost an eye. A nasty piece of work indeed. Freya wanted answers, but even without Fergus's warning, she wasn't prepared to turn up on the Cleat's doorstep and demand them like she had with Alice.

Luckily, she didn't have to. She pulled over onto the gravel when the road ran out. The small harbour at Burwick was about as far south in Orkney as you could drive. There was only one other vehicle in the car park by the ferry terminal – a white Citroen Berlingo van that seemingly had nobody in it. Stacks of creels and large concrete blocks from the tidal defences had similarly been abandoned at the point the road dropped into the sea. The ferry terminal itself – a fancy name for a one-windowed roughcast shack – looked as dead as ever. A jetty beside it ran down to the water. A single boat was moored to it.

Freya knew Alice had been lying to her about the night Michael disappeared. She wasn't sure how she knew, but something about it didn't ring true. She also knew the best way to hide a lie was to disguise it among fragments of the truth. She thought Alice was being genuine about the name of Seamus Cleat's boat. And if she was, then she had helped Freya decipher another set of initials as well.

Freya reached across the gear stick and took the notebook from the glovebox. She flicked through to the section she needed:

AT uses phone box c/o Cragiefield and Work, 3/31
AT meets SC @ Windwick, 22:49, 04/07
TDL @ Burwick, AT, SC, GL present, 00:19, 07/07
AT uses phone box c/o Cragiefield and Work, 4/31
AT meets SC @ Evie Sands, 23:30, 10/07.

She ran her finger down the page to the third line: TDL @ Burwick. The Dying Light. Here, in this harbour.

She put the notebook back and got out of the car, swatted away a swarm of flies that had descended on the hot metal of the vehicles side panels, trying to keep out of the breeze. The place was silent save for the hush of the wind and the waves, the rhythmic clunk and clatter of the boat moorings. She looked back along the road as she crossed, towards the small chapel at the head of the bay. She would be able to see from here in plenty of time if anyone was coming. She walked over to the jetty, her step quickening as she neared the boat, got as close as she could to read the name on the side of the hull, painted in swirling yellow letters:

The Braemar

She kicked a stone and it clattered off the metal barriers running down the side of the jetty, hit the water with a plop. Her spirits sank with it. But she wasn't done yet.

Across the car park from the jetty there was a path leading up onto the headland. Where it levelled out across the clifftops she stopped, looked out to sea. Watched the tankers rounding Duncansby Head in the distance, making the perilous switch from the North Sea to the North Atlantic. The coastline here was jagged with little inlets – geos, they called them here. She walked a short way along it, peering over the edge, the wind off the Firth gathering velocity as she climbed higher, hiked further around the southern curve of the island. Sweat began to drip from her, but she kept going. With every step, with each geo she peered into her sense of desperation grew. Because she knew – she'd *always* fucking known – that there would be nothing to find here. It had been far too long since her dad had seen that boat in this harbour. Far too long since any of the things she was trying to investigate had taken place. She was chasing ghosts.

But she had hoped. With all her heart, she had hoped to find something.

She dropped down, sat in the long, damp grass with her head in her hands.

It was the worst possible moment for her phone to vibrate.

A text from Kristin: 'Where are you?'

Freya felt like throwing her phone into the sea. She reached for the piercings in her ear, as she always did. Counted forwards and backwards and forwards again and it still didn't work.

She wanted to ignore it, knew there was no way she would be able to show up at work if she did. She just needed to buy herself some time.

She texted back, 'Had an interview with a source. I'll be in soon.'

She about to turn her phone off when it rang.

She cancelled the call, sent it to voicemail. Another text came within seconds of her phone falling silent. 'You've just texted me back. PICK UP!!!'

The phone rang again. Freya forced herself to answer.

'Where are you?'

Her boss sounded as mad as she'd ever heard her. She could hear raised voices in the background.

'I'm in Stromness,' Freya lied. 'Like I said, I had an interview with—'

'Was this for the council tax story?' Kristin cut her off.

'Erm … no, it—'

'The ferry disruption piece?'

'No, Kris. Look, I know they're important, but this…'

She heard a voice in the background saying, 'Ask her.' Hard to mistake who it was.

'You wouldn't happen to have been in Outertown this morning, would you? And last night?' Kristin asked.

'What's she saying?' Gill pestered in the background. 'Is she stealing my story? Because if she is—'

'We've had another complaint,' Kristin said, cutting her off.

Freya screwed her eyes shut.

Freya pinched hard on her studs. 'I can explain.'

But Kristin didn't let her. 'Apparently, this time you've been harassing some poor woman who's a carer for her very sick brother. For Christ's sake, Freya, she says you forced your way into her home.'

'I never—'

'She also says you told her your name was Gill Irvine.'

Her eyes snapped open.

'What the hell are you playing at, Freya? What's got into you?' Kristin said. She seemed less angry now, more concerned. That was worse.

'I'm sorry,' Freya said, beginning to cry. She wasn't sure if she'd said it out loud.

'Whatever this is all supposedly related to, you can't use it. She's said if she sees her name anywhere near our publication, then her words were she's going to, "sue us into the ground." And she meant it.

'I know. I'm sorry.'

'I can't have this on top of everything else we've got to contend with right now, Freya. I just can't.'

'I fucking said I'm sorry,' Freya screamed into the handset.

Then she launched her phone into the air.

It happened in a micro-second. A moment of pure rage and sadness and a thousand other emotions she couldn't name. She watched as her phone disappeared over the cliff edge, then she dropped onto her back and she screamed into the sky.

She screamed at the futility of finding out what had happened to her dad, because nothing would bring him back.

She screamed because she knew she was autistic, regardless of whether someone who knew nothing about her thought she was coping just fine, but still needed to know for sure.

She screamed because she had killed a man, and even if it was in self-defence, the fear she felt every single day at the thought of anyone ever finding out was close to unbearable.

She screamed, and when she was done screaming and her throat was scratched raw, the familiar feelings returned. Guilt. Shame. Panic when she remembered what she had done with her phone. What a fucking stupid thing to do. What a fucking stupid human being she was.

She wiped her tears on the back of her hand, crawled through the grass to the cliff edge, peered over into the geo, knowing full well the device would be long gone.

Down in the water, anchored close to the cliff face on the far side of the narrow inlet, she saw a boat.

30

Eilidh looked up as Fergus entered the CID office. 'Was that her?'

He nodded. He'd just hung up the phone to Emma Wishart. She'd told him the same things Freya had, plus a couple more. Such as Alice Harcus, one of the names on the call log, had been Michael Wishart's girlfriend at the time he disappeared.

'I now officially know what I told you unofficially,' he said. What he still didn't officially know, and so couldn't share or act upon yet, was that Rabbie Cleat was the man Peter Moss was supposed to have been meeting at the Dwarfie Stane. For that, he needed Peter Moss's notebook. But first things first.

'Good, so are you ready?' Eilidh asked.

Sergeant Fraser had done as Fergus had requested. He'd gathered everyone who was on duty and called in others who weren't. They were now all in the incident room, waiting to find out why they were about to launch a manhunt for one of their own.

'DI Muir?'

Both Fergus and Eilidh turned at the sound of the voice. Magnus was standing in the doorway with a tall woman in her mid-to-late thirties wearing a sharp blue suit. Fergus had seen her around but couldn't recall her name.

'This is DS Naomi Stewart of the Professional Standards Division,' Magnus said. 'She's going to sit in on the briefing.'

'Absolutely, sir.' Fergus shook her hand. Stewart was someone he would very much like to talk to, but he'd rather they weren't having this conversation in front of Magnus. 'Is PC Drever someone who's come up in your investigation afore now?'

'His name has appeared in connection with one or two cases we're looking at.'

'Aye, but he's been here donkeys' years, joined straight out of school. It's a small force: I'm sure any of us who are long enough in the tooth will have been connected to cases you've got your eye on.'

DS Stewart gave a tight-lipped smile, and said nothing.

'So, he's not someone you had pegged for having any kind of connection to Allan Tait?'

'With the investigation ongoing I can't say too much, but no, he wasn't one of the names at the top of our list when it comes to Tait.'

Fergus nodded, glanced at Magnus. He wondered which names were up there and if his boss's was one of them.

'Shall we get started?' Magnus asked.

Fergus thought about asking DS Stewart if Michael Wishart's case had come up so far in her investigation, but he decided to keep that name back for the briefing. He wanted it to be a nice surprise so he could see the look on his Magnus's face.

The incident room was as packed as it had been the morning those bones had come out of the ground at Skara Brae six months back. Only the vibe this time was far more tense. Angrier, even.

'What's this about, sir?' one of the uniforms in the front row of seats asked. Fergus resisted the urge to say that, if everyone would shut up, he would tell them. He didn't need the room to be against him any more than it already was.

The assembled cops began to settle. 'Thanks everyone for coming in,' he started. 'I know this is a shock to everyone and you'll have plenty of questions. Jake is one of us. A heap of you will be close to him. But if this feels personal, I promise you it isn't.' He looked at the officer who had asked him a question before, a PC named Mainland. Tried to remember his first name. Jamie, he thought. 'As you'll all know, retired inspector Peter Moss was found dead at the Dwarfie Stane four days ago. The circumstances of his death are still unknown and are being treated as suspicious. This morning, we received the text messages and call log digital forensics were able to pull off Moss's burner phone. One of the people he'd been talking to was Jake Drever.'

A murmur rumbled through the room.

'So that's it?' a voice piped up from the back. 'We're launching a manhunt for Jake because someone who probably wasn't even murdered sent him a text?'

This was another PC, one Fergus knew all too well this time. Mark Foubister. Fancied himself for a detective job one day. It would be over Fergus's dead body.

Fergus took a deep breath. 'Jake left an active incident he was attending when he found out we were coming to talk to him. And we're going to be looking into how he found that out as well.' He paused, made sure he held Foubister's gaze. 'He then drove to Kirbister Loch, abandoned his vehicle and his radio, and is now missing while on duty. I know you're not a detective just yet, PC Foubister, but to those of us who've been doing this a few years, things like that are a bit of a red flag, son.'

Out of the corner of his eye, he saw Eilidh bite her lip. That hadn't won him any favours with some of the rank and file, but he couldn't hold his tongue a second time.

'But, in answer to your question, no, that's not it,' he continued. 'This morning, we also discovered Peter Moss's reasons for being in Orkney. He was here working as a private investigator looking into a case from the late nineties – the disappearance of a teen-aged boy named Michael Wishart.'

He glanced at Magnus. The chief inspector had his head down, enthusiastically taking notes again. Fergus couldn't gauge his reaction, but he saw the look on DS Stewart's face, standing by the wall behind him. He'd wager Wishart's case was definitely on PSD's radar.

'For those of you lucky enough to be too young to remember, or too old in your case, Jim...' That got a slight ripple of laughter, and a light-hearted 'Cheeky bastard' out of PC Brannigan, but the room still wasn't fully on his side. '...Michael Wishart went missing in June, 1997. He went out to spend the night at a friend's house and never came home. The friend he'd gone to stay with was Jake Drever.'

Fergus watched the faces in the room take that in. Some of the auld guard remembered, or at the very least, the mention of

Michael's name was bringing it all back. Others seemed completely unaware of the case or Drever's connection to it.

A hand went up near the front of the room. One of the older officers. 'Would that have been the boy whose parents died in the house fire shortly after he'd gone missing?'

'One and the same. Now, at this stage, nobody's accusing Jake of anything, we simply need to get his side of things. But, above anything else, we want to know that he's safe.'

'Why wouldn't he be safe?' a voice asked from somewhere, Fergus didn't spot where.

'We still don't know if Moss died of natural causes or if someone wanted to stop him from finding out more about Michael. If it's the latter, that same someone might want Jake to keep quiet too. Another name that's come up in connection with Wishart's disappearance is Rabbie Cleat.'

Again, he looked at Magnus. His head was still lowered, but he'd stopped scribbling in his peedie notepad. 'I know that name will mean something to many of you in here. The Cleats are as slippery as they come, and twice as violent. The old boy, Seamus, spent some time inside back in the day, but we've never managed to pin anything on them since, despite all the suspicions and the rumours. If Rabbie had anything to do with Peter Moss's death, this might be the thing that finally changes that.'

Sgt Fraser was tasked with coordinating the response. Sending the cars out to find Drever, assigning officers to contact the airport and ferry companies. 'I want everyone out on this, except for PC Flynn,' Fergus told him. He looked at Kate. 'I need your help with something else.'

She looked disappointed when he told her he needed her to pull up the old Wishart files, pick out everything she could where it looked like things had been missed, or anything that might point to why Allan Tait had not wanted the boy to be found.

'I also need you to find out who's looked at that file recently,' he said to her separately as the rest of the officers began filing out of the room. 'Moss must've had help from someone within

Police Scotland to get the information he did. I'm not interested in getting them into trouble, but they might be able to help us.'

Kate nodded, but she looked upset.

'I know this feels like you're getting benched,' Fergus said. He put his hand on her shoulder. 'I promise you're not. There's folk here in this room who were around back when this case was first active. Folk who may well have had a hand in making sure whatever happened to Michael never came to light. Trouble is, I couldn't tell you who those folk might be, but I do know one or two I would certainly trust with my life. And one of them is you.'

She smiled. 'I'm on it.'

'So, what are we doing?' Eilidh asked him as the room emptied.

Fergus watched Magnus leave with DS Stewart, deep in conversation with her. 'We've got a trespassing complaint to look into.'

Eilidh frowned. 'Are you taking the piss?'

'Not a drop of it. There's a farmer in Outertown who wants to talk to us about a van.'

31

She was going to have to swim.

Scrambling down the cliff face into the geo was the easy part. The boat was anchored about fifteen metres offshore, rising and falling with each gentle sigh of the sea in the narrow inlet. Freya didn't know much about boats, but it looked a decent size. Maybe nine or ten metres. It was old, the red paint on the side faded. There might have been a name on the hull at some point, but now it was lost to the salty air.

She stood on the rocky beach, trying to decide what to do.

Really, the moment to have made this choice should've been when she was still standing on the clifftops. Now she was down here, it didn't make sense to turn back. She slipped off her coat, kicked off her shoes and socks and stood barefoot on a patch of sharp shale. She'd need to take her jeans off too. She looked up – the geo was sheltered, only visible from the coastal path if, like her, somebody got close enough to the edge to look down. And she knew there was nobody there. The air had been hot in the exposed sunlight at the harbour, but down here in the shade of the steep rock walls it was Baltic, and as the gentle waves reached her toes she cried out. The water was even colder. This was the stamping her foot on a nail analogy in reverse; she couldn't not do this. Her brain simply wouldn't let her walk away. She'd come this far, she may as well get it over with.

She pulled off her jeans and stepped into the sea.

There was a ladder at the back of the boat. The stern, she thought it was called. There was a name painted here too; she hadn't been able to see it from the shore. Her heart raced as she traced its faded shape with wet fingers: *The Dying Light.*

She felt a rush of adrenaline that made her forget the cold, but still, logically, what did she do now? Finding this boat here, in Burwick, hidden away from the harbour, confirmed that Alice had been telling the truth. It surely confirmed that she had been right about its initials being in her dad's notebooks too. But that was it. It had been over a quarter of a century since Michael had gone missing, the same length of time since her dad had seen Allan Tait, Graham Linklater, and Seamus Cleat meeting here. Whatever had happened on this boat, surely there wasn't going to be any evidence of it now.

She looked around. There were padded benches running down the side and across the stern. An open cabin ahead of her. As she'd swam alongside the hull, she'd seen portholes, suggesting there was another cabin below deck, even though the boat barely seemed big enough. While the vessel itself was clearly a few decades old, the equipment in the cabin had been updated. There was a radio, screens that looked like they might display radar and GPS data, maybe water depth too. Various dials and buttons. None of this was going to tell her a thing.

Next to the wheel there was a hatch, no doubt leading down to the cabin below deck, but again, what did she expect to find? She was beginning to regret her decision, was thinking how twenty minutes must have passed since her call with Kristin and how her boss would be expecting her through the door of the newsroom any minute. She was going to be furious when she finally showed her face.

She opened the hatch.

Steps led down into a small corridor. She could see it was lit by the portholes but was still dark, the small round windows unable to let in much light, especially in the shade of the geo. Stepping inside, she immediately clocked the smell. Bleach. The boat was spotless, she'd noticed that while she was looking around the cabin. To the right was a small bathroom, on the left a bedroom with bunks, the bedding stripped off both. Bare mattresses, no pillows or duvets. She noticed something on the wall at the head of the bed, stepped closer to look. A small metal half-loop, bolted into the wall. Now she was inside the room she saw there was another on the other side.

She lurched forward, put her hand on the far wall to steady herself as a large wave rolled under the boat. Being inside, unable to see the horizon, she was beginning to feel seasick, and the thick smell of bleach mixed with the stench of seaweed in the geo was making it worse. Backing out into the walkway, she looked up through the hatch, could see the clifftops appearing and disappearing from view as the boat rose and fell. The only other room down here was a lounge, straight across from the hatch, in the hull. This was the largest room of the three, with a long continuous sofa running around the curved walls with a table in the middle, and two portholes on either side.

Maybe it was the smell, or the nausea setting in, but her mind started playing tricks on her. Visions of Tait and his cronies meeting with Seamus Cleat down here. Was this where they met to discuss the disgusting things they were doing? Another wave rocked her sideways towards the sofa, and she steadied herself on the wall again, the palm of her hand pushing down on something cold. Same as in the bedroom, there were thick metal half-loops bolted to the sides of the cabin.

The boat tipped again. Something thumped against the hull. A wave, probably. Suddenly she felt the cold. She was soaking wet, only half dressed. It dawned on her too that the tide might be coming in. Had she left her clothes far enough up the beach? If the water was rising, there was a chance they would float away before she got back to shore. She held herself upright against the wall, tried to breathe to settle her stomach, stop the bile from rising into her throat.

And that's when she heard the thumping sound again.

It came from the stern.

Lighter this time, didn't sound like the weight of the water against the boat. If anything, she'd say it sounded like footsteps.

A deeper chill crept over her bones. Goosebumps ran across her flesh.

She ran back up the stairs, peered out through the hatch.

Looked up into the faces of the two men standing on the deck. One tall, one short. Both early forties. The closest was the shorter one. Cropped black hair and hollow pale blue eyes. An unhinged expression on his face, looked like he was caught between licking his lips in excitement and exploding with wrath-of-God rage.

'Who the fuck are you?' he asked, his voice low. Simmering.

Freya's gaze shot between them, her heart racing so fast she was struggling to breathe. Strange how the mind works, but in that moment, part of her seemed to detach and to notice with complete serenity that the tall man's clothes didn't seem to fit him. They were too small, like they belonged to someone else.

Serenity didn't last. She felt a thunderous pain in her chest as a boot stamped on her sternum and she was launched backwards into the cabin.

The short man came thundering down the stairs after her.

The last thing she heard before he grabbed her by the throat was the tall man behind him yelling, 'Rabbie, don't!'

Saturday, 21st June, 1997 - 1.57 a.m.

Nobody stopped him this time.

Nobody said a word. The five of them stood terrified in the cold light of the battery-powered lamp as Rabbie's shadow made monsters across the walls. The shrieks of his anger under the low ceiling of the farmhouse living room were suffocating. Michael felt each one like a drill being pushed into the squishy flesh at the back of his jawbone behind his ear. Every high-pitched squeal sending shards of hot pain through his teeth, into his temples, behind his eyes. He needed to sit down. He was going to throw up.

'Where … the fuck … did she … go?'

Rabbie had broken what remained of the furniture. Snapped and stamped and kicked the living shit out of it. Now it lay in sharp splinters between their shoes on the stone floor.

'I said…' Michael closed his eyes as Rabbie stepped closer, felt his face up against his. Could taste his alcohol breath as he panted, exhausted by rage. 'Where … the fuck … did she go, Wishy?'

'We don't fucking know, Rabbie,' he heard Alice reply. He opened his eyes to see Rabbie turn his head towards her.

And he wanted to kill him.

He wanted to reach out and wrap his hands around the daft little cunt's throat and squeeze the fucking life out of him.

Rabbie wasn't a big lad. Was the shortest of the three boys there. Shorter than Isla too. It wasn't his size that intimidated.

It was his eyes.

There was nothing there.

Michael had never seen anything like it. Even in a state of pure rage, those eyes were dead. Nothing behind them. Like he could skin you alive then go back to cracking jokes about your mum in the next breath. There was no fear, that's what made him dangerous. It might even have made him deadly. He was a threat that needed to be snuffed out, but even if Michael hadn't been feeling like he'd been run over by a truck, he knew he didn't have it in him to do it. But he wished with his whole heart that he did.

Rabbie was glaring at Alice. Everyone knew what was coming.

'Apologise,' he said.

Alice frowned. 'What?'

'Apologise to me for losing my dad's boat and for talking to me like you did just now.'

'Rabbie, don't be a—'

Michael's whole body seized up as Rabbie grabbed him by the throat and squeezed. Hard.

'Apologise!'

'Rabbie, stop!!!'

Jake leaped forward. Alice did too, both of them trying to pull him away. But he wouldn't let go. Michael couldn't breathe. He actually couldn't fucking breathe. Air was in his chest, couldn't get out, felt like it would burst. Felt like his head was going to blow up, like something out of a cartoon, swelling like a balloon. He realised he too was clawing at Rabbie's hands. But it was no use.

Someone was screaming.

He heard himself choking.

He wanted to fight. Wanted to punch and kick and scream but couldn't. For some reason, his mind went to his first and only fight, if you could even call it that, when he was in primary school. An older kid, Christopher James – he still remembered his name – had taken one of his shiny Panini football stickers. Murdo MacLeod in his Scotland kit. He'd been after it for ages. He wasn't going to simply let it slide, so he'd gone up to Christopher and told him to give it back. The older kid had picked him up, carried him while he was trying to fight his way free, but it was like kicking through treacle, like punching in a dream, and dumped him unceremoniously over the wall of the playground onto the pavement on the other side where he'd landed with a sickening crack.

'I'm sorry!'

He came to as he felt oxygen rush into his windpipe. He opened his eyes, everything a blur through his tears, and clutched at his throat. He was on the ground, Rabbie's feet by his head. He glanced up to see Rabbie was looking at Alice.

'See, that wasn't so hard. Now what are you going to do about getting my dad's boat back?'

When she spoke, he heard Alice was crying. 'Rabbie, it's gone. She untethered it. We tried to get it, but—'

'But you didn't try fucking hard enough!'

Rabbie howled. Something else shattered. Michael didn't think there was any furniture left to break.

'You daft cunts haven't grasped what's going to happen now, have you?' he screamed.

'Rabbie.' That was Jake. He was trying to sound calm, but Michael heard the tremor. 'We can get back. If there's someone else here, they'll have a radio we can—'

Michael flinched at the sound of Rabbie's hyena laugh. 'Back? I don't give a fuck about going back! Do you know why?'

Nobody answered.

'Do you know why?' Rabbie screamed again.

'Why?' Jake asked.

'Because, when my dad finds out what we've done with his boat, he's going to fucking kill me.' Rabbie was laughing as he said this. The unhinged cackle of the insane. He pointed at each of them in turn. 'He's going to kill me, and then you, and you, and you, and you, and you. And he'll make all of your fucking families watch and then slit their throats too.'

Silence followed. Everyone had heard the rumours. They knew about Rabbie's dad. Folk said he was connected to some gang down in Glasgow. People he'd met during his time in prison. Real nasty types, the likes of which Orkney never saw. For anyone who hadn't strayed far from these islands, it was hard to understand the levels of violence these people reached. But they could imagine. Sometimes, that was worse.

'We can get the boat back.' It hurt to talk. Michael wasn't sure they'd hear him, but everyone turned to look at him. 'If we can contact the coastguard, we can—'

That laugh exploded again. 'Oh aye, the fucking coastguard. Jesus, Wishy, shut the fuck up. I've heard enough out of you the night.'

'No, he's right,' Jake said. 'It's our only choice now.'

Jake looked down at him, held out his hand to help him up, and Michael felt a lump in his throat again. He couldn't remember the last time Jake had taken his side over Rabbie.

'How are we going to contact anyone?' Kelly asked. 'We've got no idea if the girl you saw actually has a radio.'

'I know somewhere we might find one,' Michael said.

'Where?'

As if on cue, a ghostly glow filled the window as the beam from the lighthouse swept by.

MONDAY, 9TH JUNE. PRESENT DAY.

32

Everything went dark.

Freya felt hot pain sear through the back of her skull as her head hit the table. She heard the crash of bone against wood, then the thud of heavy footsteps before hands gripped her throat. They closed around her windpipe, but immediately released as the animal who had dived on top of her was yanked away by his accomplice. The taller man shoved Rabbie Cleat up the steps to the deck, then the cabin door slammed shut.

She heard a muffled voice on the other side of the hatch.

'Rabbie, man, what the fuck are you playing at?'

No reply. Seconds later, engines roared to life.

Panic struck as the boat lurched forward. There was no way out of the cabin. No way past those men. Nowhere to escape to even if there had been, other than diving into the water then trying to climb up several metres of rock. The room began to jolt violently as the small vessel sailed out into open sea, crashing into waves. She could feel the G-force, knew they were moving quickly. With each passing second, dry land and safety fell further and further away.

She felt sick. Couldn't tell if it was the hit to the head or the rapid rise and fall of the world around her. Even without touching the back of her head, she could feel the stinging pain and sticky fresh blood. She could still hear raised voices the other side of the cabin hatch, but couldn't decipher them clearly over the sound of the engines and water thumping the hull.

She closed her eyes, tried to breathe.

Tried to count the studs in her ear, but she was way past that.

Some small sliver of hope, somewhere in the back of her mind, tried to comfort her with the idea that her car was at Burwick. Someone would see it, wonder why it had been left there. Tom would worry if she didn't contact him too, then he would call

Fergus. But as soon as she had those thoughts, they were replaced by others.

By the time Tom thinks to call anyone, it'll be too late.

She heard the engines cut out. The boat began to drift.

The cabin hatch flew open. The short one who'd kicked her came barrelling down the steps. Lying on the floor in just her t-shirt and underwear she felt completely exposed. Vulnerable. She scampered backwards into the table, pulled her knees up to her chest, her arms wrapped around her bare legs.

Rabbie Cleat scoffed. 'Don't flatter yourself, love. If I was going to rape you, you'd have been bent over that table by now.'

She screamed as he grabbed her by the hair, pulled her to her feet, dragged her out of the cabin. Her fingers clawed at his hand, but he wouldn't let go. Pain from the cut on the back of her head shot through her like a fire through tinder. She felt the slow, sticky creep of blood running down the back of her neck.

The tall man was standing on the deck. She saw only his feet as she was hauled past him. Heard him say, 'Rabbie, fucking think!'

But Rabbie didn't listen.

Freya was thrust forward. She opened her eyes to see choppy water beneath her, the South Ronald say shoreline a mile or so away. Out here the day seemed so bright, the sunlight stinging her eyes. Pain thundered through the back of her head as Rabbie held her over the edge of the stern by her hair.

'Who the fuck are you?' he shouted behind her.

She couldn't reply. Her breath was stolen away on the wind.

Her heart leaped into her throat as Rabbie lunged her forward, further over the edge.

'Who ... the FUCK ... are you?'

'I know who she is,' she heard the other one reply. 'I've seen her at the station a few times. She's that reporter.'

'So, what's she doing on my boat?'

Freya still couldn't answer. With the pain and the panic, she didn't know what to say. Couldn't form the words, even if she had wanted to. But if she didn't say something, she was in no doubt Rabbie would drop her into the water. And there was no making it back to dry land from here, no matter how good a swimmer she was.

'I said, what are you—'

'For fuck's sake, Rab.'

She felt hands grab her by the arms. She was hauled back onto the boat and fell to the deck. She almost cried with relief until she looked up at the two men standing over her, snarling at each other like two dogs fighting over a bone.

'Don't be a dickhead,' the tall one said. 'You know I won't stand here and watch you kill her.'

'How would I be killing her? She knows how to fucking swim. I'd be giving her a chance, same as we gave Wishy.'

Rabbie winked at his partner. A sick, wild-eyed grin spread like an infection across his face. It was unsettling how he swung from blind anger to unhinged delirium in a heartbeat.

The tall one didn't find it amusing. He looked down at Freya. 'Your name's Sinclair, right?'

She barely managed to nod. She was freezing now, beginning to shake.

The tall man looked at Rabbie. 'She's pals with Fergus Muir.'

Rabbie shrugged. 'And?'

'And she's Neill Spence's daughter.'

The mention of her dad's name was like another blow to the head. It seemed to have a similar effect on Rabbie. He appraised her now like a man who'd found a priceless antique among the junk in their dead auntie's loft.

The tall one went back to the wheel, picked up the radio.

'The fuck are you doing?' Rabbie yelled.

'I'm calling Maggie.'

Rabbie bristled. 'What gave you the impression you were in charge here?'

'Maggie's pure fuming at you,' the tall man shot back. 'She's ready to disown you for sending that Moss guy out to Hoy instead of ignoring him, like you were told. And now I'm—'

'Don't put that shite on me. It's not my fault he actually went out there, the fucking lunatic. I never thought he'd really go, I thought he'd fuck off and leave me alone.'

'Aye, but now the only reason CID is looking into this is because of where he showed up dead and how sodding weird it all looks. And here I am, panicking and doing a runner, because if they link Moss to Wishy and reopen that case, we're all screwed.' The tall man pointed at Freya. 'Use your head, man. If you drown a bloody journalist, especially this one, while we've got this kind of heat on us, Maggie'll not only disown you, she'll fucking disembowel you. And me as well for letting you.'

Freya saw Rabbie's hands had bunched into fists, but the tall man didn't back down.

'Don't even try it. I'm more afraid of your mother than I am of you.' He pressed the button on the side of the radio. 'Maggie, come in. It's Jake.'

A pause, then: 'Are you there already?'

'No, there's been a development. We found that reporter on the boat.'

'Where is she now?' came the reply. Freya recognised the voice. She placed it right away.

'She's here, we've got her with us out on the Pentland Firth.' Jake's eyes locked with Freya's. 'What do you want us to do with her?'

Freya tried to steady her breathing. Wanted to look away but couldn't.

'Apparently, I didn't make myself clear enough the last time,' the woman on the other end of the radio said. 'Bring her here. I'll be sure to remove any doubt.'

33

'You're not going to believe this.'

Fergus stepped out of the van holding a Papier notebook in his gloved hand, the words, 'Peter Moss, PI, is on the case,' embossed on its cover. With the other, he wafted away a handful of flies that had gathered on this side of the vehicle to shelter from the ocean breeze, and he squinted through the light rain at Eilidh. They hadn't long since got rid of the owner of the land so they could have a look through the van in peace. Eilidh was keeping lookout for him coming back. She was standing in front of the Mazda camper, her back to the sea in the distance, looking at her phone.

'What is it?' he asked.

'The autopsy report on Peter Moss is back.'

'And?'

'Give me a second. This has to be a mistake.'

He watched her eyes dart back and forth, skating over the screen, taking in the information they'd been waiting for.

'What does it say, Murray?'

She looked up. 'It says Peter Moss died of a haemorrhagic stroke.'

Fergus sighed, rubbed his eyes. 'Well, at least you were right about one thing.'

'What's that?' 'I don't bloody believe it,' he said. 'You're telling me Peter Moss died of natural causes? After we've sent the whole force out on a manhunt for another cop, just because his name was in his phone?'

Eilidh ignored him, kept reading. No doubt looking for some smidge of evidence she could use to justify keeping this investigation alive.

Fergus tossed the notebook through the open side door of the van and back onto the unmade bed, then snapped off his gloves.

There was no point bagging it as evidence, or opening it and 'finding' the proof that Peter Moss had gone to Hoy to meet Rabbie Cleat. The pain in his stomach gnawed at him, but he ignored it. It had been killing him all morning, since the dash to find Jake; he was sick of thinking about it now. He looked across the fields, over the water, to where the green camelback hills of Hoy were grazing the low band of cloud that seemed to be hanging over this side of the islands. From here he could see the valley where Peter Moss had been found four days ago. He couldn't accept that this whole thing had been a wild goose chase.

'If this is a straightforward natural death, then why did Drever run?'

Fergus glanced over at his colleague. She'd read his mind. 'Best kens, Murray. You tell me.'

'It has to be because of Michael Wishart. Even if Peter Moss wasn't murdered, he was here looking into that case because something wasn't right about it.'

Fergus said nothing. He looked back over to Hoy, thinking it through.

'This does say there's one anomaly that can't easily be explained,' Eilidh said. She'd gone back to reading the report. 'According to the tox screen, he had high levels of warfarin in his bloodstream.'

'That's a blood thinner,' Fergus said. 'It stops clots forming.'

'Aye, I know.'

'Well, I'm no doctor, but I don't think that would cause a stroke, would it? The pathologist would've said so in their report if it did.'

Eilidh looked annoyed that he wasn't sharing her excitement. 'No, but it would stop a bleed from healing once it started. It won't have helped.'

'Was warfarin mentioned in his medical records?'

'I don't remember seeing it. I'd have to double-check.'

'Aye, well you do that. In the meantime, where do we go next with this?'

Eilidh put her phone in the inside pocket of her suit jacket. Like Fergus had done, she looked across the water to Hoy, her eyes narrowed against the sun that was peeking through the clouds. Four seasons in an instant. 'Why would someone send him all the way out there?'

'Because they didn't want to be seen with him.'

'Or because they never thought he'd show up. Think about the effort he had to put in to get there – finding someone with a boat to take him, making the trek up there in the middle of the night on foot. Would you have gone to those lengths to speak to a witness, or would you have arranged something else? Whatever they had to tell him, he must really have wanted to hear it.'

He had to admit, it had struck him as a lot of trouble to go to. But having spoken to Emma Wishart earlier, he had got the feeling Peter Moss perhaps cared about her more than she knew.

He also thought it was the kind of move a man like Rabbie Cleat might pull, sending Moss on a wild goose chase in the middle of the night, knowing it would all be for nothing. Fergus had spoken to Rabbie a couple of times over the years in connection to cases he'd worked on. The slaughtering of some cattle at a farm in Burray about a year ago had been the last time. He'd never been able to make anything stick, and Rabbie had loved it. He was a cocky wee shite; sending Peter Moss out to the Dwarfie Stane just for the hell of it was precisely the kind of thing he'd do. 'There's the matter of the writing on his arm too,' Eilidh said. 'The Dying Light. We still don't know what that means.'

'That gets a mention in here,' Fergus said, reaching back inside for the notebook. He didn't bother with a new set of gloves: they could eliminate his prints, if needs be. Though he doubted the need would be. '"Ask RC about The Dying Light."'

'What does that mean?'

'RC would be Rabbie Cleat, judging by the list of names in here. It also says Rabbie was the man Peter was going to meet with in Hoy, though I don't suppose that matters now. It looks like Moss spoke to an Alice Harcus who told him to ask Rabbie about that.' The name suddenly rang a bell. 'Emma Wishart told me the morning that Alice Harcus was her brother's girlfriend.'

He saw the spark return to Eilidh's eyes. 'Okay, so which one of them do we speak to first?'

Fergus ran his free hand through his hair, chewed the inside of his cheek.

'Come on, boss,' she said. 'You have to admit the Wishart case deserves another look. Did you not see the look on the PSD woman's face when you dropped Michael's name?'

He had. And he had to admit, there was something off about what had happened to the Wishart family.

But he'd worked that case. Or the second part of it, at least. Neill had led the investigation into the fire and had found it to be an accident. Was that really the moment his friend had grown suspicious of Allan Tait? And then there was the question that truly hurt him, had done since the first moment he'd laid eyes on those notebooks a year ago – why hadn't Neill trusted him enough to tell him what was going on?

'Don't think that by calling me "boss" you'll sway me.'

Eilidh grinned. 'You know I'm right though.'

He did.

'Alice Harcus's address is in here,' he said, holding up the notebook. 'And I know where Rabbie bides.'

'Perfect. So where are we going first?' Eilidh said. 'Harcus or Cleat?'

34

The voices were distant. Freya struggled to hear them over the sound of her own shallow, rapid breaths inside the hood.

They'd brought her back to land, but she wasn't sure if she was on the Caithness side or in Orkney. The latter, she assumed, given who Jake had spoken to on the radio. Rabbie had produced the cloth sack she had over her head and the cable ties around her wrists from somewhere inside the boat's cabin, had laced the ties through one of the metal half-loops bolted into the wall. She hadn't been able to see a thing now for the past thirty minutes. Maybe less. She wasn't sure how long it had been. She'd tried to stay calm, focus on the details, stop her mind from spiralling. Straight from the boat, she had been bundled into the back of what she guessed from the hard wood floor and the smell of diesel was a van, then driven along winding roads. Before they'd stopped, she'd felt the road surface change from tarmac to dirt.

As for where she was now, she suspected she was inside a shed or a caravan somewhere, possibly on the Cleat farm. She had been hauled up a step to get in here, and the door had made a flat, tinny sound when she had been shut inside. The air felt hot against her damp legs, stuffy. Her wrists were bound to the legs of a wooden chair and she could feel gritty carpet beneath her bare feet. The sensation of it made her whole body itch, like she had insects inside her skin. It was disturbing her more than the thought of what they were going to do to her next. She could feel the moisture of her own breath on the rough cloth covering her head, could smell the stale remains of the sweat of whoever had been unfortunate enough to wear this sack last. She wondered where they were now and what had happened to them. Wondered how many people had been in her position before and had done what she was doing, telling themselves they'd get out of it, lying to themselves that it was all going to be okay.

A door opened, stiff on its hinges.

Footsteps.

The world tilted on its axis as someone stepped inside the room. She heard someone dragging something across the carpet, coming to a stop right in front of her. There was the slight creak of wood as someone sat down.

She waited. No sound but her own heart on her eardrums.

Then that voice.

'You do know it's awful bad fortune to have a rabbit on a boat, don't you, Red?'

Her breath caught in her throat at the sound of that name.

Light stung her eyes as the sack was torn from her head. She screwed them shut, flinched away like she was in pain. Little by little, she managed to peel them open again, blinked the figure in front of her into focus.

'Do you remember me?' they asked.

Like she'd thought, she was in an old caravan. Dirty dark orange curtains pulled across plastic windows gave the light a sepia hue. Everything else that must have once been in here – the bed, the kitchen, the bathroom – had all been pulled out, leaving scars in the walls and the carpet, and rendering the van little more than a hollow shell. Freya was sitting towards the back of it, an old woman sat on a wooden chair across from her. Late sixties, early seventies maybe. Long grey hair flowing over her shoulders, and bright green eyes that bore into hers. She had two threadbare towels in her lap. Freya didn't recognise her face, had never seen this woman before in her life.

But she knew the voice.

'I didna ken it was you when I saw you coming out of Eastwynd that night,' the old woman said. 'I would've been much clearer about what would happen if you came back again if I had.'

'Where am I?'

'D'ye not mind that night?' the woman asked, ignoring her question.

Freya did remember. When she had come out of Eastwynd Farm on a pitch-black night six months ago, a woman and two men had been waiting for her at the gate. She hadn't got close enough to see them, had only heard the woman shouting to her through the dark, but she would recognise that voice anywhere. The thick Orcadian accent. This was the woman Jake had spoken to on the radio. Rabbie Cleat's mother. He'd called her Maggie.

'Do you mind what I told you?' she asked.

'You said you'd made a note of my car's registration number.'

Freya almost cried when she heard the tremor in her own voice. She sounded so scared. So feeble.

'I did. And I used it to find out who you were and where you bided. That's when I knew the rumours were true, that our Peedie Red Rabbit had come home.'

Maggie smiled at the reaction she got by using one of her dad's rarer nickname for her.

Freya flinched as Maggie stood, draped one of the towels over Freya's bare legs. The other she used to press down on the back of Freya's head.

Freya winced as a sharp pain shot down her spine and through her teeth.

'That boy of mine's a bloody fool. Takes after his father,' she heard Maggie saying. 'He's made an awful mess of the back of your head.'

Freya saw the towel as Maggie took it away, took her a while to realise the deep red stain was her blood. She felt her stomach lurch at the sight of it. And she hoped to God the towel had been clean.

'What are you going to do with me?' she asked.

Maggie Cleat sat back down, held the towel in her lap. 'Well, it's a good question. What would you have me do?'

'Let me go.'

Maggie laughed. 'I suppose I should've known you'd say that. My boy wanted to drop you into the sea and let you drown. There's also been talk of burying you somewhere nobody would ever find you. Though that doesn't always work out the way folk plan it. Bodies have a nasty habit of turning up again, as well you know.'

A shudder ran through Freya. Her skin felt on fire but her insides were like ice. Maggie held her gaze for too long, and Freya wondered if that last comment was a reference to the bodies that had been unearthed at Skara Brae six months ago, or if Maggie somehow knew she lay awake at night panicking about what would happen if the corpse of the man she had pushed off a cliff at Yesnaby ever washed up on shore.

'People know where I am,' she said through chattering teeth. 'If anything happens to me, they'll know who to blame.'

'Oh aye, and I imagine you said the same thing to Tait six months back.'

Freya felt the chill within her deepen. That not only confirmed the Cleats' connection to Allan Tait, it also showed Maggie knew exactly what had happened in December.

'Tait called me that night,' Maggie went on. 'He told me how you'd marched into Alastair Sutherland's paper and told the handsome scoundrel right to his face how you knew everything. About him and Graham Linklater and Tait going to these parties and raping young girls. Bold as brass. No apparent concern for the consequences. You put us both in mind of your father.'

You don't know the first fucking thing about my dad.'

Freya knew that wasn't true from Maggie's use of her dad's nicknames for her, but she was angry. Confused. Petrified.

'Allan told me he was going to call in his lads, have you taken care of,' Maggie said, ignoring her. 'But then he was always an arrogant swine. Thought he could sweep anything under the carpet, make it all disappear, even long after he'd hung up his uniform. I told him it was a mistake, that it was too messy. That what we really ought to do was convince you to leave the past in the past, where it belongs.'

'And how do you think you'll do that?'

Maggie smiled. She leaned forward, picked up the cloth sack from where she'd dropped it at Freya's feet, then she stood and pulled it down over Freya's head again.

The world went black.

Freya's her heart rate hit the roof.

She jumped again when a hand touched her shoulder. Through the sound of her panicked breaths against the bag she heard Maggie say, 'When my boy gets back, Red, you'll find out.'

Saturday, 21st June, 1997 - 2.24 a.m.

He was struggling to contain his panic.

A searing pain, unlike anything he had ever experienced, was pounding through his head. He felt like he was about to vomit. He couldn't catch his breath. The rest of the group continued their uphill march, following the narrow track that pierced straight through untended fields, leading them to the clifftops overlooking the North Sea. Michael lagged behind, unable to match Rabbie's rapid pace. The prick was driven by rage. He turned his back to the powerful gale coming off the open sea and took deep, cleansing breaths. In the distance, he could make out the coast of Deerness through the growing twilight. Not a single light flickered in the windows of any of the farms or houses. The world was still fast asleep.

'Are you okay?'

Alice stood beside him, her presence reassuring.

Michael nodded, too scared to talk for fear that, if he opened his mouth, he might be sick.

The beam from the lighthouse washed over them. He didn't like the look of concern it lit on Alice's face. 'There'll be a radio or something in the lighthouse. Someone will come for us soon,' she said. 'Jesus, you're shivering.'

He hadn't noticed, but she was right.

She took off her thin jacket and draped it over his shoulders, glanced up the hill towards the others. 'Think you can keep going?'

'I'm fine, really.'

'You're fucking not, Wishy. None of us are.' She smiled at him, and yet somehow she looked the saddest Michael had ever seen her. 'I can't believe the one night I decided to risk leaving Ryan alone with my dad, this happens.'

'I'm so sorry.'

'Don't be. This isn't your fault, it's that daft shite's,' she said, nodding towards the group disappearing up the hill. Michael didn't need her to clarify who she meant.

'I asked you out tonight though, then I said about meeting up with Jake and the others. If it wasn't for me, you wouldn't be here.'

'And I went along with it. I just ... I wanted one night to be me, for once. One night where I got to have fun. And I wanted to spend it with you.'

Michael could've cried then. 'I wish we'd spent it alone. Anywhere but here.'

'Me too,' she said, and she took his hand. 'But there'll be other nights.'

The lighthouse was so close to the cliff edge that part of the boundary wall seemed to be hanging over it. This high up, about two hundred and fifty feet above the open water, the wind was blowing a skreever, knocking them sideways as they walked. The rusted iron gate was hanging off its hinges, and the path leading to the largest of the buildings was overgrown with weeds and moss, making picking their way to the entrance even more treacherous. Hard to believe people had actually lived here until only a few years ago when it had gone fully automated. It looked as abandoned and derelict as the rest of the buildings on the island.

There were a number of structures besides the main tower of the lighthouse – a cuboid-shaped two-storey house and several outbuildings. Michael and Alice found the door to the house open, the sound of objects clattering inside. They could see the pale blue light of the lamp flickering in one of the rooms as Rabbie and the others carried out their frantic search for a radio. Alice tried the switch on the wall, but no light came on.

'We should probably look for the generator instead of diving in with no light,' Alice said. 'Bet that stupid arsehole never thought to do that.'

'Do you think there'll still be fuel in it?' Michael asked.

Or, at least, he thought he did. He felt himself sway, heard Alice saying 'Woah,' as she caught him.

'Jesus, Mike, we need to get you to a hospital.'

He wanted to say he'd be fine, but a violent cramping in his stomach stopped him. He managed to turn away from Alice just in time before he threw up all over the threadbare carpet in the hallway. He dropped to his hands and knees, vomited again. Felt pain roll through him like a giant wave, making him sway, making the sickness ever worse.

A scream echoed down the hallway as something smashed in one of the rooms.

'The fuck are they doing?' Alice said.

Michael hauled himself to his feet. 'We should help them look.'

'You're in no fit state.'

'We need to help them. You said it yourself, I've got to get off this island.'

He was glad it was too dark inside to fully make out the look of concern on Alice's face as she nodded. He feared it might have broken him.

They found the others in a room filled with orange buoys and old fishing net. Other than that, the room was empty save for a long unit that ran the length of the far wall. Rabbie and the others had pulled out everything from the cupboards and drawers. In the light of the pale lamp, Michael could see a collection of seashells and the skulls of small animals – birds, sheep and rabbits – lined up along the worktop.

'There's fuck all here. This place is a shithole,' Rabbie yelled. He locked eyes with Michael. 'You. You said there'd be a radio.'

Michael said nothing.

'You said we'd find a radio here, so where is it?'

'We've only checked a couple of the rooms,' Jake said. 'We need to keep looking.'

There was only the one lamp, so there was no way they could split up and take different rooms. They had to go together. The next room they tried was a kitchen. A gas cooker, sink, cupboards still filled with pots and pans. An old metal kettle still sitting on the stove. Rabbie tore everything out of the drawers again, clattered cutlery onto the floor, even though it was obvious to everyone there they wouldn't find anything.

They came across a living room, children's toys still out on the rug. They looked positively creepy in the pasty blue light. Bedrooms with bare mattresses covered in plastic. Shelves with books, their spines too faded and cracked to read. A bathroom filled with rags and plasterboard and crusty cans of paint. With each room, their panic heightened. Michael could feel it. From the looks on everyone's faces, they all could. This place was a wreck, nothing here to help them. They were running out of options.

'Fuck!'

Michael flinched as Rabbie put his fist through the back of a cupboard. The stench in here was horrendous. He wanted to be sick again. He wanted to lie down. He wanted to curl up into a ball and go to sleep, and wake up and for this all to be over.

'What's in here?' they heard Isla calling from the landing.

Jake carried the lamp, found her standing next to the only door they'd come across in the whole building that was closed. There was a deadbolt on the floor, shards of wood where it had been snapped off, but the door was still shut. Jake tried the handle. It didn't budge.

'Move,' Rabbie shouted. He kicked the door just below the lock.

It shifted. Just a little.

Rabbie looked at the others. 'Did yous fucking see that?'

Michael glanced around the group. They had all seen it. The door had opened slightly then immediately slammed shut again, like it was being jammed by something behind it.

Or someone.

Rabbie looked at Michael, then at Alice. He whispered, 'She's here.'

Everyone knew who he meant. The girl who had untethered the boat. There was nowhere else on the island to go. This had to be where she was hiding.

Michael's stomach sank. He knew what Rabbie would do the second he was inside that room.

'I bet she's got a fucking radio in there,' Rabbie said, louder now.

'Rabbie, don't—' Alice started to say.

Another kick to the door. Then another. Jake joined in, the pair of them slamming their shoulders against the door and pushing with all their might. And it was opening, the crack getting wider.

Behind the door, someone screamed.

One final shove, and the door flew open.

Then everything went quiet. Michael peered through the group at what they had found inside. And his heart pounded in sheer horror.

MONDAY, 9TH JUNE. PRESENT DAY.

35

He hadn't been overly concerned before, but now he was.

Fergus stood by his car door and took a few deep breaths, tried to will the pain in his stomach away. It felt worse than being stabbed, an injury he'd only suffered the once, and even then, only superficially, but one he didn't particularly want to experience again. Still, right now, given the choice between this and taking a blade to the gut, he would've probably gone with the latter.

'You okay?'

He looked over his shoulder. Murray was watching him, worry knotting her forehead. Her eyes shot to his stomach. He realised he was clutching it with his hand.

'I'm fine.'

He waved away Eilidh's concerns and took out his phone. They were standing at the end of the single-track road in Outertown, having just been to see Alice Harcus. It had been a waste of time; she'd denied having been Michael Wishart's girlfriend or having seen him on the night he disappeared, but Fergus could tell she was lying. He didn't need nearly thirty years in the job, twenty-six of them as a detective, to tell him that. Something had happened that night and nobody had ever got to the bottom of it.

He called Sgt Fraser. 'Any news on Drever?'

'Nothing,' Fraser said. 'I'm having to pull people to go to other jobs, but we've still got most folk out looking. Might be worth going public though, getting some help with this.'

Fergus was thinking the same thing.

He hung up, sent a text to Freya telling her that Drever was on the run. He hoped either she would pick it up or she would let Gill know. Last thing he needed now was to have to deal with that Irvine woman.

'So, what now?' Eilidh said as they got into the car. 'Harcus has clearly lied to our faces. She knows more about what happened to the Wishart kid than she's letting on.'

Fergus nodded. 'Do you think she was lying about the boat as well?'

In Peter Moss's notebook, he'd written that Alice had told him to ask Rabbie Cleat about The Dying Light. Fergus's hunch was Moss had written that on his arm to remind himself, that perhaps his memory hadn't been what it used to be, and he didn't want to take the notebook with him.

'No, I absolutely think she's telling the truth about that,' Eilidh said. 'I also think she knows exactly what happened on that boat and didn't need to send Moss off to speak to Rabbie Cleat about it. I think she just wanted rid of him so she gave him the tiniest scrap of information she could think of. Same as she's done with us. She couldn't get us out of there fast enough.'

'I have to agree.' Fergus started the car. They set off driving in the direction of Stromness. 'I suppose there's nothing else for it but to go and speak to the man himself now.'

'Rabbie? You don't seem keen.'

'I'm not. His dad isn't the monster he once was, but Rabbie's vile enough, and his mother might just be the most rotten of the lot of them. If you thought Gary Seator up in Westray was unpleasant, wait until you meet—'

He was cut off by another sharp stabbing pain to his gut. The car swerved as his hand went to his stomach, the tyres catching the grass at the side of the road, but Fergus quickly got control again.

'Whoa, maybe we won't go and see Cleat yet,' Eilidh said. 'Maybe we'll take you to see a doctor.'

'It's nothing, it's just my breakfast—'

'Just your breakfast disagreeing with you? Aye, you've been saying that for a few days now.'

He had. Though this had been happening for longer than a few days. The pain was getting more intense too, and more frequent. He was probably going to have to admit defeat and go and see someone about it.

He opened the window a crack, felt better with some air coming into the car. Soon they were on the Cairston Road on the other side of town, the glistening blue water of the Loch of Stenness and the rolling hills of West Mainland opening up ahead of them, heading towards the A965. Fergus distracted himself from the niggling feeling in his stomach by thinking about that boat. The name had been bugging him. Before he'd handed them over to Freya, Fergus had gone through Neill's notebooks in forensic detail, trying to decipher their meaning. He was pretty sure he remembered a line that was something like TDL @ Burwick, followed by a list of initials. Given Burwick was a small harbour at the southern tip of South Ronaldsay, the island that was home to the Cleats' farm, it wasn't a giant leap to assume Neill was referring to this boat.

As they crossed the Churchill Barriers, waves lapping at the rust brown hulls of the sunken blockships on either side of the road, Fergus made up his mind.

'We'll head somewhere before we go and see Rabbie.'

'To your GP, I hope.'

Fergus gave her a side-eyed glance. 'Very funny.'

'Where are we going?'

'There's a harbour a little further on from the farm. Might be worth taking a look for that boat.'

'Do you really think it'll tell us anything? That's even assuming it's there.'

'Maybe. Maybe not. But, with the Cleats, it's always best to go in prepared. If we can at least confirm its existence, it'll strengthen our hand when we ask about it.'

The road rose and fell, the north coast of Scotland unfurling ahead of them as they crested the hill at St Olad's viewpoint. They'd left the rain behind, but they could see bands of it from here, crossing the Pentland Firth and drifting over Hoy. Five minutes later, they passed the small chapel at St Peter's Kirk at the head of the bay and the harbour came into view. It was quiet, as it generally was. Only the one boat bobbing in the harbour. A turquoise car and a small white van were parked near the tiny ferry terminal.

'Doesn't look like this'll take long,' Eilidh said as they pulled up alongside the car.

They got out. Eilidh started walking over towards the jetty, but Fergus hung back. He was looking at the car. A turquoise Hyundai Getz. He was sure that was Freya's.

He looked around, couldn't see any sign of life anywhere.

'You coming?' Eilidh called over to him.

'Aye, in a blink.'

He walked over to the car, placed his palm on the bonnet. It was cool, it had been sat here a while.

Something seemed off. It was like he already knew something terrible had happened to his goddaughter, but he needed to exhaust all justifications for her car being here first. If she was following the same lead as he had, then it would've taken her seconds to determine whether or not that one boat in the bay was the one they were looking for. There was no need for her car to still be here.

He took out his phone to text her again, saw the last message hadn't been read.

'Damn it,' he heard Eilidh shout. 'This isn't our boat.'

'Murray, I think—'

He wasn't entirely sure what happened next. He doubled over as pain like a searing hot blade shot through his abdomen. There was a noise like a wounded animal, he thought it might've been coming from him. Next thing he knew he was on the floor screaming in agony. A taste like hot metal on his tongue.

'Shit, shit, shit!'

He heard Eilidh's hurried footsteps as she ran over to him, was aware of her crouching over him. She was Shouting. He realised it wasn't at him.

'I need an ambulance, immediately. Like right fucking now.'

The pain struck again, like nothing he'd felt before.

'Help's coming,' he heard Eilidh saying as he started to lose consciousness, the panic in her voice visceral. 'Hold on, you daft old bugger. You're going to be okay.'

He coughed, felt something thick in the back of his throat, tasted hot metal again.

The last thing he saw before the pain dragged him under was the blood on the tarmac beside him.

The last thing he heard were Eilidh's desperate cries for help.

The last thing he felt was okay.

36

She could hear dogs barking over the sound of the wind. And voices.

Men. At least two or three, somewhere outside the door. It sounded like they were arguing.

Freya tried to hold her breath, to listen. But even when she did, all she could hear was the beat of her own heart whooshing in her ears. All she could feel was the scratch of this bag. Could taste the stench of it. She needed to move. Tried to rock. Felt the sharp plastic of the cable ties cut into the flesh at her wrists and welcomed the pain. It was something she could focus on. Something to tether her mind.

The door opened.

Soft footsteps on the mouldy carpet.

They came at a glacial pace, like water torture. Each step a slow, painful drip, drip, drip until finally someone was standing in front of her.

She couldn't hear the voices now for the sound of her own ragged breathing.

The cloth bag was pulled from her head again. When her eyes adjusted once more to the light, she saw Maggie Cleat sitting opposite her.

'I'm curious about something, Red. How did you know about our boat and where to find it?'

Freya blinked a couple more times until the woman was in focus. She didn't know how to answer.

It stunned more than stung her when Maggie slapped her across the face with the back of her hand.

'Don't make the mistake of thinking that I'm going to be nice to you because I've said it would be messy to have you killed,' she said. 'This isn't going to end with you just walking away from here Scott free, my Peedie Red—'

'Stop calling me that.'

Maggie chuckled. 'Oh, if that upsets you, dear, you're not going to like what's coming next.'

Freya screwed her eyes shut, bit her lip. She was trying desperately not to cry, but her thoughts kept drifting to Tom. She longed to be with him now, wished she had been focused on him and their dogs and their life together for the past six months and not those stupid notebooks. As much as she loved her dad, as much as she missed him, and as much as she desperately wanted the justice he deserved, none of this was going to bring him back. It wouldn't change anything. And she knew deep down this wouldn't be what he wanted for her daughter in the slightest. But she also knew there was no other possible world where she had simply walked away from this. It was in her blood. Her dad's drive to know the truth had got him killed – she might not have known the precise details of how it had happened, but she was now certain of that – and it looked like she might end up the same way. Like a curse, passed from father to daughter.

'The boat, Freya,' she heard Maggie say. 'What sent you there?'

'I'll tell you, if you tell me why you killed my dad.'

She braced herself for another slap, but none came.

'You are so very like Neill. No cards to play whatsoever, and yet you're still trying to make a deal.' Maggie leaned forward, rested her forearms on her knees, her face close to Freya's. Too close.

'I'm a simple wifey, Red. Farming's been in my family for generations, and I should hope it will be for many more generations to come. My husband on the other hand, back when he still had his wits, he was a monster of a man. Ambitious beyond belief. Farming was never going to be enough for him. Though I admired that, and I'll admit, I quite liked the violence too. It's exhilarating, isn't it? I can see there's a part of you that thinks so too. You're drawn to it in the same way I am.'

Freya said nothing.

'But do you ken what I liked most about my husband? He was never showy with it. Not like that man, Tait. Allan wanted people to fear him, but with my husband, it just came naturally.

He didn't need reputation to do it for him. We've survived out here without anyone sticking their noses into our business for decades because we keep our heads down.'

'That a few friends in the police force,' Freya said.

Maggie smiled. 'That too. The point I was making, though, is that we're private folk. My Rabbie did a stupid thing, sending that man away to the Dwarfie Stane in the middle of the night, thinking it would be funny to make him go to all that trouble for nothing, and now here you are. I'm fairly confident that's no coincidence. So, how did you find out about our boat?'

'What will you do if I tell you?'

Maggie held her hands out, palms open. 'I'll let you go.'

Freya stared at the woman sitting opposite her. 'You'll let me go?'

'Once I'm happy certain conditions have been met, aye.'

'What conditions?'

'You said afore that I didna ken your father. You're wrong, Red. Dead wrong. Folk say ignorance is bliss, but I ken very well that for that man it was a form of torture, and you're the same way. You're looking for answers, and you won't stop until you've found them.' Maggie stood up. She left the cloth bag at Freya's feet and walked towards the door. 'I need to be certain, that if you walk away from here alive, you'll stop looking for whatever it is you're searching for, and you'll not breath a word of what's happened to you and your husband this afternoon to another soul.'

Maggie opened the door, whistling, like she was calling a dog to heel.

It took a moment for Freya to realise what Maggie had just said.

Two men appeared in the doorway – Rabbie and another one Freya didn't recognise. It wasn't Jake Drever. She didn't know what had happened to him. They were dragging a third person between them.

And Freya felt her heart tear in two.

The noise she made was like nothing she'd ever heard in her life. A pitiful wail filled with horror, hopelessness. The man with a bag over his head being hauled into the caravan heard it and his legs gave way. She heard him groan into a gag. A similar sound to the one she'd made. A sound she never wanted to hear again in her life.

The two men dumped the figure onto the chair across from Freya. Freya thought she was finished, that she would tell these people anything they wanted to hear, but when the bag was taken away and she saw the pure, abject terror in Tom's eyes, she was lost. Whatever Maggie Cleat wanted, she knew she would give her.

'I'll tell you anything you want to know, please!' she heard herself howling.

Tom's eyes were heart-attack wide. He was shaking, crying. Freya couldn't look at him, but also couldn't tear her gaze away. Over and over, all she could think about was the warning Keith Clouston had given her, the fear in his voice when he'd said it.

'You have a family, don't you? People you care about?' he'd asked her when she had wanted to know who he was so afraid of, moments before he'd told her, 'For your sake and theirs, pray you never find out.'

'I was worried for a blink that I should've had my boy bring your dogs here instead of your man, but it looks like this will work,' Maggie was saying, but Freya could barely make it out. Could hardly process everything that was happening. 'Rabbie should've kicked you off our boat and threatened to report you for trespassing. It was really that simple. There was nothing to find, and you would've carried on going around and around in circles getting nowhere. But like I said, my boy's bloody moron. And now we all have to suffer the consequences.'

Rabbie stood behind Tom, staring at his feet in impotent rage as his mother chastised him.

Maggie came to stand next to Freya, put her hand on her shoulder again, peered down into her eyes. 'This is the final time I'll ask you nicely. What brought you looking for my family?' She noticed the other man who had heaved Tom into the van was holding an iron crowbar. She had no idea who he was, but he was scowling at Freya with a murderous hate in his eyes. Eyes she thought looked familiar.

If she told Maggie Cleat she'd heard about *The Dying Light* from Alice Harcus, she was as good as slitting her throat. And not only hers, Ryan's as well. She couldn't have their blood on her hands.

She didn't know what to do.

She looked up at Maggie, wide-eyed with fear.

And Maggie nodded. 'Very well.'

Maggie glanced at the ugly monster standing behind Tom. He grinned, the sickest smile Freya had ever seen. He lifted the iron bar.

Notebooks,' Freya cried out.

Maggie raised a hand for her monster to wait. 'Go on.'

Freya opened her mouth to talk, but started to cry. Deep, uncontrollable sobs that wouldn't let the words through.

She heard Tom whimper against the gag.

'You're testing my patience, Peedie Red Rabbit.'

'My ... my dad kept notebooks.' Freya wailed. 'He recorded everything that happened. You, Tait, Linklater. He wrote it all down.' It all came flooding out of her. She no longer cared. Maggie could know everything. She just wanted to go home. 'He wrote about your boat. The Dying Light at Burwick.'

She flinched as Maggie's hand touched her knee. When she looked up, Maggie was crouching next to her.

'What exactly did he write?'

'Initials. Your husband's, Allan Tait's. Times and places of meetings. He was gathering evidence about you all. He knew you were running those parties. And that's why you killed him. That's why...'

The sobs took her again. She was struggling to breathe.

Freya jumped again as Maggie wiped away her tears with her thumb. She sighed. 'Oh Freya, you silly peedie girl.' I think you've really got yourself in a right raffle.'

'I can show you the notebooks,' she cried. 'I know what you did to him! He was watching you!'

'No, he wasn't, Red,' Maggie said. 'Neill Spence was one of us.'

Saturday, 21st June, 1997 - 3.02 a.m.

Michael counted eleven women and girls, a lot of whom looked younger than him. All of them packed together in a space no bigger than his bedroom at home.

Nobody spoke. The two groups stared at each other through the doorway, uncertain what to do next.

'Who are you?' Jake asked.

None of the girls replied. They looked terrified, huddled together in the cramped space. Michael looked at each of their faces but couldn't see the girl who'd attacked him earlier, though his vision was beginning to blur. He felt dizzy. He took a few steps back, leaned against the landing wall. Slowly slid down the faded patterned wallpaper until he was sitting on the grubby carpet.

Alice looked back and saw him. 'Shit, Mike, stay awake!'

He snapped his eyes open, hadn't realised he'd closed them.

'Who the fuck are you?' Jake asked the girls again. It was fear more than anger in his voice.

One of the women in the group, one who looked older than the others, leaped forward, snatched the deadbolt off the carpet and held it behind her head, like she was going to throw it at Jake, as if it made any kind of weapon that could keep him at bay.

'Bāc tevi! Nenāc tuvāk!'

Nobody had any idea what she was saying, but Michael thought it sounded like the same language the girl on the beach had been speaking.

Alice crouched down by his side, whispered, 'This is who that girl was with.'

Michael nodded. 'Aye.' It was all he could manage to say.

'Who the hell are they? Why are they here?'

'I don't know.'

Alice chewed at her thumbnail. 'We're going to need another plan to get you out of here. We need to start a fire. Drag some of the shite from downstairs outside and set light to it. Someone will see.'

Michael nodded again, fought to keep his eyes open. He knew that plan would never work, but he couldn't be the one to say it.

The others were still shouting at each other in languages nobody could decipher when he heard someone give a loud, 'Shhhh.'

It was a command that was universally understood, because both the group he'd arrived with and the women inside the room fell silent.

He wasn't sure why someone had shushed them all quiet until he heard a banging sound downstairs.

He was awake now. His eyes fully open. He looked at the others. Everyone had heard it.

It came again. Loud. Fast. Sounded like footsteps. Moving quickly.

Torch beams sliced through the gloom. Three streaks of white light flashed across the wallpaper at the top of the stairs. There was the sound of boots on the staircase, then in the next moment three men stood on the landing.

Was this it? Were they saved?

Michael wasn't sure whether or not he was hallucinating until he looked at Alice, saw she was staring at them too, her face pale in panic.

One of the men came forward, stepped over Michael's legs and walked towards the others. As he passed, Michael saw he was a middle-aged man with a weathered face, hair clipped close to his scalp, and wild blue eyes that looked familiar.

The man walked straight towards Rabbie. For the first time in his life, Michael thought Rabbie looked afraid.

'Dad?' Rabbie said.

Then the man punched Rabbie hard in the gut.

Rabbie bent double, the wind leaving his lungs in a sickening grunt. There were screams. One of the men shouted, 'Seamus, for Christ's sake, don't!'

But Seamus Cleat didn't listen.

They all watched in impotent horror as Seamus punched Rabbie in the face, knocking him to the ground. He reigned blows down on his own son, kicks to his stomach, to his ribs, his arms and legs and spine while Rabbie curled up into a ball and tried to weather the attack. The man who had shouted said nothing. Nobody did a thing. Rabbie never fought back.

When he began to lose his breath, Seamus kicked Rabbie onto his back. In the light of the lamp, Michael could see Rabbie's face was already swollen. Cuts around his eyes. Blood from his lips. His nose misshapen. Seamus climbed on top of Rabbie, straddled his chest and pushed his knees into the tops of Rabbie's arms to pin him to the ground. More screams as the man took a knife from his pocket, flicked open a blade, held it to Rabbie's left eye.

'If you ever steal from me again, son,' Seamus Cleat said, his voice a low growl, 'I will fucking take one of your eyes out. Do you hear me, boy?'

Whimpering beneath the weight of his dad, Rabbie nodded.

'Fucking speak up.'

'Yes, Dad. I'm sorry.'

'That way,' Seamus continued, 'every time you look in a mirror, you'll mind what you did, and you'll mind what'll happen should you do it again.'

Rabbie said nothing. He had started to cry.

Seamus stood, his gaze sweeping over the others like the beam from the lighthouse. He gestured to one of the men, an absolute beast who looked like he could crush a skull with his bare hands. 'Get these locked away again,' he said, nodding towards the girls in the room.

The man came forward, grabbed back the deadbolt from one of the women and pushed her back inside the room. Nobody else said a word. Nobody dared breathe.

Michael flinched as the torch beam shone in his face.

'The fuck happened to you?'

Seamus came and stood over him, the blade still trailing from his right hand, blue in the lamp light.

'I said what happened, boy?'

'He was hit with a rock,' Alice answered for him.

Seamus kept his eyes on Michael as he spoke. 'And who did that?'

Michael looked at Alice. She was looking back at him. They both knew what would happen if they told him.

Seamus crouched down. 'I asked you a question.'

'I don't know,' Michael said.

'It was one of these bitches,' they heard Rabbie say, his voice muffled by his sobs and his already swollen lips.

Seamus kept his eyes locked on Michael. 'Which one?'

Michael couldn't answer. Fear had him by the throat.

Seamus turned, looked at the giant of the man he'd told to lock up the girls. He nodded, and the man seemed to understand.

He grabbed the woman nearest to him, the one who'd picked up the deadbolt off the floor, and dragged her by the wrist. She screamed, tried to pull herself free, but it was useless.

Seamus stood, and the man threw the woman down at his feet. Now she was closer and Michael could see her better in the torchlight, he realised, even though she was one of the oldest-looking ones, she wasn't a woman at all. She was no older than sixteen.

She whimpered as Seamus grabbed her by the hair, pulled back her head.

'Was this the one who hit you?' Seamus asked.

Michael realised when he spoke that he was crying. 'I'm sorry, I don't … I honestly don't know.'

Seamus nodded. And then he slit the girl's throat.

Fear. Panic. An explosion of emotions he'd never felt before ripped through him as the girl's eyes widened in pure, horrific dread. Her fingers clutched at her gaping neck as she dropped to the floor and began to convulse next to Michael. He turned away and threw up.

The world around him collapsed in sounds of horror.

People screaming. Crying. Pleading.

Seamus Cleat ignored it all. He pointed the knife, blood dripping from its blade, towards the cowering girls in the bedroom. 'Let that be a fucking warning to the rest of you.' He spoke again to the colossal man who'd arrived with him. 'Lock them up, clean this mess up, then follow us in the rib.'

Seamus glanced at Michael, then he turned to the third man in their group. He was still standing at the top of the staircase, his face pale, his eyes as wide as everyone else's in shock as he stared at the young girl bleeding to death on the floor.

'Snap out of it, Spence,' Seamus said. 'Make yourself useful and get everyone back on the boat.'

MONDAY, 9TH JUNE. PRESENT DAY.

37

'You don't believe me, do you?'

Freya had managed to stop crying. She stared at Maggie Cleat with wet eyes, said nothing.

'No, I didn't think you would.' Maggie turned to Rabbie. 'Back in the house, in the safe. Bring me the

Rabbie didn't look happy about being sent off to run errands by his mother 7mot, but he headed for the door without arguing.

Maggie leaned, arms folded, against the wall of the caravan. It was flimsy and bent easily under her weight, even though she was by no means a heavy-looking woman. To her ever-deepening horror, Freya realised these people weren't worried about sound being able to escape the thin walls. It wouldn't matter if it did. There was probably nobody for miles around to hear.

'I have to say, Red, these notebooks have come as a surprise to me. Though not as much as my revelation has come as a shock to you, I can tell,' Maggie said. 'I honestly thought you were going to say that Tait had told you all about us before he met his maker. He did love to run his mouth, that man. I've been waiting for you to show up these past six months.'

'Allan Tait did mention you,' Freya said. 'Just not by name.'

The former chief inspector's words from last December were playing now on a loop in her head.

We're merely small pieces in a much grander puzzle.

He'd told her there had been 'mean and rotten' people trafficking girls south through Orkney long before the parties she uncovered last winter had ever begun. He'd just never told her who those people were. Now, she got the feeling she was face-to-face with them.

'It doesn't surprise me he couldn't resist showing off,' Maggie said. 'For all the help he gave us, using his position within the police, I always felt he was a weak link in our operation, and I told my Seamus as much. Of course, he agreed. When you work with bent pigs, you'd be a fool to trust their loyalty. So I'm not sure what Neill was attempting to achieve with his notebooks, but he wasn't the only one with an insurance policy.'

'My dad wouldn't work for you or your husband,' Freya said.

'Wait till Rab gets back, then you'll see.'

Freya looked at Tom. He was still shaking, his skin pale. She wanted to hug him, or at the very least let him know it was going to be okay. She was going to get them out of this. She had got them both into this mess, but she was going to sort it.

She noticed the second man, standing at Tom's shoulder with a crowbar in his hand, was still staring at her with barely contained rage.

'You're trying to work out how you know him,' Maggie said. 'I wondered if you'd recognise him. I'm not sure you two met, but you were most certainly acquainted with his brother.'

Freya looked at the man with the misshapen nose and the familiar eyes. His brother must've been better looking, because there was no way she would forget a face that ugly. Whoever this man was, he appeared to know her.

The door to the caravan opened, letting in some much-needed air. Rabbie stepped inside, passed a black metal box to his mother, who held it in one arm and opened the lid.

'I did start to doubt if there was any point keeping this lot now, seeing as all the men in here are dead, save for my husband, and he may as well be. Lucky for you, I'm a hoarder,' Maggie said. 'These notebooks of Neill's, they mention our boat, do they?'

Freya nodded.

'Anywhere else?'

Freya tried to think, couldn't remember. She tried to picture the pages, but she felt so tired now, and this caravan had grown so hot, the smell was overbearing, and she could still feel the carpet crawling up her legs.

'There was a phone box,' Freya said.

Maggie nodded, rummaged in the box. She pulled out a photograph, placed it down on the towel over Freya's lap. Freya looked down, squinted. The photo had been taken with a powerful zoom lens. It showed a man standing in a phone box on a lonely lane, a car parked nearby. She recognised the man on the phone, although he had more meat on his bones and hair on his scalp than when Freya had met him. Allan Tait was glaring out of the phone box, almost looking at the camera, the receiver held to his ear. But it was the car that drew her attention. There was a man sitting in the driver's seat.

Freya looked away, her eyes filling with tears.

'There's more where that came from,' Maggie said, placing another photograph in her lap. This time, the shot was of a group of people arriving at a farmhouse. Could've been the Cleat farm, could've been another of Graham Linklater's secret properties. She recognised Linklater, and Tait again, but not a third man with closely cropped hair and eyes not unlike Rabbie's, though she could guess who he was. But again, it was the fourth man in the picture who her eyes picked out instantly.

The grainy image of her father's face blurred as a teardrop fell onto the glossy paper.

'I've got dozens of these,' Maggie said. 'At the height of our operation, we had anywhere from ten to fifteen girls a week coming into Orkney on our little boat. We'd sail out, meet one the bigger boats sailing over from Europe, and bring them back to Copinsay, far from any prying eyes. Doing that, keeping them locked away, and moving them on to our friends in the south is quite a trick to pull off without help.

Another photo was placed in her lap, then another. Her dad and these men who had done the most unimaginable things, together, again and again and again. It didn't make any sense.

Maggie dug in the box some more. THis time, she pulled out an old Dictaphone. 'I wonder if this still works.'

She pressed play.

Freya's heart stood still. She listened. Heavy static, then a voice. Faint but audible. 'There's a problem with one of your lot that I'm going to need you to deal with.'

'Who is it?'

Freya didn't recognise the first man, but the second one she did. When she had met Tait, she had thought that age and possibly sickness had turned his voice into a gravelly rasp. She was surprised to hear that he had always sounded that way. Not quite as severe, but close.

'A Constable. Scott. The parents of the Wishart boy have been filling him with bright ideas. Now, I hear he's asking questions he shouldn't.'

Her breath caught in her windpipe.

'Trevor?' Tait said. 'I thought the lazy bastard wouldn't want the extra paperwork, that's why I made sure he got this case in the first place.'

'Aye, well, he needs reigning in. A nice short leash.'

'Not a problem. Is it, Neill?'

A pause. More static.

Freya locked eyes with Maggie, stopped breathing.

'None whatsoever,' Neill Spence said. 'I'll make sure he understands.'

For the first time in over twenty years, Freya heard her dad's voice.

She folded in two, like she was in physical pain. She didn't know if it was the image she'd had of her father shattering into a million tiny fragments, or the simple fact that she could hear his voice after all this time, that completely and utterly destroyed her.

Seven words, that was all. And they tipped her world on its axis.

She heard a click as Maggie stopped the tape. Almost didn't want her too. Part of her longed to hear his voice again.

'Do you believe me now, Red?'

Freya didn't answer. She didn't make any noise at all. Inaudible sobs thundered through her, making her shake with desperate sadness, but not a single sound left her lips.

'It's fitting that all of this should be happening now,' Maggie was saying. 'A man comes to Orkney asking about Michael Wishart, dies in a lonely tomb, and it leads you here.'

Freya looked up, tried to catch her breath. She didn't understand.

'You see, the incident with Michael was the moment your father really proved his worth to us.' Maggie turned to look at Rabbie. 'You were there, son. Why don't you tell her. what happened that night?' Rabbie did as he was told. 'We stole my dad's boat, went to Copinsay. Your dad came out with my dad to get us back.' A glance at his mother. 'Do you want me to tell her what he did to Mikey?'

Maggie nodded. 'Tell her everything. She needs to know.'

Saturday, 21st June, 1997 - 3.27 a.m.

It was light when they got outside.

The sun wasn't up yet – there was another half an hour or so to go before it would be – but the horizon out to sea was glowing a golden green ahead of its imminent arrival.

Michael wished he could enjoy it. Instead, the light hurt his eyes. He was struggling to walk. Alice held him up on one side, the man Seamus Cleat had called Spence supported him on the other.

'We'll get you back on the boat, get that gash on your head cleaned up. Get some painkillers in you,' Spence said. 'You look like you need them.'

Michael didn't bother lying and saying he was fine this time. They all knew he wasn't. And not only because of the head injury.

Nobody spoke as they walked. Rabbie led the way, trying hard to walk without limping. Jake lagged behind him, looking back every now and then at Michael. Kelly and Isla were by his side, eyes to the ground, minds far away.

What the fuck had they just witnessed?

A cold-blooded murder, and what else? Why were those young girls locked up there? And was Seamus Cleat going to let them all walk away after what they'd seen?

The boat was back at the jetty with a small orange rib beside it. Seamus must've had a tracker fitted: that would be how he found them. As he stepped onto the beach, Michael's legs went from under him.

'Mike!'

He could hear Alice shouting, but she sounded so far away. He felt heat behind his eyes, but no pain. He felt calm. Couldn't be sure if he was still standing or lying on the wet sand. No idea where he was in space or time. He wanted to tell Alice it would all be okay, he just needed to rest.

Just needed to close his eyes for a while, then it would all be fine.

Another voice. 'Shit, he needs a doctor, quickly.'

He wasn't aware of any movement, but the next time he opened his eyes he was lying on the benches in the back of the boat. Could hear the roar of the engines, feel the acceleration of the vessel as they left Copinsay behind for good. He never wanted to set foot on it again.

'You still with us, boyo?'

He managed to open his eyes a crack. It was Spence; he was crouching down next to him. He smiled, and to Michael's surprise, he felt safe. Someone was sitting beside him on the bench, their hand on his shoulder. He rolled his eyes up to see Alice looking down at him. She was crying.

'Don't be sad,' he thought he said, though he couldn't be sure the words left his lips. 'It's going to be okay.'

It's all going to be okay.

Over the sound of the boat cutting through the water he heard the muffled sounds of sobs and voices. Everything sounded so far away. He heard the man who had murdered the young girl tell Rabbie to take the wheel.

Then he heard shouting.

'None of you were here tonight. You didn't see a bloody thing at that lighthouse, and you're not going to utter a word of this to anyone. Do you fucking understand me?'

He could tell it was Seamus. Michael tried to open his eyes, but it was getting harder and harder to do anything.

He wasn't sure if anyone replied. The next thing he heard was, 'And this one's a fucking goner. Drop him in the sea.'

'What?'

'You heard me, Spence. He's not making it back to shore. Look at the state of him.'

'He'll make it.'

'Well, I say he won't, and it's my fucking boat, so drop him.'

It took Michael a moment to realise they were talking about him.

He felt his heart suddenly begin to race. A scorching heat filled his head, burned behind his eyes. He felt like his skull was splitting in two, but survival instinct was kicking in. He needed to rally himself, needed to show them he was going to make it, but it was impossible to move. It felt like he was drowning in concrete.

He heard Alice yelling, 'Don't! He's going to be okay.'

'You, shut the fuck up. He's already dead. And what do you think is going to happen when we get back to shore with a dead body? You haven't quite grasped the level of shit you're all in yet, but you bloody will. Now Spence, I'll not tell you a third time. Either he goes over the edge, or they all do.'

Michael could feel the spray of the water on his skin.

Could smell the salt in the sea air.

He wasn't dead. Not yet.

He tried to sit up. One ultimate push to save himself.

The last thing he heard before he opened his eyes a final time, before he felt hands under his body hauling him over the side of the boat and into the deathly cold water, was the voice of the the man named Spence saying, 'I'm sorry.'

MONDAY, 9TH JUNE. PRESENT DAY.

38

Eilidh threw on the handbrake, jumped out of the car and chased the paramedics into the Emergency Department, waving her warrant card and yelling, 'Don't you bloody dare!' at a man in scrubs who made a misguided attempt to stop her.

Fergus was on a stretcher, oxygen mask over his face, conscious but in clear agony. He was pulling at the mask as Eilidh got alongside the paramedics who were fighting with him to keep it on.

'You're going to be okay, boss,' she said, gripping his hand. 'Just do everything they tell you.'

He pulled at the mask. 'Freya.'

'No, you silly git, it's Eilidh.'

'Resus One,' a doctor yelled. 'Let's get him inside.'

'You're going to have to go,' said one of the paramedics, trying to push Eilidh away from the side of the stretcher.

'The car,' Fergus panted, his face screwed up in pain.

It brought Eilidh to the verge of tears to see him like this, confused and in distress.

'I've got to go,' she said. 'But you'll be okay.'

'The car … at Burwick,' he said as they pushed him through double doors into one of the resus rooms. Eilidh could see a team of people in scrubs inside, waiting. Monitors and devices and drip stands loaded with IVs, ready to go.

As the doors closed behind him, she could've sworn she heard him say, 'Freya's car … Cleat.'

39

It wasn't true. It couldn't be. Freya screwed her eyes shut, tried to block out the world. She needed time to think. Not so much to process what she was hearing, but to work out the lie. Pick out the part she could cling to and tell herself that none of it was real.

'So Peedie Red Rabbit, what will you do now you know?' Maggie asked.

'I told you to stop fucking calling me that,' Freya howled, snapping open her eyes. She strained at the plastic straps around her wrists. The big ugly bastard behind Tom gripped the metal crowbar tighter in his shit-stained hands.

Maggie grinned. 'See, this was my concern. Knowing was never going to be enough for you. Now you'll want to do something about it. You'll want someone to pay for this anger you're feeling. Just like Michael Wishart's mother did. That's why I had to burn her alive.' She leaned in closer. 'Seamus and I offered her the same thing I'm giving you: the chance to walk away, so long as my conditions are met. But she wouldn't listen. She was convinced Jake Drever, of all people, had killed her little Mikey, and she was never going to stop trying to prove it. Told me as much, even after I'd tortured her husband right in front of her.'

Freya's eyes instinctively shot to Tom. He began to shake, began to cry.

'I don't think you're as strong-willed as Mary Wishart was, but maybe I'll be proven wrong,' Maggie said. 'I told you I couldn't simply let you walk away. I need to know you can be controlled. I need you to fully understand the pain I will inflict on you and everyone you love if I ever see your face, or if I even hear your name mentioned in the same breath as mine, again.' She glanced at the thug with the metal bar. 'My torturing days are long gone, so I'm going to leave you alone with Gary for five minutes. When

I come back, I'll decide if you're ready to go home or if you need a little longer to be convinced.'

Maggie whistled again and her bitch son came to heel, the two of them disappearing through the flimsy caravan door that closed behind them with a gentle click.

Gary stepped forward.

'I've waited months for this,' he said, his voice quivering with anger. 'This is for Darren.'

Freya stared up and this monster of a man, tried desperately to understand why he somehow looked familiar, why Maggie had said she'd met his brother.

Then it clicked.

The eyes. The same ones she saw in her dream.

The same ones she had watched looking up at her through the holes in the balaclava after she had pushed a man to his death at Yesnaby.

Her heart tried to rip a hole through her chest.

And Gary lifted the crowbar and swung.

It all happened in an instant. She heard the crack, saw the look on Tom's face as metal collided with bone. Shock more than pain at first. And then the agony hit him, like striking a match.

Ignition.

The howl that left her husband's lungs was something primal. A sound that plucked at the deepest nerve and unleashed a sense of dread and anguish she'd never experienced. His arm was bent forwards at the elbow at an angle it should never be at, his wrist lashed to the chair. He was unable to move. The sight of him in unspeakable pain tore her heart in two.

And then rage possessed her.

'You fucking piece of shit. I'm going to fucking kill you.'

The voice she heard didn't sound like her own.

Gary swung the crowbar again, hit Tom in the exact same place. His cry was unbearable.

Freya tried to haul herself forward, but the chair was held fast to her by the ties. She was trapped. All she could do was sit there and watch while this ugly lump of a man did whatever he wanted.

He lifted the crowbar a third time.

'Hit me, you fucking coward!' Freya yelled. 'It's me you want to hurt. Hit me!!'

Gary's eyes met hers, filled with hate. He was tempted.

He swung again. This time Tom made a sound like a tyre blowing out as the crowbar connected with his chest. He let out a horrible, rasping wheeze, blood spotting his lips, his body convulsing as he tried to get breath into his lungs. He was like a fish plucked from the water, drowning in air.

He was going to die.

He was going to die and Freya was going to be forced to sit here powerless and watch it happen.

She needed to act. Now.

'I'm going to fucking murder you,' she growled. 'Same way I murdered your cunt brother.'

Gary twitched, gave two rapid blinks. He had his orders, but the fucker was malfunctioning. He glared at Freya with the same visceral loathing she was giving back to him.

'I pushed that piece of shit off the cliff. You want to know where your brother is? He snapped in two against the rocks like a pathetic little twig.'

Gary's nostrils flared, his face growing redder and redder.

He lifted the crowbar again.

'And he fucking squealed when he dropped,' Freya howled. 'Crying like the little fucking bitch that he—'

Gary roared. He leaped forward, swung the metal bar down in an arc, aiming for the top of Freya's head, looking to crack her skull in two.

And Freya threw herself to her right.

The crowbar landed with a sickening crack, smashing straight through the legs of the wooden chair. She scrambled away as Gary recovered, but she couldn't go far. Not in this cramped space. There was no escape. The splintered chair legs were still lashed to her arms. She managed to pull one of them free through the cable tie on her wrist, spun around, thrust the broken end out in front of her as Gary lunged at her.

The spike missed his heart by inches as he rolled away to the side.

He cried out as the sharp wood sliced the flesh over his ribcage. He stumbled, fell against the paper-thin wall of the caravan. Almost crashed through it. Freya stood over him, the stake pointing right on his throat as he lay prone at the shitty carpet.

And the thought crossed her mind.

Do it.

'Freya.'

She didn't take her eyes off the man on the floor to look at Tom. If she did, he'd be on her in a flash.

Kill him. Before he kills you.

'Freya … please. Don't!'

She fought hard to hold on to her rage, but the sound of Tom's sobbed plea stole all the hate from her heart. Fatigue hit her like a freight train. She began to cry.

And Gary saw his chance, reached for the crowbar.

Just as the caravan door flew open.

40

The room was silent, save for the sound of Tom's gentle breathing.

Freya watched him sleep. Every now and then, his face would contort into a frown beneath the oxygen mask, and his eyes would move quickly behind shut eyelids, flicking left and right. She wondered what he was dreaming, hoped it was nothing bad, but she knew all too well how events like the kind they'd been through today came back to haunt you all over again.

There was a cast on his right arm, a probe on the forefinger of his left hand to measure the oxygen in his blood. Tubes running into veins, carrying electrolytes and pain relief. The doctor had told her Tom had a severe fracture dislocation to his right elbow, multiple broken ribs and a collapsed lung. They were merely the physical injuries. The arm would need more surgery, but everything would heal in time, the doctor said. Freya wasn't so sure about 'everything'. She had no idea how she was ever going to make this right with him. Or herself.

She kissed his forehead, stood up. She needed some air. Some space to think.

Outside, the sky above Kirkwall was turning pink as the sun began its slow descent towards the horizon. Freya hadn't even realised it had got so late. The whole afternoon had passed in a blur. It was still warm, but she zipped up her coat regardless. She wanted to be cocooned inside it. She stood on the pavement near the hospital doors and closed her eyes, breathed in the evening air. It was tinged slightly with the smell of cigarette smoke, but for once, she didn't mind it. She felt stuck somewhere between wanting to cry and feeling nothing at all. Numb. Maybe it hadn't hit her yet. She wondered what would happen when it did.

'You okay?'

She opened her eyes. Eilidh Murray was standing a few metres away, a lit cigarette between her fingers. She stubbed it out on a nearby bin and walked over.

'I'd quit these things,' she said. 'That's my first in six months and I'm not even mad at myself, I've bloody earned it.'

It had been Eilidh, not Maggie, who had come through the caravan door. She had rushed in and pepper-sprayed Gary's eyes before he'd been able to attack Freya again.

'Thank you. Again,' Freya said. 'When that door opened, I don't think I've ever been so grateful to see anyone in my life.'

'My pleasure,' said Eilidh. 'Genuinely. I've been wanting an excuse to kick Gary Seator's arse since I first met him last week. How's your husband?'

'He's sedated. He's going to be in a lot of pain for a while.'

'And how about you?' She glanced at the wound at the back of Freya's head.

'I'll be fine. I've been stitched up. It was nothing.'

'Those sick bastards.' She took out another cigarette and lit up. Freya hadn't smoked since a misguided attempt to take it up while she was at uni, but she was almost tempted to ask for one. 'We've got Seator and three of the Cleats in custody. Rabbie and his mum and dad. The dad we're going to have to let go - he's clearly not well enough to have been involved. And the mum's pulling the sweet old lady act, saying she didn't know what her forty-odd-year-old son and his pal were up to on her town land. Rabbie's claiming the same thing, taking all the blame. We're going to need a statement from you, when you're ready.'

Freya nodded, but didn't say anything.

'Why did they have you? You'd been looking for their boat, right?' Eilidh asked.

Freya looked away, tried to decide how to answer. She didn't know how much the police had managed to piece together about what had happened to Michael Wishart. Nothing at all, she hoped. And she didn't want to give them anything they didn't already have. Nobody could ever know the awful truth about the man she used to call her dad. And if it was Freya who inadvertently brought that secret to light, she didn't think she would ever forgive herself. It was another regret to add to a growing list.

'I'm sorry,' Eilidh said. 'Now's not the time, eh? Are they keeping you in tonight?'

'No, I've been discharged. I'm hanging around for Tom.'

Eilidh nodded, but looked unsure. She was probably good at sniffing out lies. The truth was the doctor had wanted Freya to stay in for observation, given the head injury and the traumatic event she had just suffered, but Freya had refused.

Something occurred to her then. 'How come you're here?'

'Ah. You don't know?'

'Know what?'

Eilidh shifted her weight between her feet, took a drag of her cigarette. 'Fergus is here. He collapsed when we got to Burwick. That's how I knew to bring everyone to the Cleat Farm. He recognised your car.'

Freya's right hand subconsciously went to the studs in her right ear. 'What's wrong with him?'

'I don't know. Nobody's told me yet. Something to do with his stomach. I came back to see him, but they said he's still in surgery.'

Freya felt her eyes flood with tears. 'Is he going to be okay?'

'Oh, yeah, I mean, he'll be fine,' Eilidh said. She was better at spotting lies than telling them.

This was too much. Freya had watched Tom being tortured, had lost her dad all over again, and now this. The tears came freely now. There was nothing she could do to hold them back.

She felt Eilidh put her arm around her, instinctively shrugged it away. She couldn't be touched right now. She needed space. But then she felt terrible at pushing away the woman who had saved her life.

'I'm sorry,' she sobbed.

'Don't be,' said Eilidh. 'Look, do you want to go get a coffee or something? Get away from here for a bit? Hospitals are sodding creepy at the best of times.'

Freya shook her head. She took a few deep breaths, pulled herself together.

'Well, if you don't want to get out of here, you might want to go back in and get a nurse to check your stitches,' Eilidh said, pointing at Freya's head. 'Looks like they've come loose. You're bleeding again.'

Freya tentatively touched the back of her neck. Her hair was sticky, her fingertips stained with fresh red blood when she took them away.

'You know, it's weird,' she said, sniffing away the last of her tears. 'It's bled really badly all day.'

'Head injuries can be nasty like that.'

'Yeah, I guess. The doctors thought it should've stopped by now.'

She was just thinking out loud, letting the words fall from her lips. She didn't really know why she was telling Eilidh any of this.

But the detective suddenly looked concerned. 'What do they think has caused it?'

'They don't know. They've taken bloods, they're doing some tests. They asked if I was on any kind of blood-thinning medication that might cause it.'

She saw a look flash across Eilidh's face.

'Are you?'

'Am I what?'

'On any medication that might cause that?'

'No.'

'Are the blood results back?'

Freya was getting worried. She didn't understand Eilidh's concern. 'No. I don't … I don't know.'

'Do you mind if we go and ask?'

'Not until you tell me why you're so bothered about this.'

Eilidh chewed her lip. 'Okay, fuck it, I'll tell you. But this isn't public knowledge yet, okay? I'm giving you a scoop here, or whatever you call it. And I suppose I'd rather tell you than that bloody woman you work with.'

Freya couldn't care less right now about getting any kind of story. She wasn't even sure she was going to have a job to go back to. And frankly, she didn't care about that either.

'Peter Moss's autopsy showed he died of a haemorrhagic stroke,' Eilidh said. 'But it also showed he had high levels of warfarin in his bloodstream. I need to recheck his medical records, but I don't think that was a medication he took.'

'You think someone tried to poison him with it?' Then it dawned on her what Eilidh was saying. 'And you think they might have tried to do the same with me?'

'You've been asking questions about Michael Wishart, right? Same as Peter Moss did. Someone clearly didn't like it. So, who have you been talking to?'

There was only one person in Freya's mind.

41

THE FRONT DOOR WAS unlocked when they tried it. A terrible sign.

Eilidh pushed it open. Called out, 'Hello?'

Nothing.

'Hello? Alice?'

No sound came from inside the house.

Eilidh stepped over the threshold, turned back and held out a hand, palm up, to stop Freya from coming in too. 'You should stay out here. In fact, you shouldn't even be here at all.'

Freya had followed Eilidh in her own car. She had to see. Had to know. She let Eilidh get a few steps along the hallway before she went in too.

Alice Harcus's house looked the same as it had this morning, only with longer shadows reaching down the hallway now it was getting late. It was quieter. No radio playing. No sound at all, save for the wind off the ocean whispering around the corners of the building. She could see brittle light coming in through the kitchen window at the end of the hallway, illuminating the tabletop. And then it struck her what one thing was most different from earlier.

'Alice? It's DS Murray. We met earlier,' Eilidh called through the closed living room door. 'Are you in there?'

Eilidh looked back along the hallway, saw Freya had followed. She shook her head, but didn't stop her from joining her. She gripped the door handle as Freya came up behind her.

One last call. 'Alice, I'm coming in.'

And she opened the door.

The living room was lit golden orange by the last light of the day. Beyond the large window, a pink sky blemished with only a handful of clouds seemed to stretch out forever. On the edge of the world, the setting sun was sitting inches above the horizon, casting its glow across the North Atlantic. And bathed in its light, Alice and Ryan Harcus lay together in the bed by the window, his hand in hers, their eyes closed.

Eilidh walked over, checked for a pulse, although she must have already known there would be none to find. Then she reached for her phone, called it in.

Freya left her to make the call. In the kitchen, the table and the worktops had been mostly cleared, save for some spent pill packets scattered on the counter near the kettle. She made sure not to touch them, but she could see the drug names written on them. Codeine. Paracetamol. The empty boxes were piled next to them. She had no doubt the warfarin packets would be in here somewhere too. There were still traces of powder on the worktop where Alice must have ground the pills down to mix into water for her and her brother to drink.

'Reinforcements are on the way,' she heard Eilidh say behind her. She turned to see her standing in the kitchen doorway, looking around. 'You'd better get out of here. You've not touched anything, have you?'

'No, but my fingerprints will be in here. I was here earlier.'

Eilidh nodded. 'Have you seen a note? There must be one somewhere.'

Freya shook her head.

'Why would she do this unless she was to blame for whatever happened to Michael?' Eilidh asked, maybe thinking out loud more than asking Freya for a response.

But Freya gave one. 'She didn't want to leave Ryan on his own.'

Eilidh nodded. 'People were asking questions. Us, you, Peter. She must've known the truth would come out eventually. I suppose she must've been worried that, when it did, we'd be coming to take her away.'

'Maybe that's why she's not left a note,' Freya said. 'Perhaps she wants the truth to die with her.'

Eilidh glanced at her, and for a moment, Freya felt like she could read her thoughts.

But all she said was, 'You'd better go.'

In her car, Freya sat for a while before starting the engine, looking out at the view. There was a haze creeping in around the base of the cliffs across the Hoy Sound as the air grew cold with night setting in. Alice Harcus knew what had happened to Michael. She knew the Cleats were trafficking girls and keeping them prisoner on Copinsay. She knew Neill Spence was helping them to do it. And she knew he had been the one to dispose of Michael's body in the North Sea, if the poor boy had even been dead at all by that point. She had witnessed it all and kept silent about it for twenty-six years. It felt like the kind of thing someone might confess before taking their own life and that of their twin brother.

Freya reached into her coat pocket, took out the folded-up note she had stolen from the kitchen table, and without reading it, she tore it in two.

WEDNESDAY, 18TH JUNE. PRESENT DAY.

42

There was a long queue already at Leigh's when Freya got there, but Fergus wasn't in it. He was sitting at the usual spot on the picnic benches by the water. He waved as Freya walked over. He looked fifty years older than the last time they had both sat here a little under two weeks ago.

He stood up, smiled. There were no hugs, as usual, though Freya did think about offering one this time.

'How are you doing?'

'A little more awake than when you saw me last,' he said. Freya had visited him several times before he was discharged from hospital last week, though often he had been dosed up on morphine to cope with the post-operative pain. 'But other than that, about the same.'

Freya nodded to the queue. 'You not eating?'

'Probably not, but don't let me stop you. I fear if I ate anything right now, if it didn't kill me, the doc would.'

She smiled. Fergus still hadn't told her what had happened to him. 'It's a stomach issue,' he'd said when she'd visited him. 'I'm not dead yet, that's the main thing.' She decided not to push him further.

'I'll grab something in a bit,' she said. 'Let the queue die down first.'

'Right you are.'

She sat across from him, enjoying the smell of the fried onions mixing with the cool sea air. It was cloudy and the temperature had dropped, mercifully, in the past week. Was back around a more amiable 12°C. Just about cool enough to wear her coat, if she kept it open. The sound of the food van's generator chugging away and the background chatter from the folk in the queue were calming. It was nice to be outside for once. Since Tom had come home from hospital, she hadn't much wanted to leave his side.

'How about you?' Fergus asked. 'How are you holding up?'

'I'm okay.'

'That's all I'm getting, is it?'

She shrugged. 'You've just got a stomach thing and I'm just okay.'

He smiled, nodded. 'Fair enough, point taken. And how's your Tom?'

'He's—'

'Let me guess. He's okay.'

Freya grinned too, but her smile faded as quickly as the sun that had momentarily broken through the clouds. 'No. No, he's not okay. He's ... well, he's in a lot of pain. Physically and mentally.'

The truth was, Tom had been a different person since he'd left The Balfour. The joy, the jokes he used to make, there was no sign of any of it. And she knew deep down that was normal, he was going to be in shock as well as in pain. She'd been through enough trauma to know it was going to take time to heal. But what hurt the most was the knowledge that it was her fault. He was no longer the happy, full-of-life man he used to be, because of her and the way she was and the things she had brought into their life as a result.

Fergus somehow read her mind. 'You can't blame yourself, Red.'

Freya only nodded.

Fergus shifted his position on the bench, winced a little. 'Look, I know you don't like small talk, so I'm going to get right to it. Eilidh's been keeping me up to date on everything at work, and there's good news and bad news.'

Freya took a deep breath. 'Okay.'

'The good news is, both Rabbie Cleat and Gary Seator have been charged with kidnap, and Seator's coughed to GBH with intent. He could get life for that. Here's hoping.'

That should've made her happy, but like at the hospital, she felt nothing.

'They're both still claiming the mother, Maggie, had nothing to do with it, even though she was in the house at the time.' Fergus ran his tongue over his teeth. 'Are you certain you never saw her the whole time you were there?'

'Positive,' Freya said.

Fergus watched her closely. She hoped she gave nothing away.

Maggie Cleat had come to visit Freya at home the morning after she'd been released from custody. Freya had only stopped in to shower after spending the night at the hospital with Tom. She was on her way to the police station to give her statement.

'Gary and my boy will go to prison, nothing can be done about that,' Maggie had said. 'But if you're thinking about mentioning my involvement, might I remind you of two things?'

The first had been that she still knew some very nasty people who made her son and Gary Seator look like playground bullies. People who would pick up where Gary had left off with her husband. People, she'd said, who would have no qualms about involving Thorfinn and Luna too.

'The second is, if you bring me into this, I will tell them everything about Neill. About his involvement with my husband's sex-trafficking operation. About him disposing of the Wishart boy off the boat,' she'd said. 'You know I've got the evidence to prove it. So, Red, I'll let you decide.'

Fergus nodded. 'Well, in any case, those two will be going behind bars for a long time.'

'So, what's the bad news?'

'We've reopened the Michael Wishart case…'

Fergus's voice disappeared then as a bright sound, like feedback, filled Freya's mind. He knew. Fergus had found out the truth about her father.

'…not saying a thing. So, it looks like it'll go nowhere.'

Freya blinked. 'What was that, sorry?'

Fergus frowned. 'Are you all right?'

'Aye, sorry, I just … I missed what you said.'

'I said Rabbie's sticking to the story that Michael stole a boat, and the others – Isla, Kelly, Jake – they're not saying a thing.'

'You've found Jake?' Freya asked. She hadn't mentioned his involvement in her kidnapping either, simply because he also knew the truth about her dad. She thought, if he was arrested, had nothing to lose, he might use that knowledge to broker a deal. She would rather he walked free than run the risk of letting him tell people what he knew.

Nobody could ever know.

'He showed up the day after he'd gone missing. I'm surprised you didn't see him. It'll have been the same day you gave your statement,' Fergus said. 'He walked back into the station, begging forgiveness. Claimed stress had been getting to him and, after Moss brought Michael up again, he was on the edge. And that morning he snapped.'

'And you believe him?'

'No. Nobody does. But there's no crime to answer for. Peter Moss died of natural causes. The fiscal says the warfarin poisoning won't have caused the stroke. It didn't help matters, it certainly quickened the bleeding, but they said, given where he was when it happened, it wouldn't have made much difference to his chances of survival. So, we can't pin his death on Harcus, either. Which begs the question: why did he run, and why did Alice kill herself and her twin brother?'

Freya knew the answer.

Alice and Jake were both accessories to murder, and witnesses to a sex-trafficking operation run by people who would kill them or their families to keep it quiet. In Alice's case, a PI and a reporter had come asking questions, and she was so desperate to stop those questions from being answered that she had tried to poison them both. She probably even thought she had killed Peter Moss. She was worried the net was closing in, and her brother would be left alone when she was taken off to jail. Or worse, she would be tied to a chair and forced to watch while the Cleats took him apart piece by piece in front of her. Freya probably would have known for certain what was going through Alice Harcus's mind if she had read the suicide note she had taken, but she had burned it in the hearth the second she had got home with it.

And as for Jake ... maybe he just panicked, like he said. If people really knew what had happened to Michael, he'd lose his job, probably his family too, and go to prison. Never a great option for a police officer.

'You're not taking a guess?' Fergus said.

'Yeah, it's got to be linked to Michael somehow, I guess. But it looks like we'll never know.'

'Exactly, and that's the bad news. It's a dead end. This is the case that put Trevor Scott and your dad on to Allan Tait. Seamus Cleat, The Dying Light, they have to be the SC and TDL initials from the notebooks. But, unless we find out what happened, I feel like we've hit a brick wall.'

Fergus inhaled sharply then, grabbed at his stomach.

'You okay?' Freya asked.

'Aye, it's just the stitches.'

Freya wasn't sure. Facial expressions weren't always her strong point, but she knew when Fergus looked worried.

'What is it?' she asked. 'There's clearly something not right with you.'

Fergus ran his hand through his thick grey hair, looked out to sea. 'I guess I won't be able to do that for much longer.'

Freya was getting annoyed. Why was he being so cryptic? 'Do what?'

He smiled, but without a drop of joy in it. 'Honestly, it's going to hurt for a week or two while it heals, but I'm on the mend. Not to worry.'

Freya knew he was lying, and that worried her all the more.

'How about you?' he asked. Freya could tell he was trying hard to sound more upbeat. 'Is that you fully ship-shape now? Are you back in work?'

'Not yet. I'm heading over there now to see Kristin, though.'

'Oh aye? Any reason?'

Freya thought about telling him her news, about all the things she'd been discussing with Tom, but if he was going to keep things so close to his chest, she could do the same. And it was probably going to upset him when he found out. She couldn't handle that right now. 'Just to apologise,' she said. 'I've been AWOL lately and I know she's been stressed about the paper not finding a buyer. I want to go in and make sure everything's okay between us. I didn't want to do it over the phone.'

'That part I can well believe,' Fergus said.

'I'd better go.'

'Right-oh. You're not getting something to eat?'

Freya looked at the queue. Three more vans full of workmen had turned up. As much as she loved a Smoke Stack, she didn't think she could eat until she'd got her conversation with Kristin out of the way.

'I'm going to have to pass.'

They stood, walked across the grass to Fergus's car, and Freya decided it was time for a change.

Fergus winced as she hugged him. 'As nice as this is, Red, watch the stitches.'

She waved as she drove away. Watched him sitting in his black Volkswagen in the rearview mirror. He didn't start the car, just sat there staring out of the window, watching her go.

She really wished he would tell her what was wrong with him.

She really wished she had been brave enough to tell him what she was about to do.

43

Fergus waved as Freya drove off. He sat alone in his car for a while after she'd gone, feeling the bite of the surgical wound in his stomach. He watched the punters in line at the van, wished he could join them.

He wondered if he should've told Freya the truth, explained what the docs had found when they had cut him open, but he wasn't sure he had the words to explain it, or the strength to do it yet without bursting into tears.

He checked his watch – not yet half past nine. There was still more than an hour until his appointment.

He reached over to the glovebox and took out the leaflet he'd been given at the hospital: *What to expect when starting chemotherapy*.

44

Freya checked the words she'd prepared one last time.

Her parking space had been free. From here, she could see Kristin's office window. She counted the studs in her ear forwards and backwards in order and read over the little speech she'd written in the Notes app on her new phone. She was going to mess this up, burst into tears, she could tell. Maybe she should just copy all of this into an email. It would be easier than handing in her resignation in person.

But she wanted to do this face to face. She felt she owed Kristin that.

She took a deep breath and opened the car door.

Walking up the staircase to the newsroom, listening to the background thrum of the printing press, she went over the words in her head again and again. She and Tom had talked long into the night about leaving Orkney when he had got home from hospital. What else could they do? The idea of living in the same islands as Maggie Cleat, having the constant threat hanging over them of seeing her somewhere or having her turn up on their doorstep, was unthinkable. They hadn't even got around to talking about Freya's confession to killing Gary Seator's brother at Yesnaby. She hoped that, given the ordeal he'd just been through, Tom might not remember. They would have to talk about it at some point, but not now, and not here. They needed a fresh start somewhere neither of them had any baggage.

She had a feeling Kristin might try and talk her out of it, and given how stressed her boss was, and how much she had contributed to that, she knew she might cave. But she had to do this. For her marriage. For herself.

She pushed open the door to find the whole team huddled around a desk.

Someone was talking, a voice she didn't know.

'…meet me at the Italian Chapel at 3 p.m. tomorrow, and you…'

Kristin turned around as Freya came through the door. 'Freya? This is a surprise. What are you doing here?'

The others turned to look. In all the versions of this moment she'd run through in her head, this had happened much more privately.

'I was hoping we could have a word,' she said.

Kristin walked over, gave her a hug. Sophie joined her too. She'd convinced herself everyone would hate her for the way she had abandoned her job in recent weeks. This open display of affection for her was too much, she was already on the edge. She couldn't hold it back, she started to cry.

She felt Kristin hug her even tighter. 'I'm so sorry about everything, chick,' she said, pulling back and looking her in the eye. Freya felt that familiar electric jolt, tried not to look away. 'I can't believe what those animals did to you and Tom. I can't…' She puffed out her cheeks. 'I can't even imagine what you've been through.'

Freya didn't know what to say, so she said nothing.

Through her sobs, she heard that voice start talking again. 'I don't know your name, but I've been told that this is where you work…'

Kristin spun around. 'Gill, bloody knock it off a minute, will you? It's not going to make any more sense listening to it a third time.'

Gill was standing next to a telephone on the desk, her face turning that familiar shade of purple. Keith was beside her. 'She looked like she was about to protest, but she pressed a button on the handset and the voice fell silent.

'What is that?' Freya asked.

Nothing important,' Kristin said. 'Let's go through to my office.'

'It might make sense to her, Kris. For all we know, it's her they're on about,' Gill was saying as they walked past. 'Do you want a listen, hen?'

Intrigue got the better of her. Freya stopped next to Gill, glanced at Kristin.

Her boss shrugged. 'Okay. One last time,' she said to Gill. 'Then we're deleting it. It's clearly nonsense.'

Gill didn't even let Kristin get to the end of her sentence before she poked a nicotine-stained finger at a button, and a recorded voice announced that a voicemail had been left today at 4.38 a.m.

'Hello,' the message started. 'I'm hoping this makes sense to one of you.'

The voice sounded like that of an older woman. At least middle-aged. What was unmistakeable was how afraid she sounded.

'I know I'm taking a risk by doing this, but I truly believe it's the right thing to do,' the message continued. 'Now, I don't know your name. All I know is you work for this paper and your father was a police detective by the name of Neill. Neill Spence…'

Freya's blood ran cold.

She looked up, realised everyone's eyes were locked on her. And they saw on her face that this meant something to her.

'I bloody knew it,' Gill said. 'This is for you, isn't it?'

The message had continued playing, but Freya missed what it had said. Gill started the whole thing again.

'…your father was a police detective by the name of Neill. Neill Spence. I know that he died. And I know that you were told that his death was an accident. But that was a lie.'

Kristin looked worried. 'Gill, turn this—'

'Shhhh.'

It was Freya who shushed Kristin quiet. It had been involuntary, but she had to hear the rest of this.

'I recently spoke to someone who witnessed what happened to your father. They never told a soul in their lifetime because they were afraid, and they regretted that. They didn't want to take that with them into the next life, and so in the moments before they died, they told me,' the voice on the answering machine went on. 'And now I want you to know too. So, if you would like to hear what I have to tell you, meet me at the Italian Chapel at 3 p.m. tomorrow, and you can finally know the truth.'

Saturday, 21st June, 1997 – 4.03 a.m.

'I'M SORRY.'

Alice wiped away her tears, looked at the man named Spence. He was crouched down beside Michael, his eyes screwed shut. Determination seemed to spread across the features of his face as he snapped his eyelids open and stood up, turned towards Rabbie's dad. The rage that burned in Seamus's eyes stopped her sobbing. She didn't dare cry in front of this man. Didn't dare breathe. But Spence stared him down.

'Think this through, Neill,' Seamus growled. 'Think about it very fucking carefully.'

'I'm sorry,' Spence said again. 'But I won't do it.'

A vein pulsed at the side of Seamus's shaved head. Alice watched his hands bunch into fists. He still had that knife.

'You're a copper,' Seamus said, simmering fury in every word. 'What do coppers do when folk turn up at hospital with a dead bairn?'

'I won't kill him.'

'He's already fucking dead,' Seamus screamed, inches from Spence's face, but the policeman didn't back away. 'You want folk knowing how he died? About the girls we've got in that lighthouse? About where they came from, and where they're going? Do you want to be telling the people we send them to why they're not coming anymore?' He pointed at Michael, lying motionless and silent beside them then looked around the boat at the terrified faces staring back at him. 'This goes away a lot easier if he's a missing boy rather than a dead one, so either one of you cops the blame for it, or he goes over the side, right here and now.'

Nobody spoke. Nobody moved.

Seamus ran his tongue over his lips. 'Aye, I didn't think so. I want all of you to remember, you made this choice together. His blood is on your hands, not mine. But if that gets too hard for you to live with, and you think about telling anyone what happened the night, you're welcome to join your pal at the bottom of the sea.' He turned to Spence. 'Dump him.'

Spence held Seamus's gaze. 'No.'

Alice longed to look away. She knew the face Seamus was pulling would haunt her forever. The anger in his eyes. The promise of ferocious violence. Seamus leaned forward, right into Spence's face. So close, Alice could barely hear him over the sound of the boat thundering across the water. He bared yellow teeth.

'You know why you're here, Neill. You know what you owe me,' Seamus said. 'You know why you're here. I can take her away just as easily as I gave her to you.'

Spence blinked. For a moment, Alice thought he was going to cave in. Those words had clearly touched a nerve. But he stood firm.

'I know my debt to you, and I'm repaying it,' Spence said. 'But not like this. You know I can't.'

Finally, Alice tore her gaze away, looked at Michael. He wasn't moving now. Wasn't breathing. Frantically, she turned to the others. Rabbie was at the helm, glancing back at his dad, undeniably terrified, his face puffy and red from the beating he'd just taken at the hands of his own father. Isla and Kelly were both in floods of tears. Jake was staring, eyes unblinking, at Michael. And right then she knew Seamus was right. If they got back to shore with Michael, questions would be asked. Sure, they could lie, but did she trust everyone here to play their part? Could Rabbie keep his cool in an interrogation? Would Isla or Kelly remember to stick to the story, or would they crack under pressure? The police would want to know what had happened, and a man like Seamus Cleat would would do anything to make sure they never found out. Alice was certain he would kill her, would kill all of them, even his own son, before allowing the truth to be known. Alice was certain he would kill her, would kill all of them, even his own son, before allowing the truth to be known.

And Ryan: if she was gone, she wouldn't be able to look after him. Nobody would. Not like she did. It would be as good as signing his death warrant too.

'Last chance,' Seamus said.

Spence shook his head. 'I'm not doing it. And, if you think you're taking my daughter away from me, you'll have to do it over my dead...'

Alice couldn't take it anymore. The tears came freely again. She stood up, scooped her hands under Michael's body. Her breath caught in her throat as he opened his eyes.

Michael looked up and, as he saw her face, his lips stretched into a smile that broke her heart. All her strength left her in an instant. What was she even thinking? Surely they could think up a lie, and the others would stick to it. They'd be too scared not to. There had to be some way to make this right, to get out of this with everyone alive.

She felt a jolt, someone pushed her aside.

She watched in horror as Jake Drever heaved his friend over the side of the boat and into the dark water.

ACKNOWLEDGEMENTS

I'm very lucky to have a whole bunch of people to thank for their kindness and support. These acknowledgements could quite easily be longer than the book you've just read, so strap in…

First, I am incredibly grateful to my wonderful agent, Ella Kahn. My intention was to start this book the second I handed over *Dark Island*, but life had other plans. It took a huge effort for me to get back to writing, but Ella helped me every step of the way, pretty much dragging this book out of me (In the nicest possible way!).

Thank you to Daisy Watt and Genevieve Pegg, for your patience and your belief in me and this story, and to all the team at HarperNorth. I owe a gigantic thank you to Dom Forbes, who has designed two incredible covers so far. If you did judge this book by its cover, I hope it lived up to the high bar Dom set for it.

To all the overseas publishers who have taken Freya to faraway shores, and to the fantastic translators who took my words and did something amazing with them, thank you so much. It's been a huge thrill to see all the different versions come to life.

You probably wouldn't have this book in your hands if it wasn't for the amazing support I've had from booksellers and libraries and reviewers. I've been blown away by how incredibly kind people have been, and how passionately people have recommended and supported my book. It seems cruel to pick people out when so many people have helped me, but I really must mention Grace at The Orcadian Bookshop, Richard at Perth Waterstones, Fiona at Durham Waterstones, Frances at Dumfries Waterstones, and Katherine at Ullapool Bookshop for their support and championing, and, in Fiona's case, for quite literally forcing the book into people's hands! A special thank you as well to Susan Green and Patricia Forsyth for recommending *Dark Island* to shops and festivals, you've made such a difference.

Speaking of forcing the book into people's hands, if you're reading this, there's at least a 50% chance my mum talked you into it! Thanks Mum for all your support and for shouting about my books at any given opportunity. Please do stop harassing strangers in the supermarket, though.

The other 50% of you probably got the book for Christmas off my neighbour, Jennie. Thank you, Jennie, for your enthusiastic championing. (We will finish that puzzle we started in 2023 at some point!)

A massive thank you to all the beautiful people of Orkney who have taken Freya to their hearts and haven't banned me from their shores. It's been a dream come true travelling there as an author and speaking to folk who've been so kind and supportive (and in some cases, downright excited!) about seeing their wonderful islands turned into a crime scene. Again, it seems cruel to pick people out, but I have to mention Steven Gough at Orkney Library, Stewart Bain and Rob Flett at Radio Orkney, Sarah Gilmour at *The Orcadian*, Piers and Simona Cain at Orkney Arts Society, Kev (and Zoe and Keegan!!), Jo and Dan Dickson (Did you read this one, Dan??), Hazel Pinner, Keely Herridge (Dylan and Maggie say thank you, too!), and Charlotte Platt.

I am blessed with the most incredible friends, who've helped me through some shitty times and been there to celebrate all the fun stuff too. Dani (Counsellor Dani Bell will get her moment!), Joe, Kirsty, Krystle (Hi Auntie Elaine!), Martyn, and Matt (Hi Ann Marie!), thank you for being amazing human beings. Thanks to Bev, Fí, Jenny, Julia, Neema, Pushp, Rebecca, and Wiz, for chats and brownies and John Wick and Love Island. To all of the awesome VWG, it is a pleasure and an honour to know you all. And to the fantastic folk I've come to know through Shut

Up And Write Glasgow, especially Cam, Isla, Jim, and Will, thank you for all the breakfasts, and a spot of writing too.

The biggest, soppiest thank you of all has to go to my incredible partner, and my favourite author, Danielle. Thank you for being there in the best and the worst moments. For believing I could do this, when I absolutely did not! This is the bit where people say things like, 'I couldn't have done it without you.' Maybe I could, maybe I couldn't; all I know is, I would never want to. The best part about all of this is that I get to share it with you. (Also, I couldn't have, let's be honest. I would have forgotten to eat and would've starved to death months ago!)

I can't end this without thanking you, the reader. Thank you for leaving reviews, ratings, telling your friends, sharing with your book club, coming to see me at events - it all makes a huge, huge difference. And to all the neurodivergent folk who've told me how much it's meant to you seeing a character like us being the hero because of who she is, THANK YOU! It has been the honour of my life to meet so many of you and hear your stories.

And last but never least, thank you to Dylan and Maggie. Who were, throughout everything, the biggest help of all.